PIERS ANTHONY'S VISUAL GUIDE TO XANTH

Piers Anthony's Visual Guide to XANTH

By
Piers Anthony and Jody Lynn Nye

Illustrated by
Todd Cameron Hamilton and James Clouse

Avon Books
New York

PIERS ANTHONY'S VISUAL GUIDE TO XANTH is an original publication of Avon Books. This work has never before appeared in book form.

AVON BOOKS
A division of
The Hearst Corporation
1350 Avenue of the Americas
New York, New York 10019

Copyright © 1989 by Bill Fawcett & Associates, Inc.
Cover illustration by Darrell K. Sweet
Published by arrangement with Bill Fawcett & Associates, Inc.
Library of Congress Catalog Card Number: 89-91277
ISBN: 0-380-75749-4

Interior Book Design by Robert T. Garcia

First Avon Books Trade Printing: November 1989

AVON TRADEMARK REG. U.S. PAT. OFF. AND IN OTHER COUNTRIES, MARCA REGISTRADA, HECHO EN U.S.A.

Printed in the U.S.A.

RRD   10 9

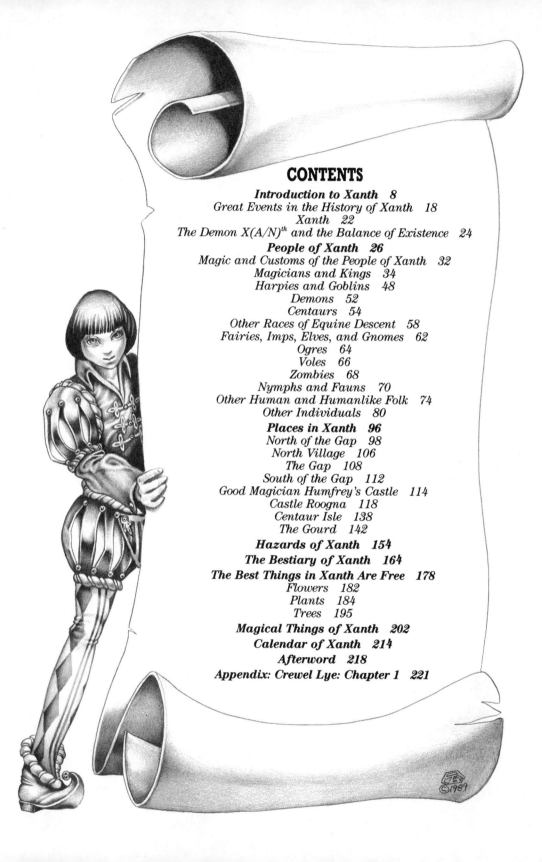

CONTENTS

PIERS ANTHONY'S VISUAL GUIDE TO XANTH

INTRODUCTION TO XANTH

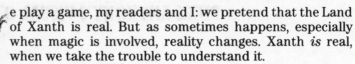

e play a game, my readers and I: we pretend that the Land of Xanth is real. But as sometimes happens, especially when magic is involved, reality changes. Xanth *is* real, when we take the trouble to understand it.

Do you know the way a computer shows you what you are typing or drawing on the screen? (In Xanth, we have Com-Pewter, which is mostly pewter and crockery, operating similarly, but for the moment let's stick to the dull Mundane version.) Well, if you want to get technical, that's illusion. You aren't really seeing what's in the computer, which is just a bunch of wires and printed circuit boards and what they call chips made out of silicon. You aren't even seeing the squintillion little switches that are all set to ON or OFF inside those chips and things. You are seeing only what the computer wants you to see, which is a picture of a little tiny part of the pattern of all those switches. But you like the way the picture looks, and you think it makes sense, so you are satisfied. You know it is fooling you, but you like to be fooled, because what's on that screen is a lot prettier than the guts of the machine. (The same is true with respect to your girlfriend: her face is prettier than her innards.) So you stick with the representation, the picture, and leave the rest alone. You prefer to settle for the illusion instead of the reality.

Well, Xanth is the picture. The reality is Mundania. In Xanth things are magic, while in Mundania they are dully scientific. If we scraped away the magic, we

would see the ugly guts of it. We would see the state of Florida, with its crowded highways, polluted rivers, and garbage dumps. But what is the point? We prefer to settle for the magic picture, which explains things in a more interesting and sensible way. The same underlying elements are in each, but one is nicer to look at than the other.

How did this Xanth picture come to be? That is dull history, but if you can stand it for a few paragraphs we'll soon get on to the good stuff.

Back in the mid 1970's I was doing two things. (Well, maybe more, if you count eating, sleeping, raising children, earning a living and such. But that is really too dull to mention.) I was setting up to move to the wilderness of central Florida, and I was making contact with a publisher. The Florida backwoods is different from Miami Beach. It is filled with oak trees and pine trees and sinkholes, instead of big hotels and white beaches. But I'm a backward kind of person, and I thought I'd feel more at home there. So we bought five acres on an old overgrown sand dune and put a cabin on it, and later we put a house on it and moved there. We had a wood stove for warmth in the winter, and fans for coolth in the summer, and we got along. We were in the middle of nature; indeed, the bugs liked to come in to join us, including a little horror of the assassin bug tribe called the bloodsucking conenose, or Mexican bedbug, whose bite raised a painful welt a week long. Remember, this was Mundania; this is the way it is there.

Meanwhile, the publisher was what in due course came to be known as Del Rey Books. I wanted to write for them (in Mundania, a singular publisher may be plural; don't ask why), but a complicated Mundanian protocol known as an Option prevented me from giving them a science fiction novel. So I tried fantasy instead, though it was generally known that fantasy was a drug on the market, and suitable mainly for lonely distaff writers, not for aggressive characters like me. I didn't expect to get rich or to have a great time, I was just operating on the principle that a writer can never have enough markets for his work. The normal condition for writers, you see, is borderline starvation; the smart ones have some other source of income, such as a rich inheritance. Also, I wanted to work with an editor who really knew what he was doing, Lester del Rey. Thus I came to sign a contract for *A Spell for Chameleon*.

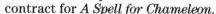

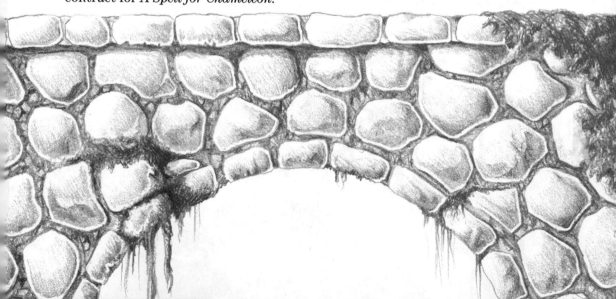

 urprise, surprise! The first surprise was that I did have a good time: I liked this type of writing. It proceeded swiftly and easily, opening out before me like the magic landscape it was. *Spell* was supposed to be a singleton novel, but it acquired a sequel, and then a third to make it a trilogy. That trilogy later expanded, until it was nine novels long. Now I'm starting a second trilogy, which may also be nine novels long. I mean, everyone knows that's the way things are done in Xanth. (Some folks poked fun at me for having a fourth novel in a trilogy, assuming that I really couldn't count. Then other writers, such as Asimov and Clarke, started doing it, and the laughter died away. But the trilogies of those others are relatively puny, running only about half a dozen or so titles.) Once I entered Xanth, I was unable to leave it. Thus I may have been the first to make that discovery, though now hundreds of thousands of readers have made it, too.

The second surprise was that I did get rich and famous from it. You see, the normal novel requires something like a year to write, and is on sale for something like ten days before being buried by a particularly ugly Mundane thing called Returns. Ask any writer! A Xanth novel requires something like three months to write, and it stays on sale forever. This is because of the associated magic; any reader who starts reading a Xanth novel breathes the magic dust between its pages and is instantly addicted. (Yes, I know, there is a grotesque exception: the reviewer. For him the magic reverses. Let's try to ignore this painful aspect.) Not only that, the reader feels compelled to proselytize: he collars his friends and makes them poke their noses in too, so they share his fate. Since a bit of money trickles down to me from each copy sold — about one-eleventh of the cover price, if you want to get technical — I keep getting more money. That's nice. It's like standing under a money tree and collecting the cash that keeps drifting down. (If, however, you buy a copy with the cover torn off, no money descends; that is an illegal sale, and the one who makes it keeps everything after paying nothing for the book. He is chopping down the money tree. If you spy one of those dealers, squeal on him to the authorities.) Xanth #1 won an award from the British Fantasy Society as the best fantasy novel of 1977, which is about my only claim to

HONK!

literary acceptance; the rest of the critical world pans Xanth. As I like to put it: as literature Xanth is a joke, but as a commercial enterprise it is about as solid as anything gets.

So I was pleasantly surprised on one or two counts (I tend to lose count; is that a trilogy?), and kept on with Xanth. But what I really set out to do, if I can remember back to the beginning of this discussion, was to clarify the origins of Xanth. These are mixed right in with the rest of this. Because I really hadn't expected to get into fantasy, I needed to start from scratch. That meant a setting, some characters, and a plot. What could I write about that hadn't been written about before?

Well, there is a fairly standard all-purpose medieval setting for fantasy, wherein men use swords, wizards do magic, and women are beautiful and useless. Bad wizard absconds with lovely maiden, hero rescues her after suffering much difficulty; as a reward, she kisses him. Anyone who wants to be successful in fantasy will do something like this; the old formula is a good one.

> **I never planned to write Xanth. I began writing fantasy at about the time Judy-Lynn del Rey began pushing fantasy. I was lucky to be able to ride the wave.**
> **— Piers Anthony**

So I started with the medieval setting, and the wizards, and a pretty girl. But there is something wrong with my mind; I get turned off by overly familiar stuff. I wanted at least one halfway original element. What could that be?

I mushed it about in my cranium, and in due course squeezed out a revelation. Suppose the magic wasn't limited to wizards, sorcerers, magicians or whatever? Suppose each person had a little? Maybe one magic talent per person. And suppose one person didn't have such a talent, so was an outcast?

That was the breakthrough, and it became the device that started Xanth's fame. It seems that the average reader can identify with being an outcast, just as I can, and also hopes for some redeeming talent. What might Joe's talent be, if he were in Xanth? What about Jane's talent? Everybody might have magic, even if it didn't amount to much. The popular fancy caught on to that, and never let go.

o here was an average young man, growing up without a talent, just as the average person in Mundania does. He was contemptuously called "Bink" because no one took him seriously. He was just coming up on 21, and if he didn't find some magic soon, he would be exiled. It was like flunking your final exam: without that passing grade, you don't graduate, and then you can't get a decent job and you are in effect exiled from our society and everybody thinks you're stupid, and you're not sure but what if they aren't right. Maybe you're really a genius, in some unknown manner —but how do you find out what that is?

Well, the editor liked the notion, but worried that it would seem too juvenile, so we had to raise Bink's age to 25. As it turned out, it didn't matter; 12-year-old readers liked him anyway. In fact, Xanth turned out to have a sizable juvenile market, and that, added to its adult market, made the series a bestseller. (As I write this, Xanth #11, *Heaven Cent*, is the #3 bestseller on the *New York Times* list; that's not bad. Of course there's always room for improvement; how come it wasn't #1? Grump. I get tired of being third-rate.) Young folk evidently understand about magic talent, and the problems of passing and failing.

The setting turned out to be a sort of peninsula. I didn't realize at first what I was doing, and when I caught on, I didn't tell the publisher, because I might have ruined the impression. Folks can be disillusioned when they discover how things are really done. There was one reader who loved Xanth, until he learned that I really work hard to make novels work, and I struggle all day, every day, taking no vacations, to get them right. That disgusted him; apparently he felt that fantasy should spring effortlessly, fully formed, from the author's lofty brow, a work of pure genius unsullied by the mundane details of plotting and characterization and spelling, or of making actual time to write when others had better uses for my time, such as shovelling manure, taking out garbage, and answering fan mail. The next novel he read was #5, *Ogre, Ogre*, and he wrote to a fanzine (amateur magazine) and roundly condemned it because, he explained, of the way the author just "pumped them out." Fortunately, no one else caught on to how hard I work at writing, so the series has continued to prosper. (If you want to know THE

dirty little secret to successful writing, it's WORK. Don't let any other writers know I told.) But you can imagine how the publisher would have reacted if they had known that I had a real model for my fantasy land, and that it hadn't originated entirely inside my bemused Mundane skull.

That model was the Mundane state of Florida. I made Xanth into exactly the same shape, with a big lake in the south and a big swamp in the north and a panhandle projection to the west. I put the North Village at the place where I hoped to build and move, Inverness, and Castle Roogna (named after a correspondent of the time in Estonia, Martin Roogna) in the general vicinity of Tampa. The entire natural landscape of the state translated into that of Xanth, with a bit of magic added. The huge drooping live oak trees with their hanging tentacles of Spanish moss became tangle trees. The bits of lighter knot wood lying on the forest floor became reverse wood, because at first I didn't know where they came from, I just knew that they burned like magic, actually melting down our fireplace grate. The occasional odd tree trunks, with red or purple moss or mold, translated almost unchanged to Xanth, while some with intriguing names, such as silver oak, became literal. After three novels I told the publisher, and by that time the series was well established, so it was too late to stop it, and the true outline of Xanth and its place names like Lake Wails, and Lake Ogre-Chobee, and the Ogre-Fen-Ogre Fen, and the Gold Coast became common knowledge.

> **Writing for me is serious. Even though much of what I write is humorous. Writing, communicating is very important to me. Even before I sold my first story, I was keeping diaries and writing just for myself. If I go too long without writing, I am uncomfortable. I do it almost compulsively; fortunately I'm successful enough that it pays well.**
> **— Piers Anthony**

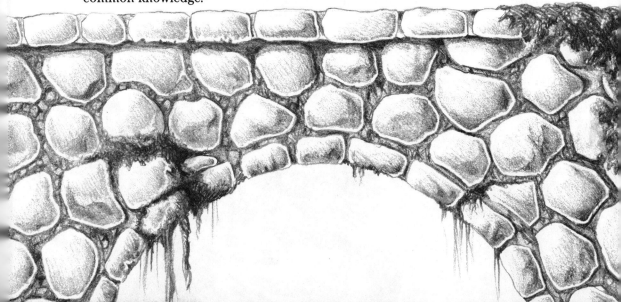

h, but what about the Gap Chasm? That doesn't show on any Mundane map of Florida! Gotcha there, huh, you chortle with the evil glee of a critic.

No you don't. The Gap Chasm is there the same way as everything else is; you just have to see it. Millions of years ago a huge long fault extended across Florida from east to west, angled somewhat. But it got buried under more recent debris: layers of sand, dirt and water, and was forgotten. Only recently did geologists discover it. In fact, they found it only after the first Xanth novel was published; I think that gave them the hint. It was too late to change the maps. But there's an even simpler explanation: the Forget Spell on the Gap Chasm made mapmakers forget to show it. Anyone who falls in it remembers, but since none of those are ever heard from again, the secret remains.

But yes, you are right: there was a more personal origin for the Gap. When we came up to explore our new five acres back in 1975 (we were buying 2½ and taking a reserve on the adjacent 2½, hoping to save the money to buy them in due course), I walked with my daughters through the forest to the east to see the railroad tracks. You see, once, in prehistoric times, there were great beasts known as Trains, very powerful and steamy, and I wanted the girls to see their ancient tracks so that they would stand in proper awe of what existed before those newfangled airplanes evolved and ate up all the passengers. We reached the place where the tracks cut through the sand dune that was now our mountain — I mean, the peak is all of 140 feet above sea level, which is pretty high for Florida — and it was an amazing gap. The steep banks descended maybe 20 feet to the bed below, and up even higher on the far side, where the excavated dirt had been thrown. That impressed all of us. Remember, we had spent our family life in Florida; there are phenomenal ranges of mountains that don't exist here. We gaped at the railroad cut. There were even trees growing down in it, and blackberries; it seemed to be another whole realm. So, slightly (the literary term for it is Hyperbole, which would you believe, is pronounced hy-PER-bo-lee, not Hyper-bole), that cut became the Gap of Xanth. Once they even ran a train up those old tracks, and stored some old

railroad cars there. Naturally the beast of the Xanth Gap had six pairs of whee—, uh, legs, and it steamed as it moved. Later yet, as the magic of Xanth granted my wish and brought me money, we managed to buy a section of that cut. It is still there, but no one remembers it. (Those who prefer more Mundane fiction about that region can read my non-Xanth novel, *Shade of the Tree*, set exactly there. Just don't tell the editor of this book that I mentioned that one; this is supposed to be limited to Xanth.)

So I had the underlying law of magic — one talent per person, similar to the one vote per person supposedly practiced in Mundania. I had the landscape, transcribed at every point from Florida. All I had to do was put together stories involving the two. But there was one more element that entered the series by surprise: the puns.

Xanth started out as light fantasy, but not *that* light. People did get hurt and killed and humiliated. But somehow humor crept in increasingly in the second and third novels, and it took over completely thereafter. The pun is said to be the lowest form of humor (which makes one wonder if the bun is the lowest form of bread). Quite a number of folks claim to hate it. But a similar number love it. I don't regard myself as a punster; Xanth just seems to lend itself to

> **T**he Gap was inspired by the railroad cut that runs through our property. Normally I find inspiration inside myself, not from the environment, but Florida did initially inspire Xanth itself.
> **— Piers Anthony**

puns. Soon readers were sending in puns for me to use in Xanth. I checked them over and used the best ones, giving credit in little Author's Notes to the originators. But this became a problem, because then folks were sending in whole pages of them, just to get their names into print. I try to answer my mail, but I was getting overwhelmed by a hundred letters a month, mostly relating to Xanth. In addition, the editor was getting fed up; he finally lopped off the entire first chapter of *Crewel Lye* to get rid of the puns in it. Something had to be done.

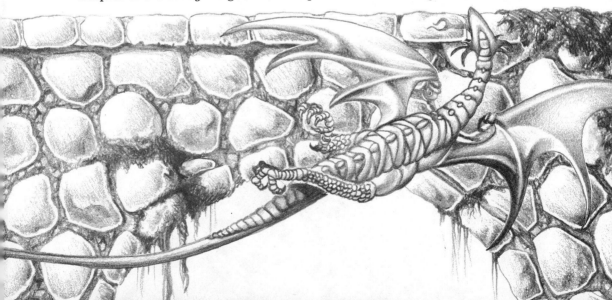

did several things. I went to a computer, so that I could answer a number of letters at one sitting, using computer cards. Once I had a string of 47 cards in one batch. But even with that speedup, there were too many; it got to the point where one month I answered 221 letters and lost half my working time to the mails. That was no good; my output would suffer if I couldn't save more time to write novels. So finally I set up with a secretary. That made my answers less personal, but it recovered some of my time. Some readers don't like that; they don't want a secretary, they don't want a computer, they insist on personal holographic (that is, written in longhand: pen and ink) letters from me. You know how much of my working time it would have taken to do that, in that worst month? All of it. Maybe that would have made those readers happy, but it wouldn't have done much for those who wanted to read my next novels, and it could have become difficult for me to earn my living. Somehow these readers seem to feel that my livelihood doesn't matter; that I owe them all personal answers. One even condemned me for saying that I didn't want even more letters. I replied that when he spent a quarter or half of his earning-a-living time for nonpaying correspondence, then he could criticize me. I didn't hear from him again.

Another thing I did was to tackle the source of the problem. I advised readers in the Author's Notes that I didn't want any more puns, and I stopped using them. *Vale of the Vole* had no reader-suggested puns and no Author's Notes. Thereafter I used a few, but did not encourage them. Xanth itself is no longer as punnish as it once was; now you know why. Oh, the mail continues, but there aren't so many pages of puns in it. Some letters, incidentally, now are from folks who were born after the first Xanth novel was published in 1977.

So Xanth is real, in ways that I didn't anticipate and don't always appreciate. But the fact remains that Xanth is the engine that powers my bestselling career. We live in a nice house now, on a nice property; my wife calls it the house that Xanth built. My daughters grew up on Xanth and are now in college because Xanth made it affordable. Don't tell me it's not real!

Last and least, what about the name? Where did I find the term "Xanth"? The word "Mundania" is adapted from the words used by fantasy fans — you know,

those things made out of bamboo and paper that blow cool air — to describe the rest of us who aren't fans. But Xanth is the magic realm, so naturally it has a phenomenal story behind it, you think. Ha — it's the most Mundanish of them all. Back in the 60's I bought some books of names for babies, which I used for naming the characters in my novels. I liked the name Xanthe, which derives from the Greek word for blond. That is, a fair-haired girl. Maybe I should have named my blond daughter that, but at first I didn't know her hair was yellow, because it was dark; only as it grew out longer did it sunbleach light. So there was this nice name. I used it in a story, "Xanthe's Heart," about a young man who loved his girlfriend Xanthe and wanted her heart; they were in a car accident together, and when he woke up, he had her heart, transplanted to replace his, which had been destroyed along with her life. That story never found a home and was duly retired. So when I needed a name for my fantasy land, I used it, only this time amputating the terminal "e." That did it; editors will buy something after it has been cut or mutilated in some way, though usually they prefer to do the chopping themselves. Thus Xanth, just a chance adaptation. At that point I didn't know there would be more than one novel, or that *A Spell for Chameleon* would sell over 700,000 copies and keep going for over a decade and maybe forever. I thought it was just another novel. I know, I know; I was criminally ignorant. But that's the way it was. Maybe if I thought about it more carefully I would have come up with a more sensible name like Oz or Narnia or Middle Earth or Amber or Shannara or The Land. Sorry about that.

Piers Anthony

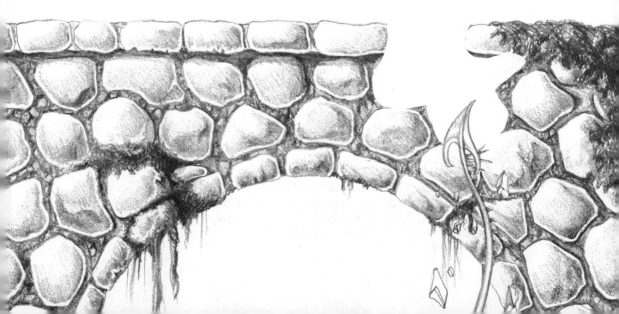

GREAT EVENTS IN THE HISTORY OF XANTH

n its earliest days, Xanth was a peaceful land in which the centaurs were the dominant species. Strong magic abounded. Magical creatures were still fairly primitive. The individual characteristics which made up the new composites hadn't yet blended into a smooth whole. The centaurs themselves appeared rough-hewn, unlike the thoroughly evolved creatures of today.

The first humans wandered into Xanth a few at a time. Most of them died there, but others eked out their livings because they didn't dare to return to Mundania. They had little effect on the land, which continued to exist in peace.

Then, a large number of humans moved into the Peninsula — the First Wave. Believing in safety in numbers, these cut down hundreds of trees, and cleared tracts of land for crops. The Firstwavers discovered that all Xanth was permeated with magic, so they built an enclosure, the first stockade, and burned all greenery and killed or chased away all animals within its confines. They brought in Mundane food and animals, and Mundane women to marry. To their surprise, their children were born with magic. The environmental effect of Xanth was to imbue each real creature born there with a talent. These humans liked the idea of children with magic, and decided to stay.

At first, there was quite enough magic to repulse them, but the denizens of Xanth were so taken aback by the brutality and ravage of the humans' invasion that they did nothing.

There was a time of foolish overreaction when it was discovered that one of the Firstwavers' children could transform lead into gold. The hills were scoured for lead. The Mundanes learned that Xanth had a surplus of gold, and stormed the stockade, killing everyone but the women, whom they married. This was the Second Wave. It was learned too late that one of the dead children was responsible for Xanth's prosperity.

Thu Lanned uv Zanth

an S.A. buy prints door

Eye live inn the Land of Xanth, witch is dis-stinked from Mundania inn that their is magic inn Xanth and 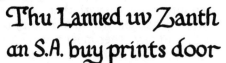 nun inn Mundania. Every won inn Xanth has his own magic talent; know to are the same. Sum khan conjure things, and others khan make a whole of illusions ore can sore threw the heir. Butt inn Mundania know won does magic sew its very dull. They're are knot any dragons their. Instead their are bare and hoarse and a grate many other monsters. Hour ruler is King Trent, whoo has rained four seventeen years. He trance-forms people two other creatures. Now won gets chaste hear; oui fair inn piece. My tail is dun.

This is the only piece of scholarship contributed by King Dor the Communicator to the body of knowledge about Xanth.

The Secondwavers were vicious thieves who committed atrocities, such as the killing of centaurs for meat. A truce was reached, but not until the centaurs had killed half the invading men.

Over time, the Secondwavers became peaceful and settled down. Several generations later, the Third Wave invaded, again killing all but the women, who were once again pressed into marriage with their conquerors. Few of the men survived long, for the women had the lesson of history before them. They killed all the men, using magic and any other means at their disposals.

Realizing that they were now left with no families in the wilderness of Xanth, the women, some old, some battle-scarred, all weary, organized to bring in new husbands. These men were of a completely different breed from the raiders. They were strong, intelligent, fearless men who knew about the history and the magic of Xanth, but remained in spite of them. Young women immigrated too, to marry some of the children, so the bloodlines would not be too closely inbred. The Fourth Wave was the beginning of human dominance of Xanth. It marked the date of a deliberate, thoughtful settlement of the land. Magician-caliber talent began to appear after the Fourth Wave.

The Fifth Wave began again the tradition of conquest and pillage. With the help of an unknown soldier (to whom a small unmarked statue exists in Castle Roogna) and a giant spider, the major assault failed when the nonhuman population of Xanth joined against the invaders. A Forget Spell was detonated in the Gap, thereby rendering it forgettable to anyone who did not live immediately within its environs.

The next seven waves lasted from a few years to several generations before those humans settled down to a life of peace in Xanth.

The Twelfth Wave was the last for 125 years before the ascent of King Trent. Fifteen years after it had ended, a Deathstone of great potency was altered by King Ebnez to form a shield around the whole of Xanth. The shield, which was visible as a sparkling haze in the sunlight, lasted 110 years before it was removed.

The Thirteenth Wave was a deliberate action on the part of the exiled Evil Magician Trent. His army was drilled to use only the force needed to secure the throne for him, and no more. He saw Xanth's isolation as stagnation, and vowed to open the border to the outer world for controlled colonization, as in the Fourth Wave.

There are records of creatures of human descent millennia before the First Wave of colonization, so humans must have been wandering into Xanth long before any numbers of them lived there. As Xanth remains isolated, humans as well as creatures change, becoming gradually more mutated by magic. New blood, Mundane blood, is necessary to Xanth's survival. Even Humfrey is becoming a true gnome as time goes by.

The Fourteenth Wave was an invasion by General Hasbinbad and his Carthaginian mercenaries who crossed the isthmus from the Po Valley in Mundania of 210 to 215 B.C.E., collaborating with a citizen of Xanth known as the Horseman. Trent was incapacitated, so he was succeeded by King Dor. The Mundanes flowed down the western edge of Xanth, taking the invisible bridge they were shown by the Horseman. The creatures of Xanth cooperated to fight them, as they had in the Fifth Wave.

When Dor fell to the power of the Horseman, he was followed by the Zombie Master Jonathan, Good Magician Humfrey, Bink, Centaur Magician Arnolde, Queen Iris, Irene, Chameleon, and the Night Mare Imbrium. In all, there were ten kings pro tem to avoid leaving the throne open for the Horseman to crown himself King. Xanth was saved by Mare Imbrium, who sacrificed herself in the Void to destroy the Horseman's short circuit.

The Time of No Magic: Royal researcher Bink freed the Demon $X(A/N)^{th}$ from its thousand-year penalty in the Game it had been playing. As all magic had issued from $X(A/N)^{th}$ all magic went with it when the Demon left. Living magical creatures gradually began to turn Mundane, and all things created by spells died or vanished. Charmed implements lost their charm, and had to be used as any similar Mundane tool would. Fairies and dragons could no longer fly, though they retained their wings.

It was also because of this Time that the Brain Coral's preservative pool was opened, and Magician Murphy and Neo-Sorceress Vadne escaped from there to Mundania, where Magician Grey (for whom the stork had been summoned on the edge of the Gap Chasm) was born.

There were other benefits to the Time. The effect of the Gorgon's gaze was reversed, so the men who had been transformed into stone were restored to flesh. The victims of Midas bugs and stone-crop also came back to life.

Shortly after Bink set him free, $X(A/N)^{th}$ returned to his cavern voluntarily, to ponder rule changes for an eon or two. (It was believed by King Trent that Bink's awesome talent for protection from magic brought $X(A/N)^{th}$ back, but his theory is not generally known.)

Though it was distressing to all the citizens of Xanth to be without their magic, they appreciate their talents as never before.

Xanth/Mundane Cooperative Ventures: Other than the waves and the odd exile, Xanth had had no official intercourse with Mundania. King Trent and Queen Iris sought to establish trade with a "beleagured Kingdom," a "body of black water" and "surrounded by hostile A's, B's and K's" (Avars, Bulgars and Khazars). While they were making peaceful overtures in the friendly kingdom of Onesti on the Black Sea they were imprisoned by a treacherous usurper. In their efforts to rescue them, King pro tem Dor, Irene, and Arnolde the Magician, a Centaur scholar, established a working relationship with a trustworthy Mundane archivist named Ichabod, who was later allowed access to the libraries of Xanth, and acted as a researcher on Xanth's behalf and friend to Arnolde. Trade agreements with Onesti were thereafter negotiated with the rightful King, Good Omen.

XANTH

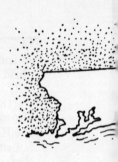

he land of Xanth is a peninsula, which moves around the face of the Earth (some say) to prevent its unique character from being diluted or subsumed by the other cultures that exist in more Mundane lands. Xanth is unusual in many ways, the most important being that it is rich in magic. Species exist there that have never been glimpsed or dreamed of outside its borders. And any child born there is endowed with his or her own magical talent. Over the thousands of years that Xanth has been a magic land, its residents have changed drastically several times. To the untrained eye, Last Wave Xanth resembled the Korean peninsula of the thirteenth century, common era. During the Mundane Era of the Punic Wars, Xanth bore a striking likeness to Italy; to the Avars near the Black Sea, it resembled the Baltic peninsula, and modern Xanth would seem to wear the face of the state of Florida in the United States of America. The human population is somewhere between two and five thousand. No official survey has ever been made of the population of the other species.

Possibly in the ancient past, Xanth was an island, and retained its unique character through complete isolation until the land bridge was formed. Access remains complicated, since Xanth is not fixed in time the way Mundane lands are. If correct timing is not observed, there is no guarantee that the era you left when you entered Xanth is the same to which you would return. Each era "window" lasts between five minutes and an hour, though the window can be left open if it is occupied by a traveler from Xanth, so that he will reenter Xanth in the same time frame he left it. The knowledgeable traveler will watch the color of the water to determine on which era the window is open. To the Mundane (non-Xanth) world at large, Xanth remains a myth, known only in stories and legends. Except during the Waves of Colonization which bring new human settlers, or in the upheaval of a wiggle swarm, it is a peaceful land — for one that uses puns as fundamental building blocks.

THE DEMON X(A/N)th AND THE BALANCE OF EXISTENCE

anth was once a magicless land just like Mundania. Its magic issues from the aura of the Demon X(A/N)th, who became trapped deep underground over a thousand years ago. X(A/N)th was compelled to serve a penalty for failing to complete a formula in the required time during the course of a multiverse-wide Game it is playing with other infinite entities. The Demon has no real name. X(A/N)th is the expressed formula that is the means by which it plays the Game and how the still-running score is determined. The entities negotiate for increases or decreases in value of their terms and exponents, which are not really numbers, but concepts such as gravity, density, luminosity, charm, and other cosmic characteristics. X(A/N)th remains in the depths of Xanth because he is currently contemplating a change of rules in the Game.

Demons are all-powerful and all-intelligent, though not omniscient. The magic that the Demon X(A/N)th emits is only a tiny trickle of his full magical power. His influence issues up through the ground in a sort of solid fountain that reaches the surface as magic dust, which is distributed by the citizens of the Magic Dust Village, situated in the middle of the Region of Madness.

X(A/N)th's magic caused changes to begin immediately in the surface world, first subtly, and then more obviously. Species of plants and animals unlike anything ever before seen began to spring up. (Some of those early ones, like dragons and manticores, escaped to the outside world, where they were described by people who were either turned off as loony or became famous storytellers as a result of their sightings of these fantastic beasts.) Love springs, the residue of X(A/N)th's magic in upwelling groundwater, caused otherwise incompatible species to mate and breed new hybrids. Very soon, combinations of men and beast, beast and beast, beast and plant (samphires), or man and plant (hamadryads) appeared. Centaur history cites the love springs as being responsible for the creation of their species.

Deathstone

Pure human beings, too, were caught in the wave of magic. Adults or children who wandered into Xanth did not acquire magic themselves, but their offspring, the second generation, showed signs of possessing spells and talents of their own. Soon another wave of humanity then found its way into Xanth, much as the first had, and added fresh blood to the population.

Periodically, over Xanth's history, the Nextwavers, or invading bands of men, have entered Xanth. Their incursions were nearly always bloody, but it was always to Xanth's benefit in the long run. Like C. S. Lewis's land of Narnia, it is not necessarily a human's land, but it is good for a human to rule. There have been fourteen waves to date.

To protect Xanth from intruders, a Magician King took a huge Deathstone and tuned it to cast a deadly shield all around the peninsula, guarding its sea borders on three sides and its land border on the fourth. The shield could be opened only briefly for some purposes by certain talented humans. Since it could no longer be diluted by Mundane blood and stimuli, the population of Xanth was in danger of becoming extinct through continual inbreeding. Magical types were not as numerous or as well developed in the early human history of Xanth than later on, and the mutations became stranger. Magic was becoming too concentrated. As before, the children of Mundane settlers had magic. Over many following generations, the adapted humans BECAME magic, evolving into giants, dwarves, gnomes, elves, or mating with other species to become new magical creatures. Over many generations, these new hybrids grew inbred and peculiar.

In the reign of King Trent, that Shieldstone was moved to the cavern of the Demon $X(A/N)^{th}$, and the border was left open to those who could find it.

THE PEOPLE OF XANTH

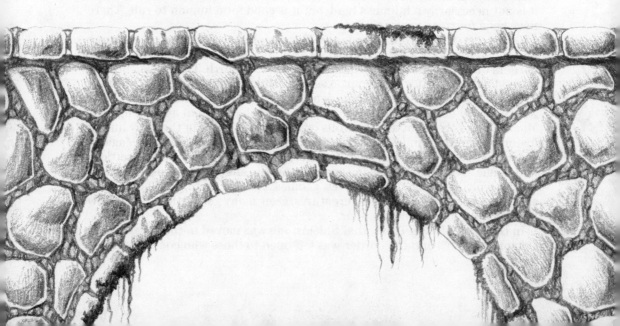

Bear in mind that the origins of Xanth are hopelessly Mundane. When I needed new characters, I just looked around and found whoever fit the part, and that person came into existence. After that, the new character would sort of run his own show. The writing of Xanth has been as much a process of discovery as of invention; it is as if I set up the rules of the game, then explored the ramifications. (Ramifications are like male sheep who run around butting down fortifications; you never can tell what will turn up in the resulting rubble. They are distantly related to the battering rams and the hydraulic rams, all of which tend to be rambunctious.) There is a listing further along of all the characters we could catch; some may have escaped, but just about anybody who is anybody agreed to pose for that occasion.

However, some of the characters developed a hidden side. I didn't set out to do it that way, it just sort of happened, in somewhat the manner of forbidden love. Thus they came to have Mundane analogues. Now in the genre when someone takes real people and writes them into fiction, it is called Tuckerization, after a writer named Wilson Tucker who did that. I never got along well with Tucker, but I give grudging credit where it is due. I didn't do that; all my characters started in Xanth, not Mundania. They just didn't quite stay there.

Well, now that I doublecheck, I see that there were a couple. There was EmJay and Ass MiKe, who compiled the Lexicon of Xanth, published in X9, *Golem in the*

Gears. I made them characters, so they could get in there and do their job. (It is very difficult for a Mundane to get into Xanth via normal channels.) That was so successful that EmJay married half of the Ass, which I suppose makes her husband half — um, maybe I can rephrase that if I think about it. They're nice people who don't deserve such irreverence. Shows you the fate of nice people, in Mundania.

There was also Joey, who made the Isles of Joey in X11, *Heaven Cent.* He didn't appear as a character, but he was named in the story. He was 11 when X11 was published, fittingly. (All things make sense; you just have to fathom how they make sense.)

My daughters could not be excluded, of course, or their horses. Tandy looks just like Cheryl as she was when I wrote *Ogre, Ogre*, and Ivy is like Penny, all the way from three to seventeen. Cheryl's white horse Misty suffered a sex change and modeled for the day horse, and Penny's black horse Sky Blue became Mare Imbri. Blue still likes to play night mare when it gets dark, because she becomes invisible. (Blue was also the model for Neysa the Unicorn in the Adept series. She gets around. The name Neysa came readily, because Blue is a neighing horse; she neighs to say hello, or to call attention to something, or she asks for fee-eee-eee-eed. She's thirty at this writing, and still spry.)

Sometimes my characters do develop in ways I don't expect. Nada Naga was meant to be a bit part and she was going to be a girl of eight. Instead she became a real character, and a girl of fourteen, which complicated everything. I found I had a real character with real problems. Now she is a major character and will be around in Xanth a long time. Grundy also started as a minor plot item and just grew into a very interesting character.
— Piers Anthony

ut mainly it was the other way around. First, of course, is the Ogre: that's me, as in *Bio of an Ogre*. I also identify to some degree with many other characters, such as Bink, who was a nonentity without a talent until he discovered an excellent hidden talent; mine turned out to be writing light fantasy, but if you passed me on the street you would see right away that in Mundania I remain painfully nonentitious. My talent doesn't show physically, you see. But I'm also the Zombie Master in that I'm thin; one article on me likened my body type to that of a praying mantis. I am also fascinated by death. But mainly I'm the vegetarian ogre who smashes down all opposition in the genre publications. Ask anyone who has ever tangled with me there, but don't tell him you're my friend or he'll punch out your lights before answering your question. My special targets for smashing are reviewers and critics; I suspect that the only good critic is a squished one. Well, isn't that obvious? But I didn't set out to pattern these characters on myself; I merely recognized aspects of myself after the characters came into being.

Sometimes I recognize aspects of other folks as I watch my characters. In X12, *Man from Mundania*, the Sorceress Tapis is a grand old lady with singular artistic and magical talent and excellent temperament. When I think of her I think of Andre Norton, who has similar qualities. I think the aspect of the 1987 World Fantasy Convention in Nashville, Mundania, that I remember most fondly are the three breakfasts I shared with her there, chatting about the things authors chat about: problems with agents, publishers and fans. If none of those folks existed, the life of writers would be a lot simpler. I have a kind of contest with her to see which of us can attend the fewest conventions; it's close, but I think I'm gaining.

Some places, too, may have Mundane parallels. There's Lake Ogre-Chobee, and the Ogre-Fen-Ogre Fen, and Lake Wails, and the No Name Key, and the With-A-Cookee River, and the Ever-Glades and who knows what else. The Isle of Illusion just happens to be where so many Mundane efforts to send ships into space occurred; naturally there were some spectacular failures, because Mundanes

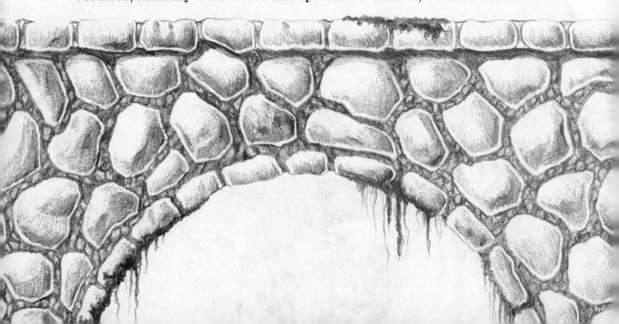

are, well, Mundanes. There's the Kiss-Mee River, where Mundane demons masquerading as the U. S. Army Corps of Engineers channelized that Kissimmee River just the way the demons did in Xanth, with similarly awful results. How much better things might be if demons would just leave the environment alone!

But perhaps the major identifications are the Good Magician Humfrey and the Gorgon. I don't know when it started, but I know it happened, because, well, because. Humfrey became my editor, Lester del Rey: small, old, grouchy, and more knowledgeable than anyone else. Humfrey married the Gorgon, and she became Judy-Lynn del Rey. Here the description is not physical, it's character. Judy-Lynn started as a nice young woman whom it was unwise to cross, and became one of the most formidable figures in the genre and indeed, in Parnassus itself. When her eye fell on something, it knew it had better get moving fast. When his knowledge and her drive combined, Del Rey Books forged to the top of the genre heap. He picked 'em, she promoted 'em, and nonentities like Stephen Donaldson, Terry Brooks, David Eddings and Piers Anthony became the bestselling fantasy authors of the day.

> **Sometimes my fictional characters take on a mundane identity. The Gorgon started without any connection and ended up being very similar to my editor.**
> **— Piers Anthony**

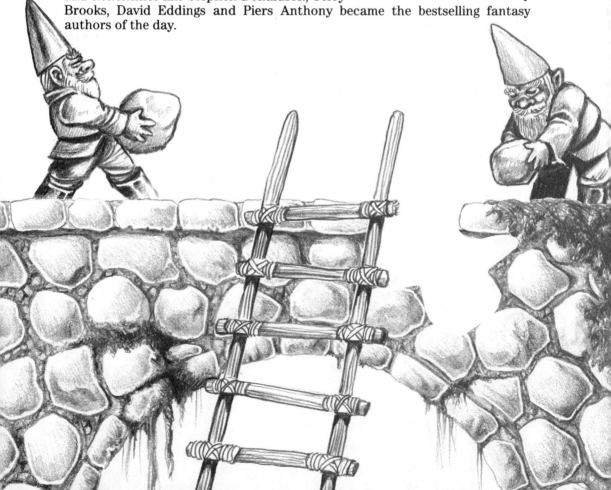

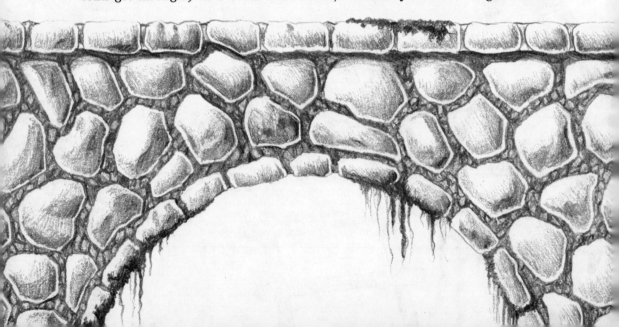

I f you check in the credits section of X7, *Dragon on a Pedestal*, you'll see Judy-Lynn del Rey listed for the Fountain of Youth and Gorgon-zola cheese. The Fountain was to enable Humfrey to live longer, and the cheese — well, you can see that Judy-Lynn knew who she was, even though I never discussed it with her. I did remark that the fans would think she was just another young fan, and she responded, "I **am** a young fan!" Right on. When I said in a Note that the publisher's gaze was like that of the Gorgon when an author was late with a manuscript, a fan wrote something to the effect that it wasn't that bad, and Judy-Lynn wrote on the letter something to the effect of "Ha!" Oh yes, she knew!

Then it soured. I put in things like the Gorgon stoning little bulls so that they turned up in Mundania as statues, but Lester del Rey edited them out. You see, Judy-Lynn had this little collection of Papal Bulls, named after prominent Popes, and one of them even had an agent, the Scott Meredith Agency. In fact, I once received a fan letter sent through that Bull. I guess Lester thought I was playing it too close. He cut that out, and later on got to cutting more. Judy-Lynn — well, there's no nice way to state this. She died. It was a surprise stroke that took her out young. After that, things sort of fell apart between Anthony and Del Rey Books, and my business went elsewhere. It was a tragedy on several levels, and not at all the fun kind of thing you see in Xanth.

Doing Xanth for a new publisher, I had a problem: what to do with Good Magician Humfrey and the Gorgon? I was no longer working with them, and there was not much way their lives could continue to parallel their Mundane versions. No good character ever truly dies in Xanth, even of old age; they just retreat gracefully into the background and let the young ones have the stage. It is part of the Xanth formula to let the protagonist (main character) go see the Good Magician, and have an awful time getting in. (I'm getting more like Humfrey in that respect; with my mail threatening to rise above a hundred letters a month, maybe way above, and people wanting to visit me, I have to slow them down some way. So my residence now has similarities to the Good Magician's castle, and only a few folks get through.) How could I have that, if Humfrey and the Gorgon faded gracefully out? But if they didn't, I would have to risk the Gorgon's death. No way.

So they departed ungracefully: they abruptly disappeared. When Esk Ogre and his companions arrived, the castle was deserted. That started a three-novel mystery — actually a four-novel mystery, because not until Xanth #14, *Question Quest*, do we get to see the whole century-long life of the Good Magician. In the interim, Xanth just has to lurch along without him, until finding a temporary replacement in X12, *Man from Mundania*. At least the challenges at the castle continue! This shows the complications that can arise when real people get tangled up with fictional characters. It is harder to write a script for real folk; they are ornery about going their own ways. I hope real folk stay out of Xanth in the future, but some may sneak in the way the others did.

There are even a few Mundane places that sneak in. Onesti and Ocna, where there is action in X4, *Centaur Aisle*, exist exactly where described: some distance in from the Black Sea (you noticed the black water?) in Rumania. Our intrepid party also ventured through the crimson tide, as far as Montgomery, Alabama, anyway, where they met Ichabod.

MAGIC AND CUSTOMS OF THE PEOPLE OF XANTH

ossession of magic is sometimes dependent upon possession of a soul. Souls manifest as infinitely delicate spheres when separated from the body, and they are infinitely precious. Creatures which do not have souls can BE magic, but as a rule do not possess a magic talent. Creatures which are magic have been magically engendered, such as griffins and dragons. Humans, and their many related races (such as harpies and goblins), have magical talents in proportion to their fraction of souls. The soul can eventually regenerate if a part of it is torn away.

In magical creatures, their magic is considered part of their nature, and not as controllable talent. At first it was believed that all people had talents that were different, but it was found that Curse Fiends all have the same talent, so perhaps they have become magical creatures after all these generations in Xanth. The discovery in the Fourteenth Wave of magical creatures who can do magic changed the existing theories of the nature of talent. Some magically spawned races, such as centaurs, have been established for so long that they have become a natural race, and so have developed their own individual talents.

An old custom among the human population demanded that a young man or woman had to show signs of talent before his or her 25th birthday. That talent didn't have to be interesting, powerful, or even useful. Some could make a colored spot appear on a wall, untangle knots by looking at them, or make roses smell of garlic. To be citizens of Xanth they simply had to have a magical ability of some kind. Nearly all children showed their talent early in life. Those who didn't usually manifested theirs during puberty. To fail to show talent was grounds for expulsion from Xanth. The custom died out around the same time the Shieldstone was removed from the border. People were thereafter accorded respect not for their magic alone, but for their other qualities.

It is considered necessary to exercise one's talent, or it will stagnate. Type of talent depends on need, environment, and personality. The strongest talents in any generation are known as Magician-caliber or Magician-class. In the past, Magicians have come forward who were capable of doing matter transformations or creative meteorology. Magic itself is neither good nor evil; it is the intent with which it is used that designates whether the user will be known as the Evil Magician, or the Good Sorceress. As Queen Irene noted, there is an ethical dimension to power, especially great power. It should be used responsibly, or not at all.

Talents tend to overlap, though with two notable exceptions no two have ever been exactly the same. The strength of talents is not hereditary except in the case of ogres, whose hereditary talents are strength and stupidity, and the Curse Fiends, who all have the same magic; there is no way to predict what type or potency of talent a human child will develop. But there is one exception: because Bink did the Demon $X(A/N)^{th}$ the favor of freeing him, the Demon (prompted by Cherie Centaur) made all of his descendants have Magician-class magic. Thus, Dor had it, and Ivy and Dolph. That was to make a big difference in the history of Xanth, and to usher in what may someday come to be known as the Golden Age, with a number of Magicians and Good Kings.

It used to be that the King was chosen by the leaders of Xanth from the available Magicians. Now, with Magicians being in the direct line of descent, it has become in effect hereditary, and women can be King too. Xanth is hopelessly oriented on male prerogatives, to Queen Irene's ire, but progress is being made. No Queen can rule, but a female King can.

Spider Queen

Of course the other species of Xanth have their own leaders, and these regard themselves as rulers of all Xanth, because they don't take much account of human politics. So the Dragon King is the supreme ruler of Xanth, and so is the Lord of the Flies, and the King of the Elves, and the Goblin King, and the King of the Basilisks, the Night Stallion of the Gourd, and so on. It's all a matter of viewpoint. Sometimes liaisons are made between royal houses, as when Prince Dolph is betrothed to Princess Nada Naga. It all works out. Since the Xanth histories that are smuggled into Mundania are for a human audience, the perspective of the human species tends to be followed, but this should not be taken too seriously.

MAGICIANS AND KINGS

The last King of the Fourth Wave was Roogna, best known for his talent, which was adapting living magic to his purposes, and as the architect of Castle Roogna, the first central seat of human government in Xanth. Roogna was a gentle, pudgy, solidly built man in coveralls who enjoyed gardening. He appeared to be an unlikely defender against the Fifth Wave, though it was under his direction that Xanth was mustered.

Roogna's contemporaries were Magician Murphy, Jonathan the Zombie Master, and Neo-Sorceress Vadne. Murphy's talent was making things go wrong. His is a subtle magic: almost nothing is immune to his influence. What can't be misdirected might just refuse to work. Murphy made a wager with Roogna that the Castle wouldn't be finished in time to stand as a defense against the Fifth Wave. He was not a traitor to Xanth; it was of academic interest to him whether he could be beaten.

Jonathan the Zombie Master was the third Magician of the era of Roogna. His talent is the power to animate the dead. If any corpse is brought to him, no matter how poor its condition, Jonathan's power causes it to move with a half-life forever, unless the zombie is torn into too many small pieces. Jonathan was a solitary child and then a solitary man until he met Millie the Maid. They fell in love and would have married if it hadn't been for the interference of Neo-Sorceress Vadne. Jonathan committed suicide and spelled himself into a zombie, which he remained for 812 years until he was disenchanted by a Restorative Elixir he had brewed and entrusted to a barbarian named Dor.

Neo-Sorceress Vadne's talent, topology magic, was not considered to be of Magician-caliber. She was able to change the form of living things without changing their nature. She was bitter that her magic didn't get the recognition she felt she deserved, and she was jealous of Millie, so she used her magic to transform the girl into the shape of a book. For her crime, she was sent

Vadne

through the vanishing hoop into the storage pool of the Brain Coral, to be preserved indefinitely.

The fourth Magician of the Fourth Wave was the Sorceress Tapis, creator of the great Castle Roogna Tapestry. Her talent was sewing tapestries that enable folks to step into their worlds. Her needlework could be entertaining or predictive, depending on need. Her picture tapestries functioned similarly to magic mirrors, displaying to those with sufficient will to control them scenes in the past or the present. At other times, the magical moving figures in the designs provide simple entertainment, showing pleasant sights of beauty and plenty. The great historical Tapestry was intended to be a gift to Zombie Master Jonathan. Her home was a large thatched cottage in the forest, near a patch of chocolate milkweed. Two trees in her garden held neatly the warp and woof of her work, so that she needed only to ply her shuttle for the picture to begin to form.

Tapis also embroidered the partially completed coverlet intended for the Sleeping Beauty whose sarcophagus was accidentally occupied by Electra, whom Tapis was using to complete the Heaven Cent. Tapis ran afoul of Magician Murphy, but survived his curse, perhaps because she was a good person.

King Gromden was the last King to occupy Castle Roogna after its construction. He ruled four hundred years after Roogna. His talent was knowing the complete history of any item he touched. After Gromden died,

the Kings of Xanth ruled from their home villages for the next four hundred years. He was succeeded by Magician Yang, who married Gromden's daughter Threnody. Threnody committed suicide soon after her marriage.

Yin-Yang were two halves of the same Magician's personality. He was King of Xanth four hundred years after King Roogna, ending the dynasty that used the Castle as the center of government. Yin, Magician of light who must always use magic positively and tell the truth, was forced to serve the half known as Yang, Magician of darkness, who always uses magic negatively and lies, after Yang won the competition for the throne set by King Gromden. After Yang became King, Castle Roogna stood empty, for Yang preferred decentralized government.

Most spells and enchanted objects in Xanth date from his reign, for his talent was making spells which, in spite of his nature, are neutral, because magic is a matter of symbolism and intent, and objects have no intent. All object spells are his, even the ones before he lived, like the Gap Forget Spell, and the others in the royal arsenal.

Xanth declined after Yang was gone, for he had managed to destroy its focus.

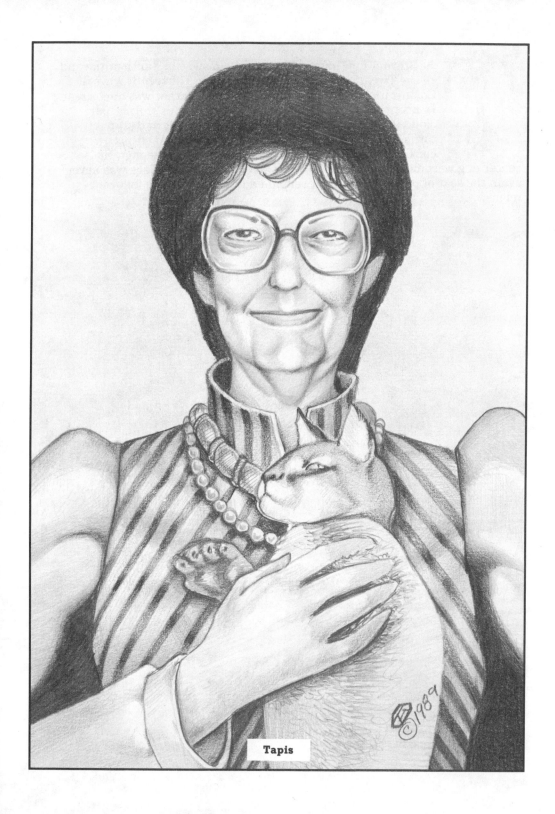

Tapis

The Storm King (name unknown) held sway in Xanth at the end of the Twelfth Wave until just before the Thirteenth Wave of Colonization. His power to control the weather was once great. In his prime he was able to conjure enormous storms, part clouds in the midst of hail, call up hurricanes and stop tornadoes, but in his old age, the talent weakened considerably. He could barely summon a light zephyr. His center of government was in the North Village. Though the village was never again the seat of power of Xanth, it remained important in the following reigns.

CLOUSE '89

uring the Thirteenth Wave, Trent the Transformer, formerly known as the Evil Magician, was the King of Xanth. He was exiled from Xanth in his twenties for trying to take the throne by treachery. He spent the next two decades in Mundania rethinking his motivations and establishing a conquering force. He married a Mundane woman and had a son by her, but both the wife and child died of a mysterious flu virus. Thereafter, Trent devoted himself to reentering Xanth and putting himself on the throne, but this time by reasonable if not peaceful means.

He was helped indirectly in his pursuit by Bink.

Few people know the actual details of Bink's talent. He was exiled by the Storm King under the old custom for having no demonstrable magic. His talent is purely defensive and probably the most complex in Xanth. Bink cannot be harmed by magic. Even when an enemy detects the nature of his talent, it will still conspire to protect him. At times, his magic has to make value judgments on what will best keep him from harm. Only a purely physical attack without the use of magic can hurt Bink.

Bink was eventually convinced of the validity of Trent's motives and willingly gave him his help. When the Evil Magician turned Good King Trent ascended the throne and judged the ramifications of Bink's talent, he made Bink the Royal Researcher of Xanth. Bink's job would be to investigate and discover the source of magic of Xanth and bring his findings to the attention of the King (see *Time of No Magic*).

The Demon $X(A/N)^{th}$ has bequeathed to all Bink's descendants the full magical talents of Magician-caliber, though neither he nor his family knows that. He has continued to explore and examine magical curiosities throughout Xanth, and also acts as a liaison between Xanth and some parts of Mundania.

Chameleon is from the Gap Village. Her talent is phasic. During a quarter of the month, she appears as Wynne, supremely beautiful, sweet, and hopelessly stupid. Her beauty fades as her intelligence increases. When she is completely average in both looks and brains, she is known as Dee. The metamorphosis continues until she is

Bink meets $X(A/N)^{th}$

absolutely ugly, bad-tempered, and brilliant. Her name in that phase is Fanchon. During the final fourth of the month, she changes to Dee on the way through to becoming Wynne again, though each time Wynne is beautiful in a different way. Chameleon has no control over her talent. Like the animals of Xanth, she appears to be magical, rather than to have controllable magic. She married Bink, who enjoys her constant variety.

The Sorceress Iris, Mistress of Illusion, is capable of creating the image of anything she wants to, down to accurate sound, smell, taste, and, to a limited

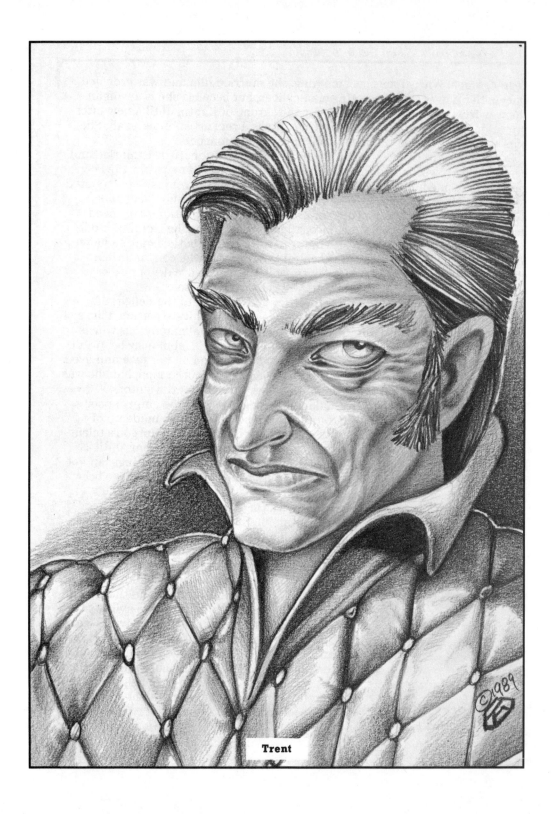

Trent

degree, touch. When Trent became King, she married him and was crowned Queen. Her power is genuine Magician-caliber, but because she is a woman, she was frustrated in her ambition for the throne of Xanth, until a new interpretation was made of the office of King. Iris is a real artist of her craft. She puts the most detailed touches to any illusion she concocts.

Good Magician Humfrey is the Magician of Information. He is a gnarled and bent old dwarf with a bad temper. No one knows how old he is, but the best guess is over one hundred years. Humfrey is an inquiring genius. He is reputed to know a hundred spells, all of which are used for uncovering facts and accruing knowledge. Many people approach him with Questions they need answered. They figure that if he doesn't know the Answer, he can find it out. Humfrey is a hermit by nature. He hates to have people bother him, so he puts as many obstacles in the way of potential Querents that he can, and then charges a year's service for one Answer. Only those who are desperate or serious enough about their Questions will get through to see him.

Early in the reign of King Trent, Humfrey got married, to the delight of everyone who had been in his service, who felt that they were getting a little of their own back by seeing Humfrey enter the bonds of matrimony. His wife is the Gorgon, a nymph from the Region of Madness. She is fabulously beautiful and shapely, but no man before Humfrey had ever gazed on her face and lived. Anyone who looked at her was turned to stone. She admired men, but she was lonely because her talent always made statues out of potential suitors. Humfrey solved the problem by making her face invisible. The empty space where her head should be is surrounded by her hair, which is made up of hundreds of tiny, hissing snakes. Like her sister the Siren, the Gorgon's talent was directed only at men. But when she matured, so did her talent, until it affected women, too, and even other living things. Had the Good Magician not made her face invisible, all living things around the Gorgon would have been stoned.

After making the Gorgon serve a year waiting for the Answer to the Question she asked ("Would you marry me?"), Humfrey married the Gorgon. Humfrey had always been using the water of the Fountain of Youth to keep himself a crochety hundred years old, but after his wedding, he youthened himself enough to father children.

Hugo, first child of Humfrey and the Gorgon (HuGo), has the unimpressive ability to conjure fruit. When enhanced by Ivy, Hugo's talent improved immensely, as did his looks and intelligence. Though each enhancement is temporary in effect, a little more improvement accrues each time. With Ivy's help, Hugo's intellect and fruit-conjuring talent stopped a wiggle swarm.

Bink

Good Magician Humfrey and Gorgon

he Fourteenth Wave: Dor, the son of Bink and Chameleon, is the Magician of Communication with the Inanimate. Any nonliving thing can speak with him. Dor is married to Irene, daughter of Trent and Iris.

Dor traveled into the Castle Roogna Tapestry to visit the era of King Roogna. His intention was to secure a Zombie Restorative from the Zombie Master so that the zombie Jonathan could live again. While he was there, he and his companion Jumper (q.v.) heroically assisted Roogna in his efforts to repulse the Fifth Wave.

When King Trent abdicated after the attack of the Horseman, Dor ascended the throne.

Irene, present Queen of Xanth, has as her talent the Green Thumb. She can make any plant grow from seed to maturity by ordering it. Her talent was not considered to be of Magician-caliber until her first pregnancy when it was enhanced by her unborn daughter, but she reigned as the eighth temporary King of Xanth during the Horseman's incursion. Irene is as beautiful as a nymph, and has fine legs, which she showed off in tantalizing glimpses during her youth. The color of her panties was a subject of much speculation among the males of the court.

Ivy is the eldest child of Dor and Irene. Her talent is that of Enhancement, a powerful and subtle magic similar in potency to her grandfather Bink's. Anything she enhances increases in the qualities she chooses. If she feels that a monster is nice, it will become nice. If she enhances the blueness of a flower, it will become more blue than any other flower that ever bloomed. She is cute and curious about everything, and always puts herself in the way of adventure. Her mother, Irene, grows tiny ivy plants for her and Dor to wear so they always know Ivy is all right.

Dolph is Ivy's younger brother. He is the Magician of Shape-change. His talent is similar to that of their other grandfather, Trent, whose magic is Transformation of Others, but directed toward himself instead of toward other living things. Although he frequently disagrees with his big sister, they love each other, and have in-jokes between themselves. Phlod Firefly, Prince Dolph's alternate identity in dragonform, is his name spelled backwards. The designation came from a game that he and Ivy played when they were children. He has also gone about in the form of Trilobyte, an armored swimming fossil arthropod with extra memory, when he visited Draco Dragon's nest. He has also taken the shape of a fire-breathing dragon, a werewolf, a tree, a tiny fly, and a food-conserving ant.

Grey Murphy is the son of Magician Murphy and Neo-Sorceress Vadne. He has hair-colored hair and neutral eyes, and his first eighteen years were dull even by Mundane standards, but he's a decent guy. He became betrothed to Ivy in the middle of a hate spring. His Magician-caliber talent is the Nullification of Magic, but his wisdom and native ability for problem solving set him to fill an important gap in Xanth. He can show many complex expressions on his face, such as I'm Saying This For Your Own Good, Now You Know This Is Foolish, and This Is Not The Time To Disabuse You Of Notions.

Dor

HARPIES AND GOBLINS

The higherarchy and lowerarchy: harpies and goblins are traditional enemies, since neither can suborn the realm of the other. The goblins hold sway under the earth and in darkness, the harpies hold sway above it and in day. In the beginning the part-human races needed to join their strengths against the early wavers, and sometimes even shared the same caves. In time, the goblins grew greedy for the harpies' space in the caves and drove them out.

Goblins are ugly humanoids half the height of a man, with large hands and feet. Their heads are as hard as stone, so it is impossible to hurt one by coshing it, but their hands and feet are very soft. They prefer to attack a victim in large numbers and under unfair circumstances. All goblins are cowards, and have nasty dispositions. No fewer than four or five will set upon a single man if he wanders accidentally into their demesne. Most modern goblins fear the light, but some still go about in full daylight, such as the Goblinate of the Golden Horde, the meanest gang north of the Gap. Goblins like to eat candied insects and bugs, or indeed any kind of meat.

The goblins blame the harpies for blighting the sight of the female goblins so they were only attracted to the weak and ugly males. Goblins claim they used to be the handsomest, smartest, strongest and bravest of the half-human races. Because of the harpy curse, in the long run only the goblin-wimps were able to find wives, so there is nothing left in the goblin caves but beautiful females and ugly males.

The harpies, on their side, are just as rude and cruel as the goblins. They blame the goblin women for stealing the harpy cocks away using the lure of their limbs. The counterspells to stop the feud were not invoked until the early Fifth Wave, after a human intervened.

Harpies have the heads and breasts of women; and the bodies, great greasy wings, and short ugly legs of vultures. They come from the love-spring cross of

Harpy

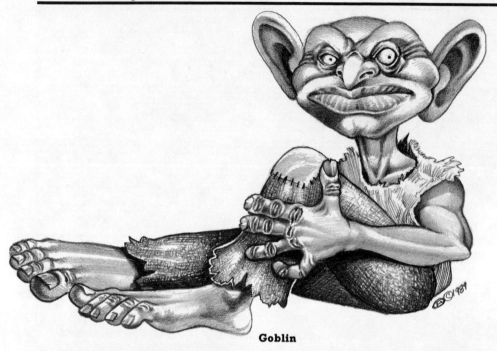

Goblin

a human and a vulture, though history does not record which sex was what species. They can fly, and their talons are sharp but usually chipped and stained from lack of personal care. They prefer the taste of meat, and will eat the entrails of humans if they can.

Most harpies are ugly and dirty, but the youngest females are beautiful and clean. It is only after decades of bitter and abusive spinsterhood that they begin to neglect themselves. A few handsome male harpies exist, but far and away (the best way to view harpies) the greatest number are female. When no male harpies have been hatched, the females propagate the species by mating in alternate generations with men and with vultures. Each flock is ruled by a Queen. All males are considered to be princes, because there are so few of them. The males must obey the Queen, but the females are reluctant to alienate the few males they have by denying their wishes.

They live in grimy holes dibbled into the sides of cliffs, and use their dung for building. They save unhatched eggs as weapons, for harpy eggs explode in an unbelievable stench, and spray mess all over the landscape.

It was discovered by Glory Goblin and Hardy Harpy that goblins and harpies, half-humans all, have "half-talents." When the appropriate pair of harpy and goblin join up, they can do magic. Glory's and Hardy's half-talents are for invisibility. The two species are negotiating an armed truce for exploring their new powers. They feel that humans have had a monopoly on magic too long, and it's their turn for a share.

The thing to remember is that Xanth was not always magic. There was a time before Demon X(A/N)th arrived when it was Mundane, unpleasant as it may be to mention this. When the Demon brought the magic, and it started filtering out into the surrounding region, the Mundane creatures and plants began to change. Many retain some semblance of their original natures, but often only their names suggest it. For example, shoe trees once supported shoes instead of producing them.

Now, with the magic strong, there is constant change. New species develop, and old ones merge. Thus, after many hundreds of years, the species of winged centaurs is arising, and Gloha the winged gobliness is born of a goblin-harpy union. There is no telling what may happen in the future!

Winged Centaur

DEMONS

emons are not very attached to their shapes. They can change their forms into anything they wish. A demon can turn into a cloud of vapor, but it can't remain in that form for long. It must be solid at least ninety percent of the time, or lose cohesion permanently. Because of their shapeshifting ability, it is difficult to hurt demons, and nearly impossible to kill them. They can become vapor to avoid a blow; or turn to steel and dent whatever is striking out at them.

A demon in its natural form is easy to distinguish. Its hind feet are hooflike, it has a long tail with barbs at the tip, and fiery, glowing eyes. Demons are interested in the sensual pleasures, and seek to share them with other creatures, willing or unwilling. Stories exist of mortals who have enjoyed the company of demon lovers. Demons can mate with other species and produce children who have characteristics of each parent. Threnody, daughter of the human king Gromden, was half-demon. She had a human's magic talent, and possessed some demon-like traits of personality.

Most demons have pointed horns, though Beauregard, Humfrey's once bottled advisor, has only vestigial ones. His tail has a soft tuft instead of a barb, and he wears glasses. Nevertheless, he is a powerful demon in the Demon Realm. Fiant, a very male demon who harassed the half-nymph Tandy, has sharp horns and a many-barbed tail. Some demons, like Metria, have only the glowing eyes, dusky skin and pointed teeth to show that they are of the demon kind.

Demons have far more sensitive hearing than humans do, and are especially bothered by the sound of hummers. In seeking to ruin the Kiss-Mee River valley to drive away its inhabitants, they managed to make it unliveable for their own kind.

They can phase in and out through walls. Very little can keep a demon out of a place it wishes to go. If one senses that it can make mischief, it will come back again and again unless physically or magically prevented. Fiant was kept from bothering Tandy again by being stuffed into the gourd, where his soul was exchanged for hers. Demons enjoy pleasing themselves at the expense of other beings.

Beauregard the Demon

CENTAURS

everal crossbred races in Xanth are descended from horses. Foremost among them are the centaurs. From the waist up, centaurs have the heads, arms and chests of humans. From the withers down, they have the four-legged body and tail of a horse. Their hooves are magically hard, to prevent chips and breakage. The centaur race was engendered many ages ago by three human men and their mares who had wandered into Xanth and drunk from a love stream.

The waist of a centaur is remarkably supple, as he might need to turn around where there isn't room to back his long horse body. Both male and female centaurs stand taller than human folk. The fillies are accustomed to being stared at by human males, for their mammary development is considered spectacular by human standards. Centaurs do not place the same stigma on natural behaviors, such as sex, nudity, or evacuation that humans do. They have other taboos which humans do not often understand.

Centaurs are fierce fighters and strong-bodied. Even a filly can hoist the weight of her equine body using only her human arms. Their faces usually show their half-heritage in the length of the nose. Centaur ladies let their hair grow down all the way to the saddle area, and wear their tails long, too. Beauty, which is a less important characteristic among centaurs than among humans, is considered more in the light of their horse-halves. Chester Centaur has a homely face, but an exceedingly handsome posterior. His wife Cherie has a beautiful human half as well.

They run in herds, and rule themselves by a council of elders which thoroughly discuss important matters and make accordingly wise decisions. Centaurs once seemed to age at approximately a quarter of the speed humans did, so that a centaur colt of twenty was still just a tot. But time can be odd in Xanth, and it later was apparent that no such ratio can be maintained. Cherie's foals Chet and Chem aged at the same rate as Chameleon's foal, uh, baby Dor, and Chem's foal Chex, being a crossbreed between a centaur and a hippogryph, aged between the human and animal rates. Thus Chex was mature and ready to mate while the human Ivy, four years older, was still a child. It's hard to tell how rapidly Chex's son Che will age, as he hasn't been

Chester Centaur

foaled yet, but the human rate seems likely. Centaur physicians are called vets.

Centaurs, though partly magic in origin, have full magical talents. However, polite centaur society considers magic to be obscene, so few of their talents have been described, let alone realized by their possessors. They use a croggle test (a pun on the Mundane Coggins test for horses, and fans who get croggled — see *fantasy fan* under *Magical Things of Xanth*) to discover whether a centaur has been infected by magic. Some are even considered Magician-caliber, such as Arnolde the Archivist, a hundred-year-old Appaloosa centaur, who now serves as the ambassador of trade between Xanth and Onesti. His talent, that of an invisible radius of magic which he can carry outside Xanth, is only observable in the absence of magic. His Centaur Aisle is of considerable use beyond the borders for any traveler who wants to employ his talent abroad. Centaurs are usually the most wise and logical of creatures. It is curious that they would not accept extant facts about themselves.

Herman the Hermit, a hero of Xanth, was a centaur of great wisdom and courage. He gave his life to save the land from the wiggle infestation in the days of King Trent. Herman could summon will-o'-the-wisps, mischievous dancing lights that could lead one into the wilderness and lose one there. He was an outcast from his own people because he recognized his talent. His nephew, Chester Centaur, possesses the ability to manifest a sweet silver flute which plays beautifully with no hand or lip touching it. Herman was the first centaur to realize that centaurs had been in Xanth so long they had become a natural species, and so were able to be born with talents.

Chester's wife Cherie grudgingly acknowledges that centaurs have magic, but refuses to come to terms with her own ability. Cherie is otherwise an excellent tutor to young Dor, who is undoubtedly a Magician. (Obscenity is tolerated in humans, who are considered a lesser species by the centaurs.) Their foals, Chet and Chem, make use of their magic, as it is not considered anathema among the humans with whom they associate. Chet can make large things small, but he can't reverse the process. The most useful facet of his talent is that he transforms rocks into calxes, which are used in calculus, so the more rocks he shrinks, the more the effect of his magic grows. Chem's talent has more widespread uses. She can manifest, in thin air, a map of any terrain she has seen.

The Centaur Isle is the center of learning in Xanth. Even the least intelligent centaur is more brilliant than any human. Scholarship is valued in centaur society. Chester, who seems to be a fool in most other matters, is an expert in mathematics, specifically horsepower applications. Most Xanth children, if they are able to, attend centaur school to get their basic education. Hobbies and other occupations are valued for letting the mind rest between studies. Centaurs play chess and other games of strategy, and practice useful handcrafts. A popular game among centaurs is people-shoes, played with stakes and the fruit of a shoe tree.

Centaurs have a high regard for honor, and a centaur's word is inviolate. They are independent in nature and have perfectly developed powers of observation. They are the humans' most important allies.

Arnolde the Archivist

OTHER RACES OF EQUINE DESCENT

 egasi are handsome winged horses who graze in the treetops. They are members of the winged monsters, a loosely organized multispecies group led by the centaur Cheiron.

Hippocampi are sea horses with the head and forefeet of horses and the tails of dolphins. The forefeet end in flippers rather than hooves, and the tail curls in a muscular loop when at rest.

Night mares appear to be nothing but sleek, pretty Mundane equines, solid black even to their hooves, except that their eyes glow faintly, and their hoofprints resemble the face of the moon.

Their home is the gourd, where they are led by the Night Stallion, Trojan, who is also known as the Dark Horse. Trojan commands all the disembodied beings of the gourd, for he rules the realm of dreams. It is the responsibility of the night mares to carry dreams crafted within the gourd to sleepers of the outside world who need them.

Trojan, who has power over all dreams, is really a prisoner in the gourd. He cannot visit the solid world as his mares do, unless he pays for it with the souls of those who lost them in the gourd. He won the job of Dark Horse by defeating the last King of Dreams to hold the office. When Smash Ogre bested Trojan, the Night Stallion offered to make him Dark Ogre in exchange for being set free, but Smash refused.

To uneasy sleepers, the night mares look like huge nebulous monsters with gleaming white eyes and glinting teeth, for they bear bad dreams to those who deserve them, or who need them when solving problems. The purpose of night mares is to force a dreaming mind to suffer the pangs of conscience or regret, the realization of the consequences of evil. The immortal night mares "guard constantly against spiritual degradation" (*Ogre, Ogre*, p. 258). For example, a misogynist, a man who hates women, was once visited with a horrible bad dream of being loved to death by a score of beautiful mermaids. To some, that

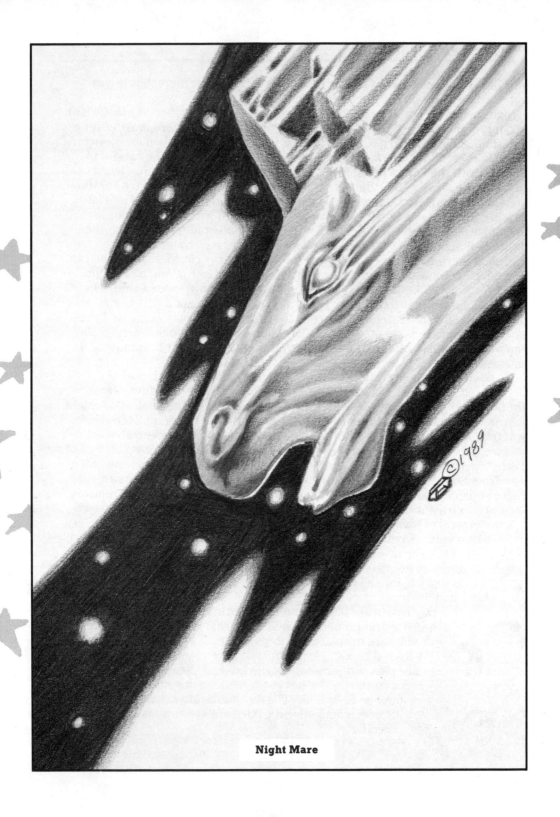

Night Mare

may be a wonderful dream rather than the gift of a night mare, but it was appropriate to prod that dreamer's conscience.

Night mares do not have souls. Those who gain souls soon become inefficient. It is not in the nature of souls to be truly brutal, as a night mare must be on occasion. Those who earn souls turn them in to the Night Stallion for storage and bonus credit for extraordinary service. A night mare must be careful to frighten with the fewest possible images so that the dreamer will not learn to consider dragons or other dangers passe. Night mares are immortal until they are foolish enough to keep a soul. Then they assume the liabilities of mortality, as Mare Imbrium did. Some may eventually get bored with their jobs and seek to change occupations. If they choose, they may mate and foal and turn the position of night mare over to their offspring.

A night mare is not actually solid while outside of the gourd, though one can be ridden by someone who is asleep. A rider need not fear falling off a night mare, for if she consents to carry you (and the price is high: half a soul), the mare will always be the right size. Night mares cannot speak aloud, but make dreamlets of a nonfrightening nature in the mind of an awake being, and those say what the mare wishes to express. They only come when one is asleep. They can phase through solid matter under cover of darkness, be it a shadow or a smokescreen.

On each mare's hoofprint, that sea which was named in her honor is highlighted: i.e., Mare Crisium (called Cris or Crisis), Mare Imbrium, Mare Humerum, Mare Nubium, Mare Frigoris, Mare Nectaris, Mare Australe. A night mare's moon hoofprint fades as the moon changes into lesser quarters. She will tend to slip because of the lack of traction unless she concentrates.

Mare Imbrium, known as Imbri, whose name means "Sea of Rains," or "Sea of Tears," was once a night mare, and an artist at her craft. After receiving half a soul from Smash Ogre, she was transferred to daydream duty by her sire, the Night Stallion. It was a kindness, for she had always wanted to see the rainbow, but also extra duty, because she was now expected to act as liaison between the Powers of Night and the Powers of the Day during the rise of the Fourteenth Wave. She defeated the Horseman by sacrificing her body in the Void. Because she had a soul, she was restored to life, and continues her career as a true day mare. She is perhaps better suited to this job, for she has a gentler nature than she needs for handling bad dreams.

Day mares are happy, careless creatures who do not work at the same frantic pace as their nocturnal counterparts. If their dreams are misplaced or forgotten, or if a double supply is delivered to a single dreamer, it doesn't matter. Daydreams are pleasant fancies, designed to rest the mind in contentment. Unlike a night mare, a day mare has a soul, but she is invisible. The day mares are ruled by the Day Horse, a magnificent golden stallion, who is a very casual leader.

Pegasus

FAIRIES, IMPS, ELVES AND GNOMES

airies and imps are the smallest of the humanlike creatures in Xanth. They are delicate and dainty, measuring no more than the size of a man's hand. Their wings have colorful flowerlike images on them which sometimes change. Fairies who are destined to fall in love display the glow of love at first touch. Fairies do fine craftwork, though always on a very tiny scale. Imps make small magic items out of ephemeral materials, such as mirrors from soap bubbles.

Elves are the next largest. They live in organized tribes, each led by a King. The elves have been known to come forward to help defend Xanth. They are known by their traditional battle attire, which is always green.

Gnomes are about one third the size of men. They are short-armed and short-legged, leaving their bodies somewhat out of proportion to their size. Female gnomes are called gnomides. Gnomes are extremely forthright, but temper their bluntness with occasional civility. The gnomides are much nicer than their menfolk.

Like goblins, gnomes have been known to eat intruders if they look tasty. Gnomes favor red clothing and battle attire. The hat is one item of wear which no gnome will ever be found without. They hang on to their hats to keep the aversion spells they wear there, to drive away monsters. One underground village of the gnomes can be reached through a hollow artis-tree in the forests near the site of Threnody's ancient cottage, northwest of Castle Roogna. Their job is mining. They hollow endless tunnels in the rock below Xanth.

OGRES

gres talk in simple rhyme, though unrhymed speech would save them time. When ogres are hungry for some meat, any flesh is thought good to eat. Normal-sized ogres stand twice man-height tall, wear their own shaggy skin and nothing else at all. An ogre's strength is legendary; no limit to what he can carry. Ogres' arms are like tough gnarled wood, and their faces do not look even that good. Hairy muscles knot like the boles of old trees, and they can wrestle a full-sized dragon to its knees. Even the handsome ones are grotesque; the ugly ones are a horrible mess. Bad storms and spoiled food are ogres' delight, they also like to shout and fight. Their hands and feet are huge, their voices a roar, their manners are awful, and all of them snore. They're so dirty bugs live in their pelt, but skin is so tough raises never a welt. They like jokes that are easy to tell, as ogres don't think very well.

The best of all the ogre bunch, they call he by the name of Crunch. All ogres gnaw on human bone, 'cept Crunch because of Fiend Curse thrown. Crunch is a good cook of vegetarian fare — humans are his friends; let their foes beware. Crunch found she with face like mush, whose smile could make a zombie blush. A Curse Fiend all made up was she, no time to explain when carried off by he. They wed; an ogret arrived with a crash. In ogre fashion, they named him Smash. Smash is half-human, which his folks think is dandy. When he grew up, he married half-nymph Tandy. Ogre courtship is rather rough, so it takes a she who is quite tough.

Ogrets are tougher than little dragons. Except that it is impossible to keep ogrets out of trouble, they are easy to care for. They eat anything, and it is nearly impossible to hurt one.

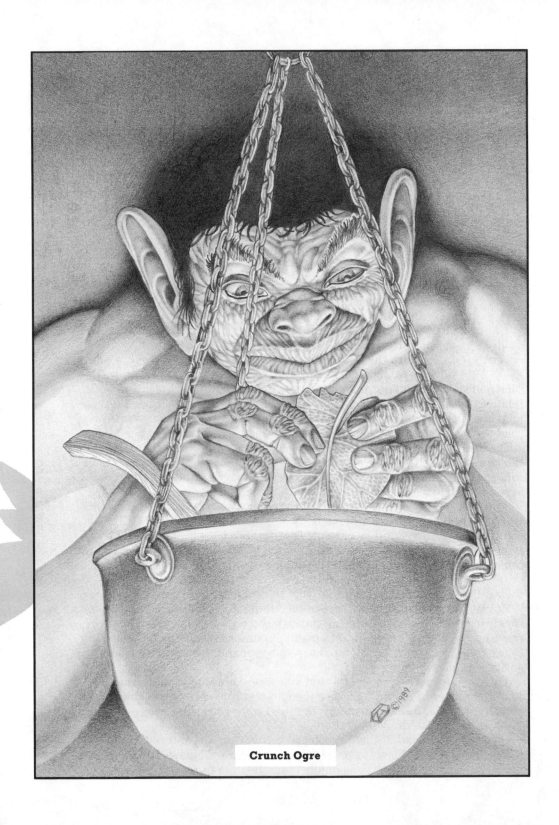

Crunch Ogre

VOLES

oles are lemon-shaped furry animals that live in the wilderness to the east on the Kiss-Mee River, which connects Lake Kiss-Mee and Lake Ogre-Chobee. A mature vole looks like a quadruped with sharp, curved claws. Immature ones resemble jointed worms of varying sizes, from tiny to immense.

They are the finest excavators under Xanth. It is in the nature of voles to dig quickly and well, creating passageways through rock and soil that will not fall in under any circumstances. Voles and their relatives bore magically through rock. They can leave a tunnel behind them, or no trace of their passage at all, according to their mood, but most leave it solid for the pleasure of digging through the same rock again and again.

The lesser forms of voles are called wiggles, squiggles and diggles. Diggles, the largest, range the huge expanses of bedrock far below the surface; squiggles, the loose earth and stone above; and wiggles, the superhard metal ores and rocks.

Squiggles resemble voles more than the other two breeds do. They have whiskers, and are more flexible in body and mind than the diggles. The squiggles are curious and intelligent. They tend to be solitary, and do not swarm. They have a highly developed society deep underground. Squiggles use directional pebbles to help them find their way, with an increasingly bad taste to tell them that they are going in the correct direction. Often the only sign of their recent presence is a mound of dirt that wasn't there a moment ago.

Diggles look like worms, and are of mere animal intelligence. They move slowly beneath the earth, phasing through the rock without affecting it. They move by elongating and contracting and expanding segments of their bodies. Diggles will work only for a song. Both squiggles and diggles are harmless to surface-dwellers.

Their history records a legend that voles were created by the Demon L(I/T)ho, Maker of Earth, who gave the choicest region to them. Voles, the archetype, were the chosen of L(I/T)ho, and were given free choice of their habitat, and chose the Vale of the Vole.

Civilized voles lived in the Gap Chasm before humans entered Xanth. They use artificial hollow claws to protect their own natural claws from wearing down. Such artifacts are occasionally found by human researchers.

Vole

ZOMBIES

ombies are the corpses of beings animated to half-life by the Magician Jonathan, beginning in the time of the Fourth Wave, and then again from the end of the Twelfth Wave on. Zombies lose material continually without losing mass, but generally, they grow more decrepit over time. A zombie makes a very faithful servant, but can only perform the simplest tasks without supervision, because its brain is rotten, and ideas fall right out. Zombies make good guardians, since nothing can hurt what is already dead. They have to be hacked apart to be stopped. And most creatures have a fear of the dead, so even a fairly deteriorated zombie makes a useful deterrent. Most are human, but any species can be reanimated.

NYMPHS
AND FAUNS

ymphs and fauns are innocent, pleasure-loving magical
creatures, perfect in form, but possessing no long-term
memories or extraordinary intelligence. Every day is new
to them. They quickly forget any hurt they have suffered,
and it is as if any of their number that die or disappear
have never lived. Like the other magical species, they are
thought to have no souls. There are several varieties in
Xanth that evolved from earlier forms present during the early Waves of
Colonization.

Nymphs are slim, lovely female creatures who resemble teenage girls of
extraordinary beauty. By and large, they have little intelligence, and do not
possess souls. Children are not supposed to see them up close, but adult men
pursue them, hoping to catch them.

Fauns were the original counterpart of nymphs: handsome, slender young
male beings. Dry land fauns, or dryfauns, had greenish hair and dark brown
fur on their legs and lower body in the manner of the trees they associate
with. On their heads were hornlike tufts of hair, hooked to allow them to draw
down fruit from the trees, and their toenails resembled hooves. In time,
dryfauns throughout Xanth became satyrs, with entirely goatlike nether
portions, and goatlike horns on their heads. Dryads were nymphs of the
forest, with green hair and graceful movements. Dryads and hamadryads have
become more attached over time to single trees, with whom they share a
symbiotic life.

For the naiads, the water-going nymphs, there were naifauns who had
flattened flipper hooves and horns which pointed straight up like spears. On
their legs they had delicate scales instead of hair. The naiads became
mermaids, and the naifauns changed over time into tritons. Their horns
disappeared, and they began to carry trident spears. The flipperlike hooves
and the naiads' feet became tails like those of fish.

Faun

Oreads and orefauns, nymphs and fauns of the mountains, have all but disappeared in greater Xanth. The orefauns had powerful furry legs with hooves like those of a deer, and hooflike hands which allowed them to run easily up the sides of mountains. Their horns were curled like those of a Mundane ram.

Nerefauns and nereids lived in the sea. They had webbed hands, scales along the lower halves of their bodies, and flipper feet which evolved into the powerful tails of sea fish. They have become merwomen and mermen. Merwomen are more mature than mermaids, and are somewhat better fleshed. They are excellent housewives. Merwomen remain youthful in appearance throughout their long lives, but the males grow old and grizzled unless they counter the ravages of time with a protective magical charm, such as a firewater opal.

Merfolk can interbreed with other races, to produce halflings, which are brought by the storkfish. Merwomen frequently mate with sailors after their mermen have lost interest in stork-summoning. Some sailors who are reported drowned are happy beneath the sea, protected by their merwomen lovers, and do not want to go back to dry land.

There is one valley in Xanth where the various kinds of nymphs and fauns live as they did in the distant past. There they are protected by a Monster Under the Bed named Snortimer, who settled there to find romance.

Nymphs and fairies are believed to have no souls. They are magical beings who exist because of X(A/N)th's magic. Nymphs are capable of mating with humans and producing offspring. Tandy, daughter of Crombie the soldier and Jewel the Nymph, is half-human, and so possesses a half-soul. Tandy's magical talent is her ability to throw tantrums, which pack enough punch to knock out a demon.

The Siren, whose magnificent singing voice and magic dulcimer lured many men to their doom in the face of her sister the Gorgon, is also a nymph. Once deprived of her magical musical instrument, she became merely a mermaid of spectacular beauty who offered no compulsion to men but her normal nymphly charms. When she wishes to, she can separate her tail into a pair of human legs. She married a triton named Morris the Merman who lives in the Water Wing. They have a son, Cyrus, who can also change from triton's tail to human legs at will.

Mermaid

OTHER HUMANS AND HUMANLIKE FOLK

Millie the Ghost: Millie's talent, which provoked her first death, is Sex Appeal. She came from the West Stockade, a very small community. As a slim, lovely young maid of seventeen with long, golden hair, Millie left the employ of the Sorceress Tapis to seek employment as a chambermaid at Castle Roogna. There, she was ensorcelled by Neo-Sorceress Vadne, who molded Millie's body into the form of a book, *The Skeleton in the Closet*, thereby squeezing the life out of her. Millie spent 800 years sadly haunting the abandoned Castle Roogna. She was restored to life with the help of Bink and Humfrey. The stress of being a ghost for 800 years darkened her hair to black. It soon grew out blond again, after she was once again fully alive.

After her restoration, she spent twelve years as maid and nurse to Dor until she married Zombie Master Jonathan and moved with him to Castle Zombie. They have twins, their son and daughter, Hiatus and Lacuna. Both of them inherited the lanky physique of their father, so at a distance it is difficult to tell which is which.

Their children have talents that seem positively intended for mischief. Lacuna can change printed text to read anything she wants. Hiatus's talent of Manifesting Sensory Organs allows him to give the walls ears.

Grundy the Golem was once formed of bits of string, clay and wood, but began to change into an elf when he learned to care. The final alteration to living reality was done by the Demon X(A/N)th when Grundy fulfilled a challenge to give X(A/N)th an advantage over his fellow demons, which he did by teaching the Demon about enlightened cooperation, where giving away advantages helps a player to win in the end.

Millie the Ghost

Grundy's magic talent dovetails neatly with that of King Dor's: he can understand and speak the languages of all living things. There is only one main language in Xanth, but the various creatures, plants, and organisms speak it in different ways. Grundy is usually rather tactless, and flavors his translations with crude insults. He has a natural turn for invective, and his mouth lands him in as many or more trials as his talent for communication is capable of getting him out of. He keeps company with Rapunzel, once Ivy's pun-pal, whose ability to shrink and grow her own body to any size she wishes brought her down to Grundy's level.

Rapunzel was imprisoned in the Ivory Tower by the Sea Hag until freed by Grundy and his companions. Her talent is her hair. Rapunzel's tresses are infinitely long, silky, black at the roots shading to purest white at the ends. She can compress her hair so it weighs nothing at all while it is bound up on her head. She is genetically able to make herself larger or smaller at will, as she is descended from generations of interbreeding between elves and humans. Her eyes shift colors. She is a many times descendant of Bluebell Elf and Jordan the Barbarian.

Because they were pun-pals before either of them could write, Rapunzel and Ivy used a magic box called a tress-ract to correspond with one another (though it was marked PUNDORA on the side). Ivy sent her ordinary things like stones and flowers; in exchange, Rapunzel conveyed physical puns, such as puncils that write lines on the air (and can erase same), a messy pig-pun filled with smelly earth, a puncushion full of sharp-pointed puns, and delicious hot cross puns with white icing faces that smile when the puns are eaten. She also sent Ivy a pair of Puns and Judy dolls, a pair of snake eyes on small cubes made of part of the substance of the Ivory Tower, and two simple captured-noise spells in globes: an outcry and a sound-of-mind.

Roland, Headman of the Council of Elders in the North Village, is Bink's father. His talent is the Stun Gaze. One special glance from him, and whatever he was looking at is frozen in place, alive but immobile, until he chooses to release it. The Council of Elders take care of administrative chores that are too routine to merit the King's attention. Roland is personally consulted by the King on numerous occasions; for he appreciates Roland's wisdom and clear-minded thinking. Roland's wife is Bianca, who can replay five seconds of time.

Rapunzel and Grundy

Jordan was a barbarian of the Fen Village, who lived in the reign of King Gromden. His talent was Healing Himself. He was the victim of a cruel lie which cost him his first life. He was the hero of a prophecy which predicted the appearance of a young, well-formed barbarian riding a pooka he had tamed, who would take the Hero's Challenge, which was to judge whose magic of the twin magicians, Yin or Yang, was more effective in practice as he sought to fetch Threnody to Castle Roogna. The outcome would determine which half of Yin-Yang would serve the dominant half as King. He was never to find true love until his flesh had rotted. Renee appeared, and he was happy with her, not knowing for years that she was Threnody.

Threnody is the illegitimate half-demon daughter of King Gromden. She bore a curse put on her by the Queen that if she ever returned to Castle Roogna, the castle would fall. She has midnight hair and eyes. Her birth disgraced the King so that his courtiers began to drift away from Castle Roogna. Her talent is Demon-Striation. She can diffuse from supersolidity to insubstance over time, grow big or small, and change shape to any form she wishes, but each change takes an hour. She married Magician Yang but suicided near Castle Roogna because she was unhappy and secretly loved Jordan, whom she had cut to pieces to save him from Yang's more harmful attention.

Jordan was restored to life by Ivy, who sought out where his bones had been hidden, and the two of them found a way to bring Threnody back to life, too. Jordan and Threnody travel throughout Xanth. The curse on her still holds against Castle Roogna, so they have never visited the human capital.

Threnody

OTHER INDIVIDUALS

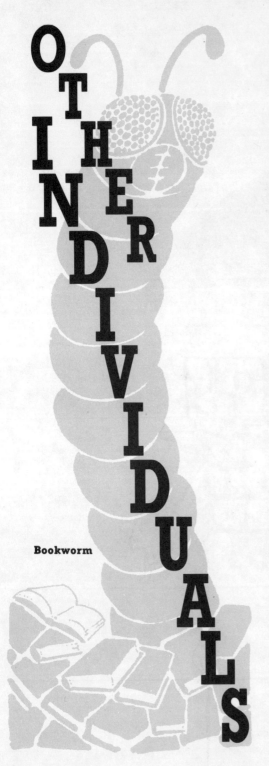

Bookworm

Agenda Andrews: The first girl sent to Grey Murphy by Com-Pewter. She has brown hair and is excruciatingly well organized.

Agent Orange: A vaguely catlike orange creature who works for the Catapult in the Region of Madness. It withers and kills plants wherever it passes.

Alister: A boy of the Gap Village whose talent is finding things.

Anorexia Nervosa: Grey's second girlfriend. She is very thin, and always dieting.

Arrowhead: An elf of the tribe of Flower Elves, who carries a bow and quiver of arrows for protection.

Awl: An elf of the Tool Tribe.

Belo: A ruffian of the South Village. His talent allows him to block any one of a person's seven senses.

Beryl Bluebird: The Bluebird of Happiness of the Magic Dust Village.

Bloodroot: An elf of the tribe of Flower Elves, who carries a red bag containing blood-poison as a weapon.

Bluebell Elf: Dainty lady elf of Flower Elves who chose to exchange favors with Jordan the Barbarian; she is an ancestress of Rapunzel.

Blythe, formerly Blyght: A brassie of the City of Brassies in the gourd. Has a mysterious dent about her person, dealt her by Smash Ogre.

Bookworm: A giant purple worm who lives in the depths of a complicated maze which can only be negotiated by solving the riddles which appear on its walls in glowing letters. The bookworm cannot speak aloud. Its thoughts are translated to printed words on the walls of its domain. It nests on a huge mound of old books, which it keeps in order by means of the Dewy Decimal System, tiny droplets of moisture on the bindings which only it can read. When the bindings wear out, it spins new ones for them. A voracious reader, it eats leaves of irreparable books.

Buster

Brain Coral: A stationary entity of great intelligence, magic, and conscience that lives at the bottom of an underground pool. It acts as the guardian of the Demon $X(A/N)^{th}$. Over the ages it has absorbed power and thought from the Demon, and is one of the most magically powerful entities in the land. It can take control of a creature by giving it powerful suggestions that are enough like its own behavior that it finds nothing objectionable in its instructions. The coral acts as a buffer between the Demon and the rest of the world, for if the Demon were disturbed (as it was by Bink, shortly before the Time of No Magic), $X(A/N)^{th}$'s influence would disappear from the land, and all magic would swiftly leach away.

Boy (1): Witness at Grace'l's trial; doesn't like girls.

Boy (2): Child who got lost in forest and was rescued by Girard Giant. No relation to Boy (1).

Bria Brassie: A lost Brassie girl with an Accommodation Spell to enable her to marry Esk Ogre; daughter of Blythe Brassie.

Brick Bat: Guardian of Draco's nest.

Brida: Alister's best friend in the Gap Village. Her talent is becoming a tabby were-cat.

Brunswick Bluebird: The Bluebird of Happiness of the South Village.

Bucktooth Goblin: Member of the Goblinate of the Golden Horde.

Bulls and Bears: Mundane animals that trade with one another and fight for dominance of the stockyard, a place where a little action can raise a big stink. The Bulls always go up, the Bears always go down.

Buster: Short for Filibuster. Senior village elder of the South Village whose talent is the manifestation of a huge red balloon capable of carrying up to four people in a basket below it. He fuels the balloon by generating enough hot air to lift it. Buster is a great talker.

Cactus: An elf of the tribe of Flower Elves, who carries a cactus thorn as a weapon.

Cat O'Moran: A water-going cat boat lent to Fortinbrass by the cats at Lake Ogre-Chobee.

Centurion: Centaur who comes to the Oracle for advice about his talent. He has one hundred fine arrows.

Charl: The centaur schoolmaster of the Gap Village.

Che: Colt of Cheiron and Chex Centaur.

Cheiron: A winged centaur, leader of the winged monsters. He is very handsome and well muscled, has silver wings and golden hooves, and can really fly. Cheiron is Chex's mate.

Chex: Winged centaur filly, daughter of Chem Centaur and Xap Hippogryph. Her eyes and wings are grey and her hair, mane, and coat are brown. Her talent is in her tail, which makes things light when it flicks them. With its aid, she can fly. Her wings are not normally strong enough to support her weight.

Chilk: A boy of the North Village, whose talent is the invisible wall.

Chisel: An elf of the Tool Tribe.

Clem: Centaur schoolmaster of the South Village.

Com-Pewter: In an air-conditioned cave sits a metallic box with a series of buttons and a pane of glass on its front. It can revise the script of reality to conform to its liking. Everything it prints on its glass screen happens. Created by the Muses of Parnassus to help with their work in recording reality, but they erred in the design. It is frequently foiled in Xanth, but has freer rein in Mundania, where free will is less valued. It uses a Worm Program to set up Sending, an emulation which it uses to introduce Ivy to Grey Murphy, as part of the insidious, heinous, and successful plot to make them like each other. Similarly successful plots have occurred elsewhere in Mundania, as married folk know.

Controlla: A female troll who is headwoman of the Magic Dust Village.

Cowslip Elf: Cousin of Oleander, of the Flower Elves.

Craven: Sub-chief of the Chasm Clan of Goblins in the days of the Fourth Wave.

Crombie the Soldier: His talent is direction. He can whirl and point to anything he wants to find. He hates and distrusts women. He claims that it is because his mother could read minds and made life miserable for him and his father. He is married to Jewel the Nymph, whom he considers to be an exception to his rule about women, because nymphs aren't really women. He was once changed into a griffin to enable him to be more helpful on a quest.

Crool: A goblin of Craven's clan.

Crown-of-Thorns: King of the Flower Elves.

King Cumulo Fracto Nimbus: Lord of the Air, Thunderhead, a cloud who crowned himself, is a puffed-up bag of winds who believes he rules Xanth, but he is all wet. He has inflated vanity and a stormy temper, and likes to ruin events held outside. Fracto carries grudges clear across Xanth, but he is prone to flattery and can be thwarted by reverse psychology. He is an ill wind that blows no one good.

Cumulo Fracto Nimbus

Dogwood: An elf of the tribe of Flower Elves, who goes armed with a canine-tooth tipped spear.

Dolph: See *Ivy*.

Donald the Shade: The ghost of a man who died seeking wealth to feed his family. His discovery of a silver tree would have gone unknown if it had not been for the intervention of Bink, who helped him complete his mission. Donald was able to go to his rest, knowing that his family would be provided for. His talent was flying.

Donkey: Centaur who resembles a donkey, being small and grey, with big ears. Friend to Ivy and Grey and Electra. His talent is to change the color of his hooves.

Doris: Curse Fiend girl with nice legs.

Draco Dragon: Possessor of the Firewater Opal. His nest is in Mt. Etamin, part of a constellation of mountains. Not a bad sort, if you like flying dragons.

Dungeon Master of Hurts: In charge of the painful aspect of bad dreams.

Duke Dragontail of Dimwit: Guest at Chex's wedding.

Dolph and Electra

Dyslexia: Grey's third girlfriend: a blue-eyed blonde who has trouble reading because she sees things backwards.

Egor Ogre: Servant to Jonathan in the days of the Fifth Wave invasion.

Electra: She substituted for the sleeping princess, owing to Murphy's Curse, and was betrothed to Prince Dolph when he woke her. She's a nice girl who once had a thing about her father, but now loves Dolph desperately, despite the fact that he is three years younger than she (no father fixation there!), but he is betrothed to her only to keep her from dying. She is the size and form of a child with freckles, and her eyes are the color of wonder. Her talent is electricity; she can give a person quite a jolt.

Elsie: Citizen of Xanth 400 years ago, first girlfriend of Jordan. Taught Jordan how to send messages to the stork regarding offspring. Her talent was turning water into wine by touching the liquid with her finger. X8

EmJay and her Ass MiKe (Michael and Keith): Researchers who prepared a lexicon so Mundanes would know about Xanth. X9

Eskil: Son of Tandy Nymph and Smash Ogre, half-human of which half is curse fiend, one-quarter nymph, and one-quarter ogre. Rather ordinary looking, with brown hair and grey eyes. His talent is protesting. If he says, "No!" he can stop a creature from doing to him what it intends without understanding why. He can become quite ogrish if provoked.

Euphoria: Grey's fourth girlfriend. Hypnotically intense eyes, swirling black hair, lush figure, but she's into mind-bending substances.

Fairulter: A faun who frequents the Flee Market; friend to Glim.

Fates: Brida's cerberus; he and Marbles sing in a Barkershop Quartet.

Ferdinand: King of the Cowboys, a kindly ruler.

Fireoak: The nymph of the fireoak tree. Fireoak is also the name for the wood which, though it looks as if it's burning, makes good fireproofing.

Fortinbrass: A brassie of Brassilia. He left the gourd to study in the soft world. His fiancee is Patchricia, an animate rag doll.

Fulsome Fee: Duck-footed leader of the Fee, who need to interbreed with others to increase their stock.

Furies: Tisiphone, Alecto, and Megaera, old women with the hideous faces of dogs: furry ears, projecting snouts, and bloodshot eyes on the sides of their heads. They have hair coiled like the bodies of zombie snakes, not pleasantly alive like the Gorgon's; and huge ribbed bats' wings that serve them as cloak and hood. They scourge victims with shame and guilt, driving them nearly to suicide by blaming them for neglecting their parents. Their weapons are guilt, sorrow, and suffering. The Furies are armed with brass-studded staves hung with whip-like thorns. The whips are poisoned, drawing copious blood and agony, leaving festering wounds that will not heal. They can throw one curse of misfortune apiece, which makes a victim wish that he were dead. They call themselves the daughters of Mother Earth, but they have none of their own. They sprang from the blood of their murdered father.

Galatea: Ivory statue of the loveliest of pigs, being carved by the sculptor Pyg Malion.

Ghost Writer: His talent is the ability to create realistic phantoms, steamy pot-boilers and illusory ghosts. His aim is to control the folks of Xanth through their emotions. He lives on the Phantom Ranch in the Plain of Grasses in the swamplands north of the Centaur Isle.

Prince Gimlet: Leader of the Tool Tribe of Elves. His body was temporarily occupied by the Sea Hag's spirit.

Gina: Lady invisible giant, originally the figment of a dream, now Girard's girl.

Girard: Invisible giant, trapped in the realm of the gourd, where he is visible. He was bound and bleeding for a long time in the gourd as the source of the River of Blood, until rescued by Grey.

Glim: Proprietor of a bookstall in the Flee Market. He will stall as long as he can to keep from selling a book; he loves them so much he hates to part with any.

Gloha: Daughter of Glory Goblin and Hardy Harpy; a winged goblin girl who participates in the festivities of Chex's wedding.

Glory Goblin: The petite, dark-haired, lovely youngest daughter of Gorbage Goblin of the North Slope Gap goblins. Glory is in love with Hardy Harpy. She has incredibly shapely legs. Their joint talent is invisibility.

Gnasty Gnomad: A gnome of the Gnobody Gnomes.

Gnaughty: An elderly gnomide of the Gnobody Gnomes.

Gnifty Gnomide: A nice female of the Gnobody Gnomes.

Gnitwit: A gnome of the Gnobody Gnomes.

Gnymph: A young gnomide of the Gnobody Gnomes.

Goldy Goblin: Daughter of Gorbage, a very beautiful goblin miss with long golden hair and great legs. She possesses a magic wand which allows her to levitate objects or people.

Goody: Goblin, unconscionably polite, cured by a session with curse burrs.

Gorbage Goblin: Chief of the Rim Goblins of the Gap; father of Goldy and Glory.

Grabraham: New, young, timid Bed Monster under Ivy's bed, known as Grabby for short. He replaces Snortimer, who found romance.

Grace'l Ossian: Female walking skeleton, Marrow's girlfriend. She has nice bones, and is the source of the Skeleton Key.

Grabaham

Gromden

Gromden: King of Xanth 400 years after Roogna, whose talent is that he can hold any object and divine its entire history, seeing and hearing it.

Grotesk: Goblin chief of the Goblinate of the Golden Horde. Mean, even by goblin standards.

Haggy Harpy: Leader of the Gap Harpy flock.

Handy: Dolph's regular Bed Monster.

Hannah Harpy: A harpy of the Gap Flock.

Hardy Harpy: Handsome harpy in love with Glory Goblin.

Harold Harpy: A prince who had been exiled by a rival to the harpy crown and preserved for three centuries by the Brain Coral, and only released when asked for by Dor.

Hatty Harpy: A harpy stoned by the Gorgon.

Baron Haulass of Shetland: A guest at Chex's wedding.

Heavenly Helen Harpy: The most beautiful harpy, whose downy feathers, clean lovely face, and shining brass claws made her First Concubine to Prince Harold Harpy.

Henrietta Harpy: A harpy of the Gap flock.

Henry: A deaf man who helps Ivy practice sign language.

Hoe: An Elf of the Tool Tribe.

Horace Centaur: A centaur zombie who died of an unfortunate accident during a game of people-shoes. His speech is slurred and his hide moldy and his face wormy, but he is not too far gone, and Ivy likes him, which counts for a lot.

Horsejaw: Tactless bully who lives near Castle Roogna.

The Horseman: First perceived by the Night Stallion as a threat to Xanth. A true were-horse who wanted to conquer Xanth. He is the son of a stallion and a human woman who drank from a love stream. In his horse form, he's a white stallion who wears a brass band about one ankle. As a human, the circlet is around his left wrist. This brass band is a short circuit which diverts power from its proper avenue. He is a consummate equestrian who can ride any steed, willing or unwilling. His talent is to form a line-of-sight connection between any two places, which he used to join the gaze of all the Kings during the Fourteenth Wave with the peephole of a hypnogourd.

Hotbox: A blue female wyvern at Chex's wedding.

Hugo: See *Humphrey*.

Ichabod: Arnolde's buddy, a researcher and scholar from the library in a southern American city of the modern era. He is considered to be the best historian in the state of Alabama.

Ignor Amus: Very stupid juror at Grace'l's trial.

Invisible giant: A heroic giant who died in the wiggle swarm halted by King Trent and a salamander-transformed Bink. This giant was known to be 60 feet tall, though he was never seen.

Itchlips: One of the Mt. Etamin goblins.

Jama: Obnoxious youth of the North Village, whose talent is the manifestation of a sword.

Jennifer: A female dog.

Jewel the Nymph: She lives in the cavern beneath the Vortex, south of the Magic Dust Village. She is unusual among nymphs, for she has wit and purpose. Most nymphs are purely decorative, and have only one signal talent. Jewel is perfectly lovely, but she has an important job to do as well. Her job is to deliver all the gems of Xanth to their proper places in the depths of the earth. Her keg of gems is self-renewing, so that whenever some are removed from it, more appear. She rides a diggle who can phase through the rock so long as she sings to it. It works for a song. She places the crystalline gems that the diggle has left behind in their proper setting once the diggle has stopped moving. Pearls are thrown into oyster beds, where the oysters swallow them. Jewel's talent is the generation of scents and smells according to her mood.

Joan: A male fairy who lives in Birdland. He got a name at birth which was intended for a female fairy, but until he met John was unable to switch for the right one.

Jody Lynn Nye: Nymph who makes Xanth gamebooks such as *The Encyclopedia of Xanth* and *Ghost of a Chance*. Some of the punniest puns have taken refuge with her. She kept coming up with so many formerly unknown folk, creatures and things that the regular Xanth author finally collaborated with her on a *Visual Guide to,*

to, it's right at the tip of my, well, anyway, it's a pretty good listing of whatever in connection with something.

John: A small female fairy who accidentally got the wrong name at birth. She didn't get the correct name until her wings were burned beyond healing. She and Joan experienced love at first touch, so she stays with him in Birdland.

Jumper

Jumper: A tiny spider of the Phidippus Variegatus Salticidae, the most handsome and sophisticated of the spider clans, who became Dor's valiant companion while he was in the Castle Roogna Tapestry searching for Zombie Master Jonathan. Jumper was rather beautiful in spider terms, though he could be considered formidable in appearance. His fur was green, with variegations of black, grey, and white on his abdomen that form the face of a smiling bearded man. Because of the size magic which put Dor into the Tapestry, Jumper appeared to be eight feet high instead of his usual quarter-inch height. He was also of great intelligence, and his wisdom guided Dor through many dangers. He knew how to balloon with silk, a talent some but not all spiders have.

Justin Tree: A man of the North Village transformed into a tree by Evil Magician Trent before his exile. His talent was ventriloquism, so he still has a voice. As a tree, Justin's leaves resemble flattened human hands, its sap is blood red, and its bark is the color of a deep tan. When Trent returned, he offered to change Justin back, but Justin preferred to remain a tree.

Knock-Kneed Knights: These empty suits of armor control the fertile pastures under the fields of the cowboys. In exchange for the sacrifice of the finest young bullocks and heifers every year, the Knights allow the cowfolk to graze in the nether pastures. They consider themselves to be creatures of chivalry, allowing the young cowfolk to try and defeat their Knight Tourney Champion in the labyrinth during the Running of the Gauntlet, but none ever do defeat him, because it is not a fair fight. The Knight has an armored horse, a sword and a lance, and the cowboys are forced to fight empty-handed and on foot. The Knights' armor is empty, for without honor, they are nothing at all.

Knotweed: An elf of the tribe of Flower Elves who goes armed with a knotted rope.

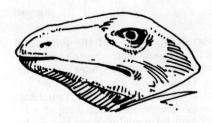

Komodo li Zard

Komodo li Zard: Guest at Chex's wedding, prince of the Isles of Indon Esia.

Lathe: An elf of the Tool Tribe.

Latia: A homely old woman of the Curse Fiends who is so ugly and so talented with stage makeup that she is able to best an ogress by using her face to curdle water instead of milk. She accompanied Esk to the Vale of the Vole. Her talent is flawed: one out of every three curses she throws turns out to be a blessing instead, probably because she is a good person.

Leonardo the Lion-Tamer: Huge lion that tames other animals (including humans), tiger lilies and dande-lions, with a whip and hoop.

Lily: A woman of the Gap Village.

Liza: A woman of the South Village whose talent is embroidery. She is the finest liar in the stockade.

Lyman: A man of the South Village. His talent is twosight, which is only half as accurate as foresight. Half of his predictions come true.

Mae: One of the maenads of Mt. Parnassus. A wild woman who didn't fit because she doesn't like blood. She became a priestess of the oracle. Her eyes glow like candle flames when she is excited.

Magistrate: Curse Fiend official.

Maiden: A pretty girl who comes to the Good Magician's castle for advice about love.

Mallet: An elf of the Tool Tribe.

Manticora: A monster whom Bink met at the castle of Good Magician Humfrey while serving a year for the Answer to his Question. The Manticora is the size of a horse with the head of a man, the body and mane of a lion, wings of a dragon, tail of a scorpion, three rows of iron teeth one inside the other, and a surprisingly beautiful musical voice.

Marbles: Rock hound belonging to Alister.

Mare Frigoris: A night mare, after whom the Sea of Cold on the moon is named. She is a 300-year veteran. She testified at Grace'l's trial.

Marrow Bones: Walking skeleton who was lost on a path in the gourd. Originally used to frighten sleepers in dreams, he got lost. Like all magic skeletons, he can disassemble his bones and reassemble them in assorted useful configurations. He was chosen by Dolph as his Adult Companion on his Quest.

Max: Man of the South Village, the local animal doctor. His talent is his lantern jaw.

Mela Merwoman: Full name Melantha. Captor of Prince Dolph. She resembles a mermaid, but lives in salt water and is more voluptuous. She has no panties (few mermaids do).

Jewel the Nymph's Jewels

Mermaid: One of twenty lovesick mermaids in the dream realm, in a scene to love a misogynist to death.

Merwin Merman: Mela's dead husband. He had a difference with a dragon and got toasted at point-blank range.

Meto Nymy: Juror with attributes, at Grace'l's trial.

Metria: Rude demoness who wanted to take over Esk's comfortable hidey-hole. She has trouble remembering the specific colloquialism for what she wants to say.

Mike

Mike: A Mundane or barbarian (the distinction is moot) warrior, with the standard huge thews, whose body Dor inhabits when he visits the past of 800 years gone via the Tapestry.

Mitchell: One of Trent's Mundane soldiers, who settled down in the Gap Village.

The Monster Under the Bed: A creature made up entirely of large, hairy hands that lives on dust mice and must remain in shadow, for sunlight kills it. It grabs for the tender ankles of children, but is otherwise completely harmless. Adults can't see them. They travel only at night. They feel insecure when in the open. See also *Snortimer*, *Zomonster*, *Handicraft (Handy)* and *Grabraham*.

Moola: Cowchild, whose talent is speaking the humanoid language.

Monster of the Sea: Huge creature that hunts off the east coast of Xanth, finding damsels in distress to liberate. Flexible pink snout, bulging nostrils, cauliflower ears, bloodshot saucers for eyes, huge flippers, serpentine tail, scaly skin, and wide blubbery body, it eats only plankton. Many thousands of years old, it rescued Andromeda from the rocks only to be wounded and then slandered by Perseus, who wanted credit for saving her.

Nabob: King of the Naga serpent-folk. His head is human, his body serpentine.

Nada: Princess of the Naga, Prince Dolph's betrothed, by advice of the Good Magician Humfrey who told the naga "Marry what Draco brings." She can assume either human or serpent form in addition to her natural one, and is cute in all three. Dolph loves her but she can't love him because she is five years older than he is. Nada is a close friend of Ivy's.

Naldo: Prince of the Naga, Nada's big brother. Charming and handsome in all forms: human, snake, or naga.

Numbo: Boy of the North Village, whose talent is the hotseat.

Oleander Elf: Leader of the tribe of Flower Elves.

Onda: A voluptuous young woman of the South Village, who has red hair and blue eyes. Her talent is the map she can manifest on the back of her hand.

Onoma Topoeia: Juror at Grace'l's trial who looks the way she sounds.

Ortant: An Imp, Quieta's father, whom Smash rescued from an alligator clip. He may be addressed as Imp Ortant.

Oxy Moron: Juror at Grace'l's trial; a stupidly clever ox.

Peek: Ghost mare who was in the service of the Knock-Kneed Knights, as a knight-mare.

Perrin Piranha: Chivalrous guardian of Draco's nest.

Black Pete

Black Pete: Proprietor of Thieves' Isle, not to be trusted unless one has an excellent memory.

Pook the Ghost Horse: Friend and companion of Jordan the Barbarian. Hung with chains, he is solid part of the time and insubstantial the rest of the time.

Potipher: A youth of the North Village whose talent is creating a cloud of poison gas.

Princess: Originally supposed to eat a bit of apple she carried with her, and sleep for a thousand years until a handsome young prince kissed her awake so she could marry him and live happily ever after, but she was foiled by Murphy's curse and had to settle for King Roogna. Electra bit the apple instead.

Puck: Ghost foal of Pook and Peek.

Pyg Malion: A pig who is a talented sculptor. He carved an ivory statue of Galatea, with whom he is in love. He is a juror at Grace'l's trial.

Querca: Hamadryad of one of the oldest oak trees in Xanth. She runs the Crooked B-Ranch, where the plane tree grove lies.

Quieta the Imp: A tiny person who makes tinier magic mirrors from the film of soap bubbles.

Ringmaster: His real name is Bailey. He is in charge of everything under the Big Top. He is made of clanking metal rings stacked up to make limbs, fingers, toes, head, and torso. His brother, Barnum, is also a ringman. They own the Big Top.

Sabrina: Bink's former girlfriend. Her talent is singing holographs into existence. She is devious and not particularly faithful. (She was ready to father her unborn baby on Crombie to trap him into marriage, but he found out about it first.)

Salmonella: Grey's fifth girlfriend. She's a great cook, but the food is contaminated.

Screwdriver: An elf of the Tool Tribe.

Sea Hag: This wicked old woman crafted the Ivory Tower from the tusks of innocent sea creatures. Her talent is eternal life, which she gets by taking over a new body when the one she occupies dies. She is a ghost only a few hours before beginning a new life. The Hag can only occupy a body that allows her to enter, and she can cloud minds to make one allow it. She is limited by the knowledge and intelligence of her host body, so it is in her interests to pick the most intelligent and well-informed body she can find. Rapunzel, an orphan she raised for the purpose of inhabiting her body, called her Mother Sweetness.

Sea Hag

Sending: The emulation of Com-Pewter set up by the Worm on Grey Murphy's Mundane computer. It later made use of one of the magic screens around Xanth to further its own plans.

Siegfried: Father of Onda. They live in the South Village.

Simurgh: Ageless, is the wisest bird alive. She is said to have seen the destruction of the universe three times and has the knowledge of the ages. She is the Guardian of the Tree of Seeds.

Slug: A giant firebreathing slug looking for a slugfest.

Smokey of Stover: Guest at Chex's wedding. Once better known in Mundane comics.

Snagglesnoot of Syncromesh: Guest at Chex's wedding.

Snortimer: The Monster under Ivy's bed who accompanied Grundy Golem on a quest to rescue Rapunzel and save Stanley Steamer. Along the way, he found romance.

Stacey Steamer: The Gap Dragon's mate and locum tenens. Also called Stella, since she is a star of dragondom.

Stanley Steamer: The youthened Gap Dragon, who was enhanced by Ivy and became her playmate.

Stunk: A goblin haunted by bad dreams carried by Imbri.

Synec Doche: Juror at Grace'l's trial; concerned with parts and the whole.

Tangleman: Once a tangle tree who was transformed to a man by King Emeritus Trent when he threatened Ivy. In his humanoid form Tangleman is quite a jolly green giant. He has tentacles for hair, barklike clothing, and green skin. (This episode was in the deleted Chapter 1 of *Crewel Lye*, which was axed because it was badly infested with puns.)

The Time Being: An elflike humanoid who can jump backward or forward in time as he pleases. He acts as mediator in any dispute when adversaries agree to cooperate "for the Time Being."

Toto: Wrong fantasy series; see the Land of Oz.

Tristran Troll: Scheduled for a really bad dream, as punishment for releasing a succulent girl.

Trolla: Female troll, leader of the Magic Dust Village.

Trowel: An elf of the Tool Tribe.

Truculent Troll: A witness at Grace'l's trial.

Turn Key: A human, the Keeper of the Gate at No Name Key, where the night mares depart Xanth to carry bad dreams to Mundanes.

Ivy and Stanley Steamer

Winged Demon

Urmund: Son of Liza. A mischief-maker, his talent is camouflage. He can make topographic features appear to be there that aren't, and vice versa. N2

Victrolla: A troll woman of the Magic Dust Village. She is Controlla's younger sister.

Vida Vila: Nature nymph who would like to marry Prince Dolph. She can change forms and is diligent in the protection of her land.

Volney: Civilized vole of medium-large size with grey fur and brown eyes while above ground, and brown fur with grey eyes below ground. Volney carries silver talons that fit over his own. He can tunnel amazingly fast with them on. He speaks normally, but all other creatures have trouble with their S's. Thus when he says "Sale of the Soul," they hear "Vale of the Vole."

Waya: An elder of the Gap Village whose talent is the invisible fence. She uses it to protect small children and animals from falling into the Gap.

Wilda Wiggle: Female wiggle with a taste for air-flavored stone, a curiosity among her kind. Her swarm helped to save the Vale of the Vole from the demons. Very petite and attractive, for a vole.

Wrench: An elf of the Tool Tribe.

Xanthippe: Wicked witch of the wilderness, whose power is instant hypnotism.

Xap: A golden hippogryph, mate of Chem Centaur and companion to Xavier.

Xavier: Son of Xanthippe, handsome, tan, muscular, golden hair and beard, who loves to fly on his steed, Xap the hippogryph. Xavier's talent is the zap, a light springing from his finger which stuns or kills targets.

Zink: A boy of the North Village whose talent was manifesting mirage holes in the ground.

Zomonster: The zombie Monster under Lacuna's bed.

Zora Zombie: Heroic female zombie who improved in appearance so much with love and a glance from the Gorgon, that she became beautiful and almost whole. She carried the seeds of Doubt, Dissension and War without effect, and bore three curses for her friends.

Prince Naldo

PLACES IN XANTH

Xanth is real. As real as a computer screen's image. The bright and dark points of light mean nothing until your mind interprets them. Xanth is Florida, but a different Florida than the one most people see. It is Florida seen through a mind that sees magic instead of mundane bits of light. Even beyond the puns, Xanth is real the same way that Santa Claus is real. It all depends on how you look at what you read and see.

— Piers Anthony

It is difficult to draw an accurate map of Xanth, because many places remain undiscovered, while others are elusive. Some have spells of obscurity on them. Chem is the map-projecting centaur, but when she was ostracized for mating with a non-centaur she became a bit taciturn and no longer cooperates very well. However, we were able to contact the Xanth PinUp Calendar folks, who had somehow gotten information from Chem, and so are able to present a fairly complete description here.

CLOUSE '89

anth is a land of beauty, full of exotic forests and jungles, mountains, lakes, caverns and meadows. Because of the Demon's magical influence, the features of the land are more aware of their position, needs, and appearance than those in Mundania, and are able to alter themselves magically if they choose. The face of the land changes subtly every day.

Xanth's main point of contact with Mundania is the Isthmus. At times throughout history, this narrow neck of land has been crossed by fourteen major Waves of Colonization and several times by single creatures or groups of creatures who found their way into Xanth by chance. It is possible to determine when and where you are going by the color of the water around the Isthmus. If the water is black, Xanth is tied at that moment to the land around the Black Sea in Asia. When the tide turns crimson, Xanth is close to Montgomery, Alabama, Mundania.

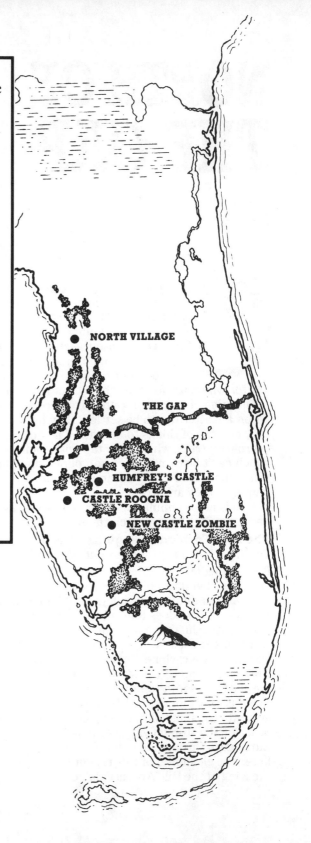

NORTH VILLAGE

THE GAP

HUMFREY'S CASTLE

CASTLE ROOGNA

NEW CASTLE ZOMBIE

NORTH OF THE GAP

 **gre-Fen-Ogre Fen:** Home of the Ancestral Ogres. This swamp is the northernmost feature of Xanth east of the Isthmus. It is an ugly place, obviously inhabited by ogres, for what else could explain the bluewood and redwood trees twisted into the shape of pretzels and huge boulders with the imprints of hairy fists knocked into them. Dragons live here, but they are terrified of anything on two legs, no matter what size, for even the ogrets who live here are fierce and terrible.

The tribe of Ancestral Ogres live here according to their own ancient laws. When a matter has to be settled, they fight it out, bashing each other until they run out of things to hit with. The only trees left standing are the beerbarrel trees, which they tap with their fists, and the ironwood trees, which can't be torn down by an ogre using only casual strength. He has to think about it to rip apart an ironwood, and no ogre likes to think. They are as stupid as they are strong.

This is not a popular spot for sightseers, as the ogres will happily eat passersby if they can catch them.

The Five Forbidden Regions: This province lies directly south of the Ogre-Fen-Ogre Fen. From south to north, the regions are:

Air: Immediately inside the border of the Region of Air, dust storms roil and tumble. There is no vegetation, no life here, just sand in dunes and valleys, and stone cliffs. The Big Winds rule here. Tornadoes tear and cyclones careen, driving sand against the cliffs to make more sand. A blast of the gritty air can tear exposed flesh from one's bones. The region is bounded by a cyclone fence.

Earth: As soon as you step across the border from south to north, the wind stops. Relief is only momentary, because the ground is quaking under your feet. It does occasionally stop moving, because Earth goes through all of its phases here. The elemental of this region is the King of the Hill. An unscalable

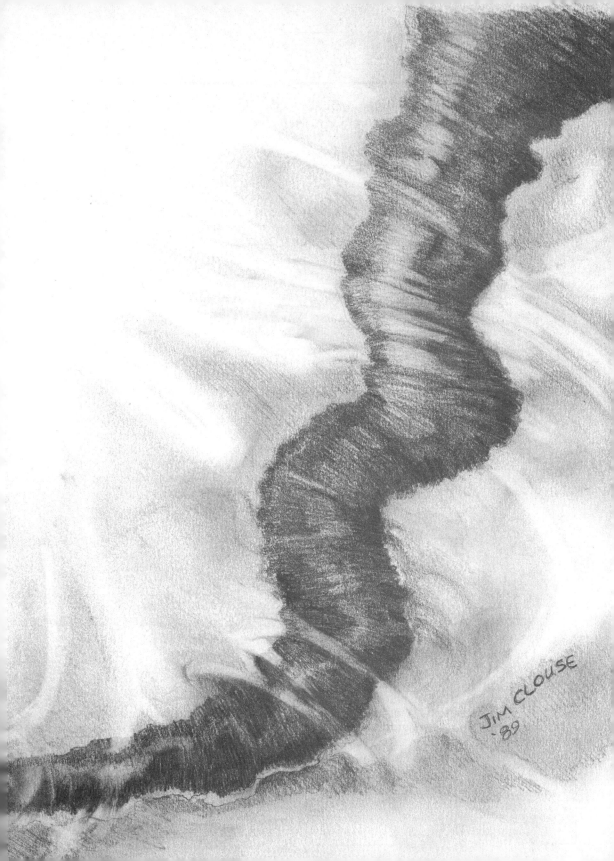

JIM CLOUSE
'89

mountain range is visible to the northeast, and a huge volcano spewing lava can be seen at the northern end of the region, on the border between Earth and Fire. Only rock plants and other sturdy growths are produced in the soils, which range from barren to wildly fertile. As you get closer to the Region of Fire, walking becomes hazardous, because the ground becomes unstable, and plates of land skate along the surface of the lava from the volcano.

Fire: A ring of fire rages along the border of this region. The land beyond it is burned and the air is full of ash. To the north, an eternal forest fire rages. To the west, a lake of fire occasionally belches up mushroom clouds of flame. To the east is a field of fire from which columns of flame rise occasionally as gas puffs up from fumaroles and ignites. New plants push up through the ashes, only to be consumed because they are so desiccated that they haven't enough water in their tissues to resist the flames. The heat is on here, and the place is ruled by the Laws of Thermodynamics.

Water: At the north end of the realm of Fire, the firewall at the flaming border raises a hot cloud of steam, which coalesces on the other side into clouds. The Water Wing has a tendency toward weather. Strong rainfall is common here, as are sleet and snow. Water abounds in all its states.

There is almost no dry land in the Wing. What topography exists is there mainly to redistribute the water that flows in cataracts and torrents. A huge snow mountain rises out of the center of the region. An Abominable Snowman has been sighted there. There are herds of snow bunnies and a few snowbirds. In a pleasant lake on the western fringe of the mountain, a few middle-aged mermaids and tritons live, enjoying the cool water and the flavored icicles which grow down beside the waterfalls of melting snow.

The Void: Beyond the border of Earth is an imperceptible swirl of nothingness. No landmarks can be seen from outside. Inside, it is a smooth, gently sloping valley. Perception is confused here. One sees what one wishes to see; it is all illusion. The Void is the absence of all physical reality. Even real things which enter are subject to misperception. Once having entered, it is difficult to leave the Void. An invisible one-way stone wall prevents you from turning back once you have come in a certain distance. Footprints glow in the Void. They can be seen in a color appropriate to the creature who made them: a centaur's are brown, an ogre's are black, a human's are red. Any beings encountered are perceived at first as of one's own species. Only by concentrating can a person distinguish the true images.

The land itself is carnivorous; it consumes travelers that wander in. Nothing is permitted to leave. The only way to escape is to transport or be conjured, or to ride a night mare out of the Void, although night mares themselves can be trapped there, too, as Mare Imbrium was.

At the southernmost extremity of the Five Forbidden Regions, just north of the Gap, is a wall of flypaper.

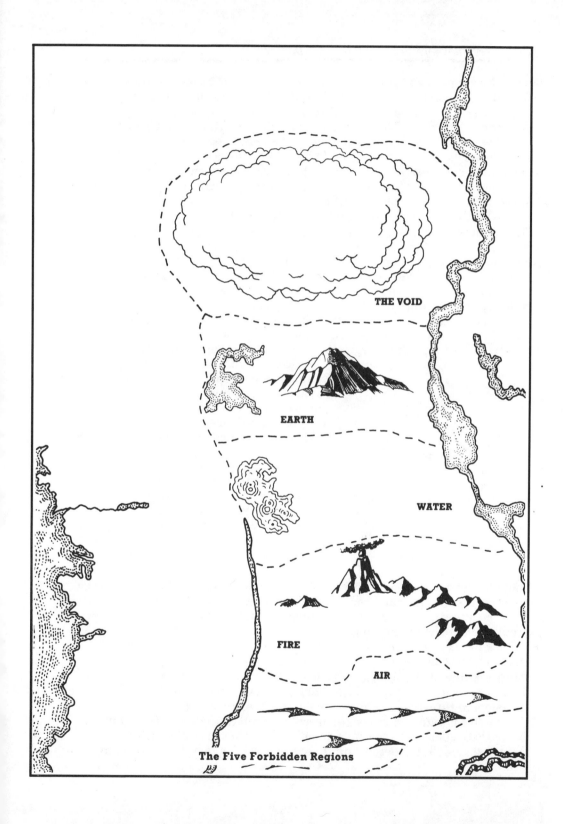

THE VOID

EARTH

WATER

FIRE

AIR

The Five Forbidden Regions

The Kingdom of the Flies: Just beyond the wall of flypaper live swarms of flies of all kinds: stingflies, worker flies, deerflies, horseflies, dragonflies, fiddler flies, and fair damselflies. Sweat gnats, itchflies, bleederflies, and fly-bys keep the air buzzing with gossip about all goings-on throughout Xanth. Shoeflies march up, bowflies shoot arrows, sawflies, hammerflies, screwdriverflies work furiously on fly-by-night construction schemes. The kingdom is ruled over by the Lord of the Flies, a huge demonic fly with multiple-facet eyes, who sits on a throne made of fly ash and flypaper. His soldiers are guardflies and spearflies.

His favorite book is *The Sting* by A. Wasp.

Dragonland: Located east of the Region of Air. The trees are crosshatched with claw-marks from dragons sharpening their talons on them. Droves of dragons roam here. Their leader is the scintillating Dragon Lady, who reigns supreme, supine on her nest of diamonds under a dragonet (dum de dum dum). Her tail is blue and barbed, and she has a bright red neck. While she reclines, she likes to read the latest number of Monster Comics.

There is a high range of mountains known as the Dragon Range. The peak at the tip of the nose is called Mount Etamin, where Draco Dragon lives in his cavern nest. Chasing the Dragon Range is another constellation of mountains

in the shape of a bear called Ursa. Mount Etamin is a steeply sloped peak scorched bare of vegetation. The cave entrance is narrow, but it leads to a large cavern system within. The passage gradually widens into a stalactite-rimmed chamber in which half the floor is taken up by a black pool of water. Draco's home can only be reached by diving into the pool and under the stone wall of the cave. This is hazardous, for the water is infested with piranhas. The cave beyond is patrolled by bats. High up on a ledge is the dragon's nest, furnished with the very latest and most tasteful in gems and other valuables.

Naga Caverns: Another cave entrance leads to the realm of the naga. Nagas are serpents with human heads, and can change shape to either of the component parts of their natures, human or snake. When nagas hiss, they produce clouds of noxious fog.

Since nagas can slither through small tunnels, the passages between the chambers of their realm are narrow.

Region of the Goblins: Located east of the Region of Fire. The goblins here follow strictly the code of behavior laid down over the centuries. Travelers are waylaid and threatened, and cheated if possible. Anything or anyone that looks edible is eaten. In case of danger, run. Profanity comes as easily to the lips of these goblins as their own names. Most goblins are illiterate, ill-tempered, and ill-mannered, and these are sterling examples of goblinkind.

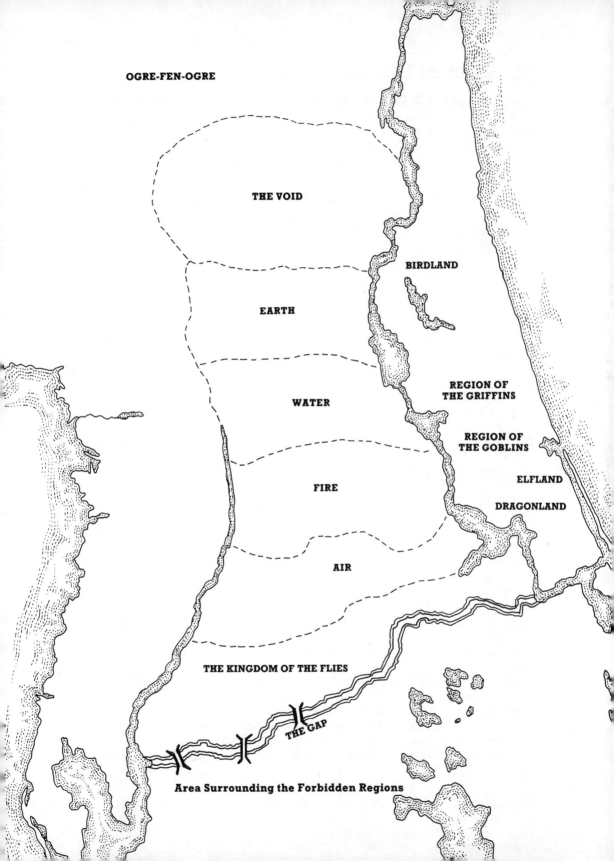

OGRE-FEN-OGRE

THE VOID

BIRDLAND

EARTH

WATER

REGION OF
THE GRIFFINS

REGION OF
THE GOBLINS

FIRE

ELFLAND

DRAGONLAND

AIR

THE KINGDOM OF THE FLIES

THE GAP

Area Surrounding the Forbidden Regions

The Home of the Callicantzari: Found underneath the Goblinland, the Callicantzari lives in a cavern lined with rainbow fungus. This beast is a grotesquely deformed man-shaped thing. It regards the world from two great eyeslits arranged over a bulbous nose in a furry face from which protrude

Callicantzari

twisted tusks. Its arms have bulging muscles, but they appear to be attached to them backwards, and some of the bones in its torso look as though they are in the wrong places. The Callicantzari exudes a stench like a putrid cloud, which helps victims keep away from it in the dark, for it is a meat-eater, and prefers to wear out its prey in the underground maze.

Elfland is south of the Region of Goblins. Elves are group hunters and respect one another's property, but unclaimed animals or creatures traveling alone are fair game. Elves make their camps only around elf elms, because an elf's strength increases the nearer he is to one. When danger threatens, the women and children flee to the tree's heights, while the warriors ring the base.

When at peace, the elves live simply. They use leaves for bowls and plates. Mice and grasshoppers are hunted for meat, which is incorporated into stew made with vegetables, nuts and fruit. To guests, the elves are most hospitable, and provide wonderful entertainment. Elfin grog is an amazing brew which makes it possible even for humans to climb trees and perform unusual feats of strength.

Region of Griffins: Northern neighbors of the goblins, against whom they defend their terrain fiercely. They have royal lineages and are fussy about protocol and neatness. Baby griffins hatch from eggs in big nests in low-branching trees. They are the color of shoe polish (making them black, brown, oxblood, white, and grey).

Birdland: Found north of the Region of Griffins and east of the Region of Earth. The road through here is a private thoroughfare, and travelers passing through have to pay a 20 percent toll tax. According to the parrot who collects it, one out of every five who pass through this land must stay here. The birds need slaves to plant and harvest seeds for the huge winged population who roost here.

Birdland is ruled by the Bird of a Feather, who keeps abreast of important topics by reading. (His latest book is *Avian Artifacts* by Ornith O'Logy.) The Bird cares for his slaves, and sees that they are well treated. They lack nothing except their freedom. Inside Birdland, near a small waterfall pool stocked with perch and lined with birds-nest fern, is a colony of fairies who were cast out of Fairyland and have found a happy home here (*Ogre, Ogre*, p. 210).

Birdland

JIM CLOUSE '89

NORTH VILLAGE

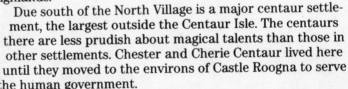

ntil Castle Roogna was reopened, the Storm King's palace in the North Village was the most recent center of human government in Xanth. This village is the largest in Xanth, composed of approximately 500 human beings. This village is home to Bink and his parents, Roland and Bianca.

The village is built within a stockade, which protects the inhabitants against the encroaching wilderness. In the center of the common green is Justin Tree, one of the North Village's most enduring and wise inhabitants. There is a market square where folks from all over the north of Xanth come to trade their goods.

There are in or near the stockade perhaps fifty houses, made of wood, stone, and clay. The roofs are thatch or boughs grown on roof-trees. Sanitary facilities are "out back" from the main dwellings. Roland's home is the largest and finest, grown from fine, glossy wall-nuts.

Outside the stockade, farmers till fields of crops. One of the most useful crops is light bulbs, which are used for interior lighting in houses. Milkweed pods are cultivated, too, to ensure a fresh supply for children, as the pods expire after about a week. Cheesefruit, hot-potatoes, and any desirable foodstuff that does not naturally grow nearby is sown by the farmers to feed the large population of the North Village. Young people with a talent for finding things forage in the jungle for other necessities, but only during the day. The wilderness of Xanth is too dangerous at night. From a boulder known as Lookout Rock, just outside the village, you can see about a quarter of Xanth. The Rock is not particularly high, but its magic is increased perspective, which makes it an appealing spot to sit and work out knotty problems. It uses its placement and its own ugliness as protective integration, so that no one would consider breaking it up to use for any other purpose. Lookout Rock is a metamorphic upthrust of the type seen in Mundania in the New England highlands.

Due south of the North Village is a major centaur settlement, the largest outside the Centaur Isle. The centaurs there are less prudish about magical talents than those in other settlements. Chester and Cherie Centaur lived here until they moved to the environs of Castle Roogna to serve the human government.

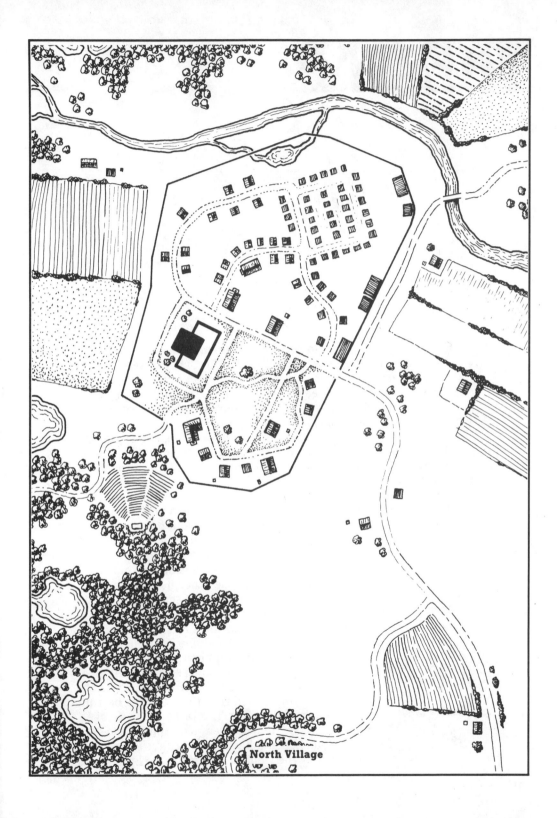

North Village

THE GAP

This vast crevice would certainly be memorable, except that it has a formidable Forget Spell on it. The Chasm stretches across Xanth from west coast to east coast, preventing anything without wings from easily crossing it. It resembles a jagged lightning bolt that splits Xanth. On closer observation, the Chasm proves to be fractile, with small jags branching off from the large jags, and smaller from each of those, and so on ad infinitum, until you might step over a tiny irregular gash an inch wide and an inch deep in the earth miles away from the Gap, and never know what it was.

There is a footpath down into the Gap east of the Gap Village, down where the Gap is shallower than at almost any other point, but it is a hard and twisted trail. The southern slope is gentler than the northern at that point, so it is easier coming from the south to get into the crevice than to get out. Vegetation is thick along the sides, providing handholds for the near-vertical ascent and some camouflage from the dangers within the Gap.

Rivers cross the Gap, flowing down one side into the Chasm, and magically defying gravity as they flow up the other side into the other half of Xanth. It is possible to escape from the Gap by swimming along one of these rivers. The Gap is guarded by the Gap Dragon, a huge steamer with a sinuous body and three pairs of stubby legs. Like most Xanthian dragons, it has metallic scales. Very supple, no rigid backbone, and the ground *whomps* when the dragon moves. The Gap Dragon has six legs and very handsome scales of shimmery blue, green, and iron grey. He (or she) is admirable, but it is recommended that the admiring be done from a good distance. The Dragon has a huge appetite for fresh meat steamed right off the bone. The Good Magician has warned that the Dragon is important to the welfare of the Gap, so Stanley or

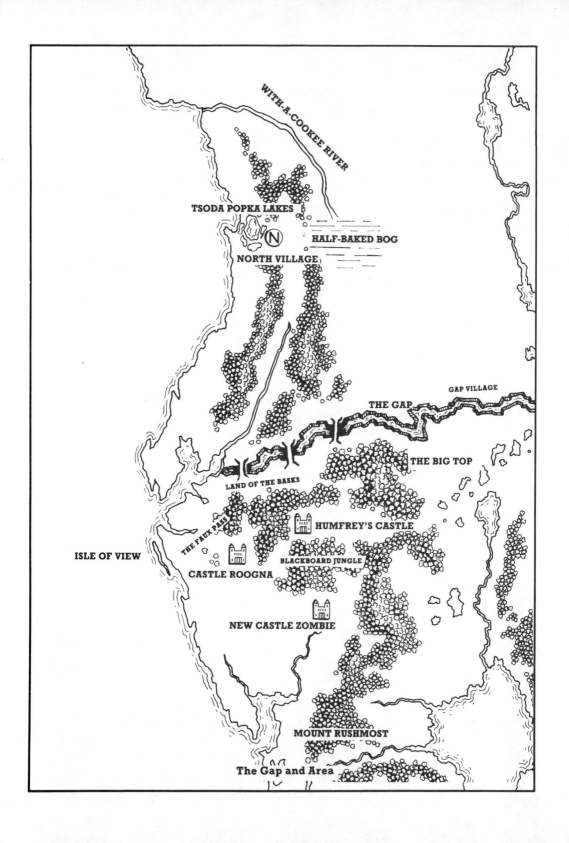

WITH-A-COOKEE RIVER

TSODA POPKA LAKES

HALF-BAKED BOG

NORTH VILLAGE

THE GAP   GAP VILLAGE

THE BIG TOP

LAND OF THE BASKS

THE FAUX PASS

HUMFREY'S CASTLE

ISLE OF VIEW

BLACKBOARD JUNGLE

CASTLE ROOGNA

NEW CASTLE ZOMBIE

MOUNT RUSHMOST

The Gap and Area

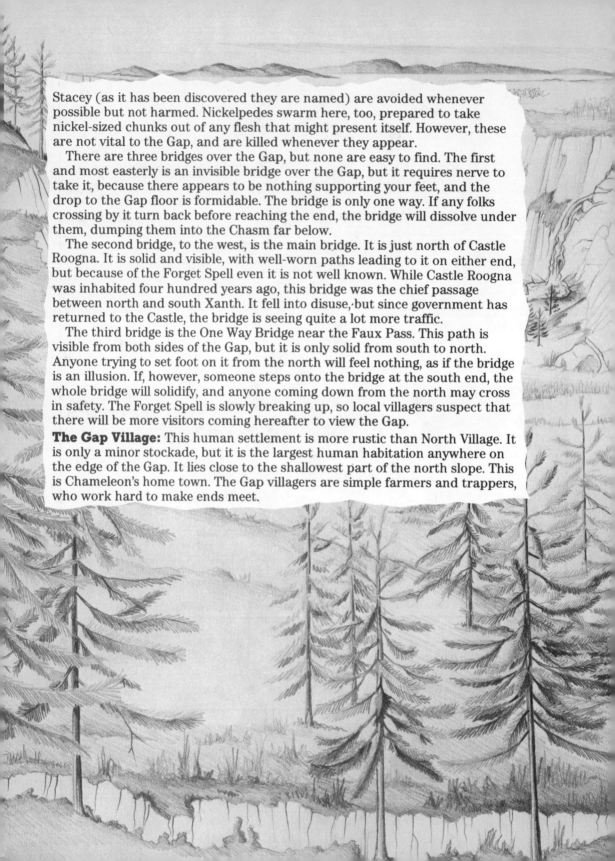

Stacey (as it has been discovered they are named) are avoided whenever possible but not harmed. Nickelpedes swarm here, too, prepared to take nickel-sized chunks out of any flesh that might present itself. However, these are not vital to the Gap, and are killed whenever they appear.

There are three bridges over the Gap, but none are easy to find. The first and most easterly is an invisible bridge over the Gap, but it requires nerve to take it, because there appears to be nothing supporting your feet, and the drop to the Gap floor is formidable. The bridge is only one way. If any folks crossing by it turn back before reaching the end, the bridge will dissolve under them, dumping them into the Chasm far below.

The second bridge, to the west, is the main bridge. It is just north of Castle Roogna. It is solid and visible, with well-worn paths leading to it on either end, but because of the Forget Spell even it is not well known. While Castle Roogna was inhabited four hundred years ago, this bridge was the chief passage between north and south Xanth. It fell into disuse, but since government has returned to the Castle, the bridge is seeing quite a lot more traffic.

The third bridge is the One Way Bridge near the Faux Pass. This path is visible from both sides of the Gap, but it is only solid from south to north. Anyone trying to set foot on it from the north will feel nothing, as if the bridge is an illusion. If, however, someone steps onto the bridge at the south end, the whole bridge will solidify, and anyone coming down from the north may cross in safety. The Forget Spell is slowly breaking up, so local villagers suspect that there will be more visitors coming hereafter to view the Gap.

The Gap Village: This human settlement is more rustic than North Village. It is only a minor stockade, but it is the largest human habitation anywhere on the edge of the Gap. It lies close to the shallowest part of the north slope. This is Chameleon's home town. The Gap villagers are simple farmers and trappers, who work hard to make ends meet.

CLOUSE '89

SOUTH OF THE GAP

he Faux Pass: This landmark was formed as the result of a giant misstep by the giant Faux (pronounced FOE), who was reputed to be so big that clouds blew around his knees as he walked. Once while tramping north from his normal stomping grounds (and we do mean stomp), Faux failed to observe a mountain range. He caught his left foot in it and tripped. He didn't fall, but his kick knocked a huge gap out of the mountain range, leaving a way through for lesser creatures.

The Isle of Illusion: This island lies in the sea on the east coast of Xanth almost directly across from the edge of the Gap Chasm. The Sorceress Iris lived there in a palace made beautiful by illusion. In reality, the house was a small, shabby shack no better than those owned by the poor farmers of Xanth. The island has been deserted since Iris married King Trent. When she was not keeping a close watch on her talent, it stole away back to the island, and had to be retrieved.

The Big Top: Lies south of the Gap, in the Winter Garden. Among ice plants, snowball bushes, and Christmas dagger plants, a huge, colorful, humming top spins like a mountainous toy. A cerberus barker guards the entrance. You need a ticket to get in, otherwise the troll roustabouts will throw you out. If you decide not to pay and sneak in under the edge of the tent, you run a risk of brushing against the bottom of the bleachers, which will drain all the color from your hair and clothes. There is a freak show inside, as well as a concession stand, a high wire-grass act, rides, and of course, the attractions in the center ring, surrounded by the bleachers. There is also a display of fantastic artifacts, which at one time included one of the volumes of the *Encyclopedia of Xanth*. The Big Top is run by the Ringmaster, a man made entirely of clanking metal rings.

Isle of Illusion

J. CLOUSE '89

GOOD MAGICIAN HUMFREY'S CASTLE

This edifice was once the ancient home of the Zombie Master. It was guarded by zombie plants and creatures, a zombie tangle tree, and had a zombie sea-serpent in the slime-filled moat. Guard-zombies were at one time stationed all around to prevent the castle from being approached unaware. The Zombie Master led a spartan existence here in the first half of its life. The castle was in only marginally better shape than its 700-year-old protectors until Good Magician Humfrey compelled a hundred centaurs to refurbish it for his use.

In what was left of the walls, stones had fallen away to reveal rotting support beams. Shreds of curtains hung in the windows like dead eyelids over empty sockets. The drawbridge had long since fallen in, but even at its best, it could just barely hold together, and the doors and gates all sag tiredly from their hinges. This castle fell into ruin over the centuries Jonathan spent as a zombie, and was abandoned to his house zombies, who happily occupied its remains. When Humfrey's work force of centaurs was through, the castle stood tall and slender with stout outer ramparts, and boasted a high inner tower topped by ramparts and embrasures.

It has all of the features such a wizard's castle might reasonably have. It is completely surrounded by a moat filled with murky water. The castle was built expressly to Humfrey's design in service for the Answer to a Question put him by the Elders of the Centaur Isle. Humfrey hates visitors or anything having to do with socializing, so there are always three perils through which one must pass to enter. They are always changing, depending on Humfrey's whim and the particular creatures who are serving out their year's indenture, though the first usually has something to do with whatever is occupying the moat. Humfrey periodically moves the castle or scrambles the paths, so that it is harder yet to find. Not only that, but the whole building is bespelled so its shape can be changed completely into one of ten different floor plans.

Good Magician Humfrey's Study

Once you have penetrated inside the castle, the character of the place changes from forbidding to friendly. The Gorgon is in charge of the interior, except for Humfrey's study, which no one else ever touches. The dining room is handsome and well appointed. The kitchen is somewhat old-fashioned in construction, but equipped with all the latest spells for cooking and cleaning. In the pantry, the Gorgon keeps delicacies, such as partially petrified Gorgonzola cheese, which she makes herself.

Humfrey's study is tiny and cluttered. Over the century-plus that the gnomish Good Magician has all but lived in it, this room has become stuffed with old tomes, multicolored bottles, magic mirrors, dirty socks, and assorted unidentifiable artifacts. Humfrey studies a book written by the Muse Thalia that keeps track of history, recording events as they happen. (Whenever he likes, he peers into the future or the past.) On the shelves are copies of the many magical texts about Xanth that have been leaked to Mundania.

A glass-fronted set of shelves with a lock holds hundreds of little glass bottles in which Humfrey keeps some of his spells. Uncorking one unleashes the spell within. These vials are useful to Humfrey when he travels, since he can pack up all his information books in one for easy conveyance. One of the largest stoppered jars contains several mothballs, magical devices which sheathe articles in grey-white streamers that spread out into a filmy tent which can protect the articles for up to a hundred years. Humfrey uses them to seal up the castle when there will be no one there for a long time.

The cave canem, a cave spell which turns men who enter it into dogs; a bag of wind; one vial of spy-I's, the rubber bands (presumably intended for entertainment); a book of Words of Power; and a squash were all used up in the dynasty battle against the Horseman.

The squash is a tiny cucurbit that grows into a giant vegetable. When the vial is opened and thrown into the air, it comes down SQUASH! The Words of Power included such words as *schnezl*, which causes uncontrollable sneezing. *Amnsha* causes forgetfulness, *skonk* emits bilious clouds of the most powerful bad smell, *krokk* changes men into gators with real teeth, and *bansh* makes people disappear.

One of Humfrey's historical accounts mentions that he once had the River Elba tied up in a coil as a useful article of magic. On a label tied to it was printed, "Able was I ere I saw elbow," which is probably how the bespeller captured and bound up the whole watery strand. Still on the shelf somewhere are the paper dollies, insubstantial nymphs which look like the real thing but disappear when punctured; a ham sandwich lunch reputed to be over a hundred years old; eighteen pairs of new, clean socks; a traveling magic mirror; a metal detector spell; and a copy of the *Mundane Information Please Almanac*. If there is any question which Humfrey can't answer from the pages of the books in his study, he knows where he can go to get the solution.

In the upper reaches of the castle are the bedchambers, furnished in a gracious style to suit the Gorgon's taste. One of them was redecorated as a nursery to accommodate Hugo, though it has been altered to suit a young Magician rather than an infant.

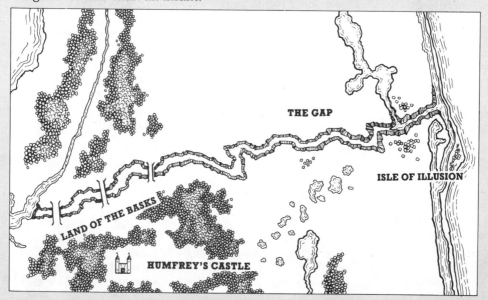

THE GAP

ISLE OF ILLUSION

LAND OF THE BASKS

HUMFREY'S CASTLE

CASTLE ROOGNA

o the southwest of Humfrey's castle, halfway between it and the chain of islands on the west coast of Xanth, lies the seat of human government and the social and magical center of Xanth, established by King Roogna during the inception of the Fifth Wave. Surrounded by a moat and 30-foot-tall ramparts is the castle, a massive edifice in stone built by centaur architects. The castle's gate is protected with an iron portcullis. The building is roughly square, its outer ramparts 100 feet on a side, braced by four great square towers on the corners, projecting halfway out from the main frame. In the center of each side is a small round tower, also half-protruding.

Originally, it had no windows, but some were cut in the walls after Trent reopened it. The strength and beauty of the walls and towers show the quality of work put into them by the centaur crew that built the castle. The extensive gardens were laid out by Roogna himself, who was a keen gardener.

Castle Roogna was built on a wager. If King Roogna failed to overcome Magician Murphy's curse and couldn't build the castle within a year, the throne would pass to Murphy. Roogna did overcome everything that went wrong, including the transformation of his newest chambermaid, to finish the job. When Gromden, who was King 400 years after Roogna, died, the beautiful palace was deserted and then forgotten.

The castle has its own magic bestowed upon it by Roogna, whose talent was adaptation — it sought a new Magician to rule as King. The castle itself is devoted to harmony, magic, jungle, and mankind.

The castle is haunted by ghosts who, unlike shades, can have no direct effect on the lives of living beings. There were six, among them Millie the Ghost, who was brought back to life by Bink; Doreen; Jordan the Barbarian, whose bones were found and reassembled by Bink's granddaughter Ivy; Button, a child of six; and Renee, otherwise known as Threnody, who had to leave the castle once she had been restored to life, because of a curse laid on

CLOUSE 89

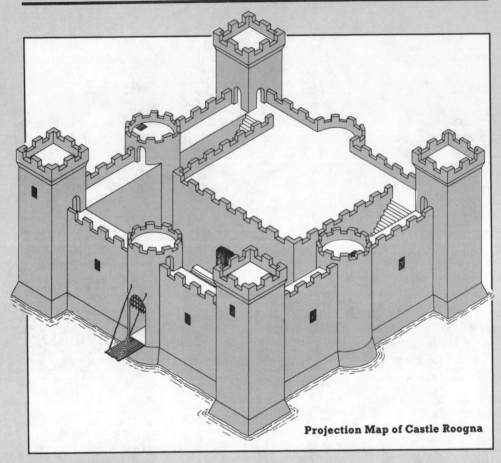

Projection Map of Castle Roogna

her by her stepmother. Roogna also has a host of zombie servitors, rats, and vampire bats.

The path to the castle goes through the gardens overlooking the orchard. Beyond the drawbridge, the main entrance leads into an anteroom where visitors wait until the King is ready to see them. Double doors open into the great hall, a majestic chamber with a high, vaulted ceiling and tall, narrow windows. There are small drawing rooms on the first floor. One of them, in which the centaur schoolmistress holds classes, overlooks the pool and long fountain in the gardens.

On the floor above the great hall is the library. This room is filled with tomes of great importance, histories, records, and information on magic and magical creatures. It is a quiet room, with wooden paneling, to which the King can withdraw for privacy.

In the upstairs drawing room nearby hangs a gigantic Tapestry, a woven magical moving picture depicting Xanth of 800 years past. It shows great adventures and episodes of love, battles with dragons, wars, scenes of peace, all in miniature and at the same pace as contemporary life, so that a day in the Tapestry appears to take the normal twenty-four hours. Princess Ivy had the Tapestry moved to her chamber for more convenient viewing. The scenes on the Tapestry can be enlarged to focus on a specific event, or rerun depending on the wishes of its audience.

Magic mirrors adorn some walls of the castle, and serve as communication devices. One of them is used by Ivy and Dolph to call home to their parents when they are away (though that one was stolen for a time by Com-Pewter).

The Royal Nursery is on the uppermost floor of the keep. The other bedchambers are on the next floor below, to muffle the sound of juvenile tears and tantrums, when there are any children. As children grow up, they move to more suitable adult chambers in the rest of the castle.

The kitchens are at the back of the castle, and their walls are spelled to keep the odor of kitchen garbage from leaking into the formal chambers. There is a dumbwaiter in the kitchen, which is used to convey food from the kitchen to the dining room above, though it played a part in the mystery of Millie's disappearance eight centuries ago.

Beneath the castle is a cellar in which good wines are kept, as well as curious magical beverages that have been distilled or brewed by one of the kitchen staff, and were not naturally grown in trees or flowers. These include boot rear, a drink that gives one a real kick, distilled from the sap of the shoefly tree. Injure jail, a concoction of incarcerated water, puts one behind bars and roughs one up. There is also card hider, after drinking which the imbiber will find pasteboards up his sleeves; club soda, a dangerous knockout punch, and droft sink, which makes you disappear through the floor.

These beverages are frequently made for parties, since the unexpected effects are considered to be great icebreakers. (It's as well to be cautious when sampling the offerings at a party in Xanth.) A few other barrels contain seam croda, poot frunch, and June pruice, though their magical effects haven't yet been noted. A very large keg to one side bears a sign that warns not to drink the contents. It contains drapple ink, which is used to sign indelibly all official documents. The dark purple-blue stain never comes off whatever it has touched.

Next to the wine cellar is the Royal Treasury. The Royal Treasury of Castle Roogna has contained a goodly number of curious weapons and spells over the centuries. Thanks to King Dor's talent of communication with the inanimate, none are now unidentified. Some fall into everyday use, such as the flying carpets, the most comfortable way to travel.

The library in Castle Roogna has books of spells and information on the older magical paraphernalia. The Escape Hoop was once a two-inch ring that was expanded to two feet in diameter by Vadne over 800 years ago. Anything passing through it finds itself in the preservative pool of the Brain Coral. The Pathfinder Spell, which looks like a small bit of wire, works only once for one person, and was meant to adapt to how much time one has to make one's way, has already been used up, but its niche on the shelf of spells is still marked, as are the places once occupied by the Melt Spell and the Forget Spell.

The Forget Spell, which was created by Magician Yin-Yang four hundred years ago, was detonated over the Gap by Dor during the Fifth Wave invasion eight hundred years ago so that the creatures he was leading toward it would forget it was there and be unable to resume their hostilities. (Forget-whorls are pieces of the decaying Forget Spell on the Gap that break off and randomly wander loose over the landscape.) The time paradox involved here is recorded in one of the books in the Royal Library.

The sunspot, a glowing globe which lights up as brightly as the sun on command, rests in a bracket depending from the ceiling of the chamber. It was once used on an adventure by Irene, but has since been returned. Magical swords, shields, and armor lie in tidy heaps in one part of the room. Gold and silver are of little use in Xanth, since there is no traditional monetary unit, but a modest glittering hoard of both metals is on hand here, along with a small keg of gems, for trade with Mundania.

Castle Roogna's defenses are not all immediately perceivable. The castle's own early-warning system of trumpet-vines, tattlesnakes, and sen-trees keep the inhabitants well apprised in advance of visitors or intruders. Glass trees provide spy-glass for maintaining a lookout over the castle walls, and a young female moat monster swims in the deep moat waters. A contingent of zombies occupy a graveyard in the castle grounds, and a few of them will be found patroling at all hours. Protective plants, like club ferns and spear grass, provide defense from attackers trying to sneak into the castle grounds over the wall. Some of them, like the cherry-bomb trees, are as old as the castle. Others were grown more recently by Irene.

Along the shortest path from Castle Roogna toward the Ogre-Fen-Ogre Fen is the Looking Glass Land. Beyond the one-way mirror which blocks the path, everything is made of glass. Glass cows graze on glass grass, and men of glass live in glass houses, though there are no stones hereabout to throw, save glass ones. The soil in which glass plants grow is, of course, ground glass. Vitreous birds fly through the air, and pretty glass unicorns live in the fragile glades.

Also in the region of Castle Roogna is the Musical Forest. The trees have radiating spokes that angle into the constant stiff wind. Each spoke produces its own sustained note, and each tree its pattern of notes. The larger the tree, the more complex the chord it plays. When a person walks through the forest, interrupting the flow of wind over the spokes, it is like playing a tune in the trees.

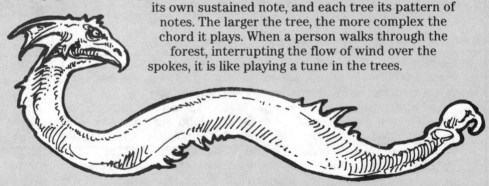

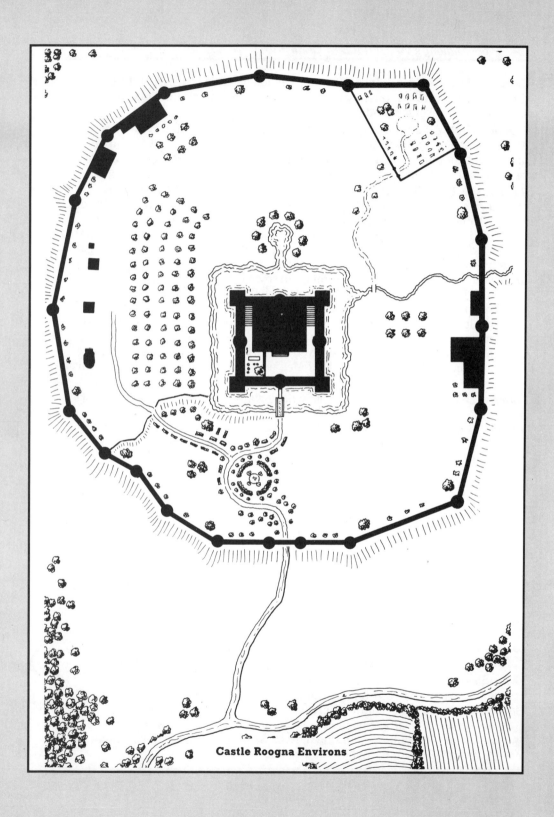

Castle Roogna Environs

Ever-Glades: Endless tracks of swampy fields, islands of trees, and tall grass through which one will pass over and over again forever unless rescued by someone with reverse wood.

Flee Market: A fast-moving, mobile bazaar seen rushing all around Xanth. Anything one wants may be bought and sold here. The Market is usually preceded by a pair of giant foot-balls that clear the way. Depending on how well the Market is going, it varies in speed from a swift trot to rapid flight.

Vale of the Vole: The Kiss-Mee River Valley once contained the friendly curved river that was home to the civilized voles in the eastern wilderness of Xanth (though for some reason they don't consider it to be in Xanth). The Kiss-Mee is so friendly that anyone who touches the water must kiss the first person he or she meets. Demons moved in and pulled it straight, depriving it of its friendly curves, which made it unfriendly to the land it passed through, drying out the land and flooding some burrows it previously missed. It was called the Kill-Mee River briefly. The voles tried to correct the straight banks, but the demons had posted guards to prevent meddling with their meddling. As a result of the demonic interference, the hummers which live there bred into unbearably large populations and drove the demons crazy. The same thing happened to the Kissimmee River in Florida, by no coincidence. Unlike the Mundane river, however, the Kiss-Mee was allowed to return to its natural state.

Demon Lake: A huge square cavern whose walls are carved to resemble brick buildings, very like a Mundane city. Rubber-tired vehicles prowl the streets, and one requires a ticket to roam the Demon Realm. There is a rum refinery in the Realm, where demon rum is made up and packaged in rum wraps. The Magistrate of the Demon Realm is Beauregard, Humfrey's former assistant.

Not-Really-In-Xanth-But-Should-Be-Mentioned-Dept.

Mundania: Since little magic exists in Mundania, apart from rainbows, there's nothing there but terrain, animals and people, none of which are interesting enough to mention here, except perhaps Squeedunk, which had the distinction of being Magician Grey's home town. No one who had a choice would live in Mundania. The name derives from the Fantasy Fans' name for the realm of nonfans. Synonym: Dreary.

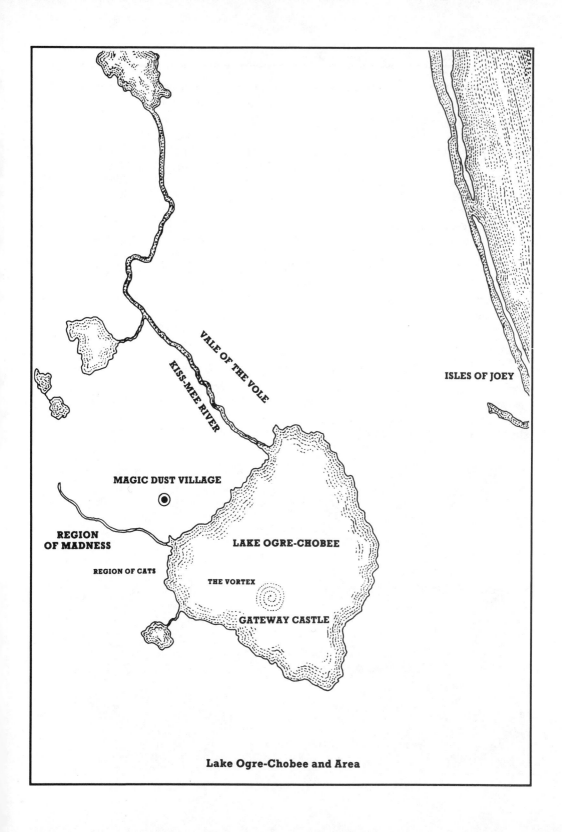

ISLES OF JOEY

VALE OF THE VOLE

KISS-MEE RIVER

MAGIC DUST VILLAGE

REGION
OF MADNESS

REGION OF CATS

LAKE OGRE-CHOBEE

THE VORTEX

GATEWAY CASTLE

Lake Ogre-Chobee and Area

Lake Ogre-Chobee: The shores of this lake are the first ancestral home of the ogres, who moved from there to the Ogre-Fen-Ogre Fen.

Faun and Nymph Retreat: A handsome lake and a lovely mountain surrounded by thick forest, enclosed by a ring of mountains south of Lake Ogre-Chobee is the last preserve of the ancient fauns and nymphs. All the breeds but nerefauns and nereids live here: dryads and dryfauns in the forest, oreads and orefauns in the caves and on the mountainside, and naiads and naifauns in the lake. They spend all day in innocent pleasure, full of love and happiness, playing, eating, laughing, chatting merrily.

By their very nature, fauns and nymphs are without defense. They do not understand hate, and when the sun goes down, it wipes out all memory of the day before, so they can't remember their fellows who were killed or kidnapped. These eternal children are helpless before any predator. Every day is new to them. The mountains and Snortimer the Bed Monster are their only protection from incursions by goblin hordes and others that would enslave or eat them.

The Fountain of Youth: In exactly the same place as on the corresponding map of Florida lies a magic pool whose water causes any living thing to grow younger. The water does not need to be drunk for the magic to take effect; it can work its magic through the skin. The Fountain is in a forest of box elders, which derive their strength from it and the youth of any unsuspecting passersby they can catch. The placement of the Fountain is kept a secret by Humfrey from everyone in Xanth, who believes that if the knowledge should slip out, the water would be generally misused. Humfrey uses the Fountain's waters to keep himself at about 100 years of age.

Fountain of Youth

Faun and Nymph Retreat

Land of the Basks: North of Castle Roogna and due east of the Faux Pass, the basilisks and cockatrices live with their families, henatrices and chickatrices. This area is not visited much by humans. Cockatrices and basilisks are by nature solitary beasts, for though they have the power to turn other creatures to stone, they are physically weak. Still, Baskland is a dangerous place to go.

New Castle Zombie: Zombie Master Jonathan and his family lived with Good Magician Humfrey in Jonathan's old castle for ten years, until the new home was completed. He and Millie now live in a castle especially decorated with slime and moss to Jonathan's taste in the southern uncharted wilderness of Xanth. In this castle, which was built to his liking, the outside is constructed of slimestone, and surrounded by a green and sludgy moat filled with zombie guardian monsters. It was built by his zombies, which means that the construction was very slow, and had to be personally overseen much of the time by Jonathan. The castle already looks centuries old. The wooden drawbridge is warped and unsteady.

The ghoulish decor does not extend beyond the gates, however, as his wife Millie has taken over the inside and beautified it. In this castle, as in Humfrey's, the feminine touch has left its mark. Tapestries and draperies cover the stone walls, giving them a pleasant warmth. The floors are spotlessly clean, and each room is tastefully furnished. Jonathan's study is sparse, with simple wooden chairs and tables, as he prefers it, but the rest of the castle furniture is suitably padded for the comfort of guests.

Hiatus and Lacuna, the Zombie Master's children, have bedrooms on the second floor of the castle, but share a sitting room between them where stands the "jerk box," a large cabinet from Mundania that plays raucous and discordant music at incredible volume.

The Blackboard Jungle: Not far from Castle Roogna, the jungle is full of magic slates on easels and stands. Each blackboard grows up with different words and pictures on it. This curious thicket is frequently torn apart by ogres, who usually can't read, and are angry that there is something here that they can't understand.

Spectre Lake: A misty body of water inhabited by ghosts, and a popular haunt of vacationing zombies.

The West Stockade: This enclosed village is on the western shore of Xanth "Where the gaze-gourds grow." This is a minor human settlement, significant only because it is from here that Millie the Maid comes.

New Castle Zombie

Isle of View: An affectionate island where the sleeping princess was supposed to wait. Just speaking its name in the company of the opposite sex can lead to interesting complications. The Love-Lies-Bleeding Monument was originally set here to mark the place of the sleeping princess, but it was stolen. Visible on the shore from the Isle is a monument marking King Trent's landing, decorated with a gourd and a never-fading purple amaranth flower. The monument was guarded by an argus, a catoblepas, and a harpy. They take it in turns to look after the monument, a day at a time. There are also a land kraken and magic vegetables to assist. The three monsters are assured unending life as long as the monument stands unmolested.

Isles of Joey: A group of islands: Thieves' Isle, where travelers forget about the valuables they bring with them, so they fall to Black Pete, the island hotel's dishonest proprietor. He uses mustard seeds soaked in Forget-Whorl to steal. His talent is dishonesty. Beauty, whose natural splendor is so complete and perfect that it would seem illusory, but it is real. However, it is populated by one hundred one and a half monsters, each worse than the last. Horror, which resembles one of the more frightening haunted scenes in the gourd. Water, where the water worm turns all it touches to water. The isle, which is made of dry water, looks like a single broad scintillating patch of water in the midst of the sea. Fake Isle is used as cover by a gigantic female kraken who eats the innocent prey that approaches. Food Isle is a huge cake with ice cream, chocolate sauce and all the trimmings. Children who find this isle forget all about good manners or decent nutrition. There are believed to be other Isles of Joey as yet undiscovered.

The Gold Coast: Several days' sailing south of the Isle of Illusion is the Gold Coast, where the sands, trees, plants, fruit and rocks are pure gold. There stands the Ivory Tower, on a lonely promontory, where Rapunzel was once imprisoned by the Sea Hag. From its top, a magic light swings around and around, illuminating the shore, then the water, then the shore again. The Tower is only accessible on foot at lowest tide. Otherwise, it is cut off by swift-moving tides and dangerous golden rocks.

Fee: Inland from the Gold Coast is the region of the Fee. In this glade live stunningly beautiful humans, mostly young women in flowing white, who are all marred by a single animal feature, such as hawk talons, dog paws, or a snake's tail. Their leader is Fulsome Fee, a handsome young man with duck feet. The Fee seek to breed with outsiders to revive their diminishing population. It is a place for travelers to avoid, for the Fee insist that they mate for life.

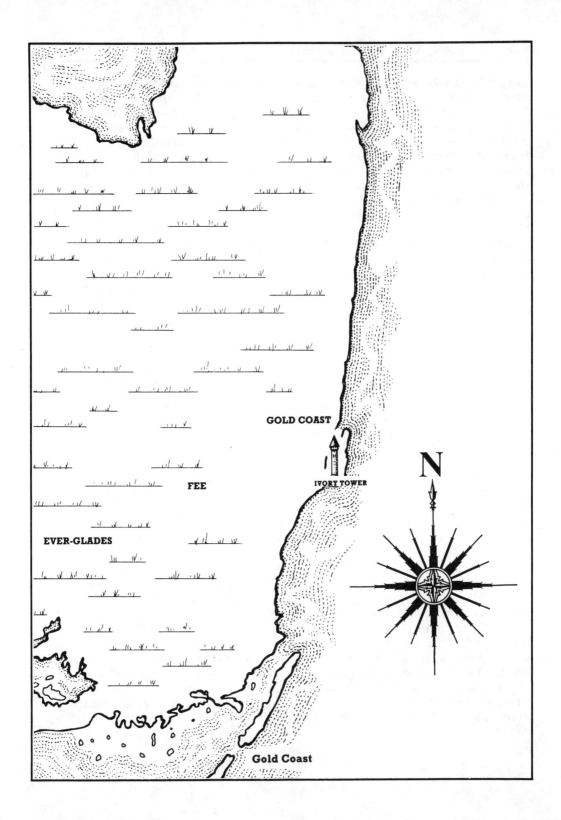

GOLD COAST

IVORY TOWER

N

FEE

EVER-GLADES

Gold Coast

Magic Dust Village: The Village was once a normal stockade where humans lived, sacking and distributing the magic dust which welled up there from the Source of Magic. Rocs beating their powerful wings drive the dust upward so that the prevailing northwesterly winds will carry it away into the rest of Xanth. The Siren arrived one day on one of the two small islands in the nearby lake, and began to lure away all the males in the Village. None of the men ever came back, and no one knew why. As the population declined, the women of the Village sent out messages asking for others to come help them with their most vital task, for without their continued work, magic would build to a disproportionate concentration there, and the rest of Xanth would revert slowly to Mundanity.

In answer to the plea, couples of other intelligent species came to stay, to help with the task, but all of those males were soon under the Siren's spell. Any females who tried to follow were consumed by a gigantic tangler which had made a deal with the Siren to take the women and let the men pass. Soon, there was nothing in the Village but the females, who kept up with their task, but mourned for their lost men.

Headwoman

It took the efforts of Bink and the Good Magician Humfrey and their companions to discover that the actual reason for the continued absence of their menfolk was that the Siren's sister, the Gorgon, was magically rendering them all into stone statues. Once the Siren's magic dulcimer was destroyed, the threat to the Village ended, and the citizens went on with their work. All the races live together there in peace.

It is dangerous to use one's talent within the Magic Dust Village, for the raw, concentrated power of the dust floating around in the air may cause an overload. As a result, the villagers do most of their work by hand, and build houses and cook food in the old-fashioned way, without the use of magic. Since the days of the Siren, the headwoman of the Village has always been a female troll, because of her hard-headed approach to common sense. Short of that of an ogress, a trolless has the hardest head of any species in Xanth.

The Source of Magic: Far below the Magic Dust Village, beneath the pool of the Brain Coral, is the giant cavern where the Demon $X(A/N)^{th}$ has remained during its Game with the other infinite entities. The vortexes of its thought are placed throughout the cavern so it is possible for anyone to wander into one and experience it. The Brain Coral's pool preserves unharmed in its brine anything which falls into it. Before the Time of No Magic, it was a plain cavern, and the Demon was entombed in a wall, but afterward, it was transformed into a palatial setting with fountains and a throne of solid diamond upon which the Demon ponders at its ease, considering how to better its advantage in the Game. A deadly Shieldstone now prevents anyone from entering the cavern.

The Demon X(A/N)th

Region of Madness lies all around the southeast edge of the Magic Dust Village. It is devoid of intelligent life because the high concentration of fallout from the airborne dust plays chaos with the ecology, and drives anything living there mad. The constellations as seen from this region appear to be alive, and behave irrationally. They can hear clearly anything addressed to them (or said about them). The centaur archer constellation we know as Sagittarius can fire its starry arrows down into Xanth.

Region of Cats falls just within the area bounded by the Region of Madness. On a catwalk, a catamount crouches, guarding the way. If one falls into the catalytic water around the catwalk, one is visited with catarrh, catatonia, and catalepsy.

Catbirds and catfish live in this area. The path leads through cattails growing in catsup where cattle graze, fattening up against future cataclysm. At the end of the path is a catacomb cared for by a caterpillar, containing catnip. Inside the catacomb, the catastrophe can be found on the wall, flanked by bright catseyes. Beyond the cataract is a catapult, a feline the size of a sphinx, which can be bribed to throw travelers in a basket clear across the Region of Madness, in exchange for catnip.

Gateway Castle straddles a vortex underneath the lake in the Region of Madness. The vortex, a whirlpool, is a one-way route to an underground cavern on the shore of a glowing lake of warm water. The complex within is the realm of the Curse Fiend theatrical troupes, so the theatre auditorium, practice halls, makeup and costume chambers take up most of the floor space. There is a suitable dungeon for getting Curse Fiend actors in the mood for gloomy portrayals, which can also be used for incarcerating the odd unwanted guest. A well-appointed kitchen provides meals handsome enough to be used on stage.

The large individual chambers for principal players and smaller dormitories for bit parts and walk-ons resemble dressing rooms more than simple bedchambers.

Catapult

Gateway Castle

Mount Parnassus: This fabled twin-peaked mount is hidden in the illiterate wilderness. Around the foot of Mount Parnassus is a dry channel of small round stones. Among them slinks the dipsas, a small serpent whose bite causes one to become endlessly and unquenchably thirsty. Its victims will drink until they explode, thirst unabated. One of its former victims drank this riverbed dry. Other perils haunt the slopes of the mountain, for at the peaks are the two greatest magical trees in Xanth.

At the apex of its south peak is the Tree of Seeds, guarded by the Simurgh, the wisest bird in the world, who is female, for only females are the keepers of seeds. On the tree grow all seeds of every type ever known in Xanth, many unknown ones, and just as many that no longer exist there, like the ex-seed, pro-seed, inter-seed. There are also seeds which could be used for evil, such as the seeds of Doubt, a nebulously shaped kernel; Dissension, a sharp-spined burr; and War, a mushroom-cloud shape.

On the south slope of the south peak is a beautifully carved stone palace of ornate columns and smooth walls etched with the incised figures of people and animals. Here live the nine Muses. Clio, the Muse of History, is eternally engaged in writing texts, among them the magic texts which Humfrey and the centaur scholars use. Thalia, Muse of Comedy and Planting, rules all forms of humor, including irony. It is she who assists visitors to reach the Simurgh.

In a cave on the same slope is the Oracle. The priestesses of the Oracle, known as Pythia, sniff intoxicating vapors that rise from crevasses and fissures in the rock and make crazy prophecies in gibberish, which are interpreted for supplicants who have questions. The Oracle is guarded by the Python, the original serpent of desire, who is wise in the fallibilities of man.

Eternally young and beautiful Maenads range the north slope. These naked nymphlike creatures tear apart and eat any creature they catch. Some they capture by pretending to be nice, sweet girls, luring males into reach. They drink from a flowing wine-spring which when restored by Magician Grey became blood-flavored wine, so that the Maenads could satisfy both of their hungers at once.

The Tree of Immortality grows on the north peak. It is necessary only to consume one leaf of that tree to live forever, but it is almost impossible to reach the tree without getting killed.

Mount Rushmost: The meeting place of the winged monsters. Their leader, Cheiron, holds court here. Its peak is broad and flat. Here gather creatures that fly: griffins, rocs, harpies, hippogryphs, winged donkeys, dragons, fireflies, dragonflies, chimerae, and manticora. Several individuals of rarer species, such as winged centaurs like Cheiron himself and his bride Chex, winged mermaids, the phoenix, winged goblins, and flying fish, also gather here. No creature without wings may land on the peak. Even Cumulo Fracto Nimbus may be driven away by the assembled. The Simurgh attends to perform weddings, and is most honored among all monsters for her wisdom.

Palace of the Muses

CENTAUR ISLE

n independent island off the southern tip of Xanth. It is actually a merging of hundreds of tiny "keys" into one big isle. The centaurs who live there consider themselves allies to the human King of Xanth, not his subjects. Gerome Centaur is the chief Elder of the Isle.

Centaurs are one of the oldest intelligent magic species in Xanth. The earliest ones were engendered 800 years before the first human settlement in Xanth by three men and their mares, who all drank from a love spring. Their descendants bred with one another, keeping the gene pool small. There have been few crosses outside the centaur line, and they prefer it that way.

The centaurs live a most civilized life, depending on magic as little as possible. Their culture is highly developed. They prefer peace, and would rather barter for what they need than fight for it.

There are not many human visitors to the isle. Human guests who are invited to stay are placed in comfortable guest rooms that are made to their size and configuration. The centaurs of the isle are always ready to welcome the King or his representatives, but few others are welcomed. For guests from one of the centaur settlements to the north, they provide stables equipped with water trough, hay rack, and salt block. Some of these accommodations have lovely views of well-kept pasture land.

The wide streets are of hard-packed earth, and banked on the curves for galloping safety. Here and there, low scrapers are placed for clearing mud from the hooves. It is easy to tell that deep consideration went into every phase of planning the construction.

Some of the buildings are made to accommodate the human side of centaurs; some the horsy side. The metalworking section of town has silversmiths and coppersmiths working on beautiful items to please the aesthetic eye. A blacksmith makes more everyday items which may be used to

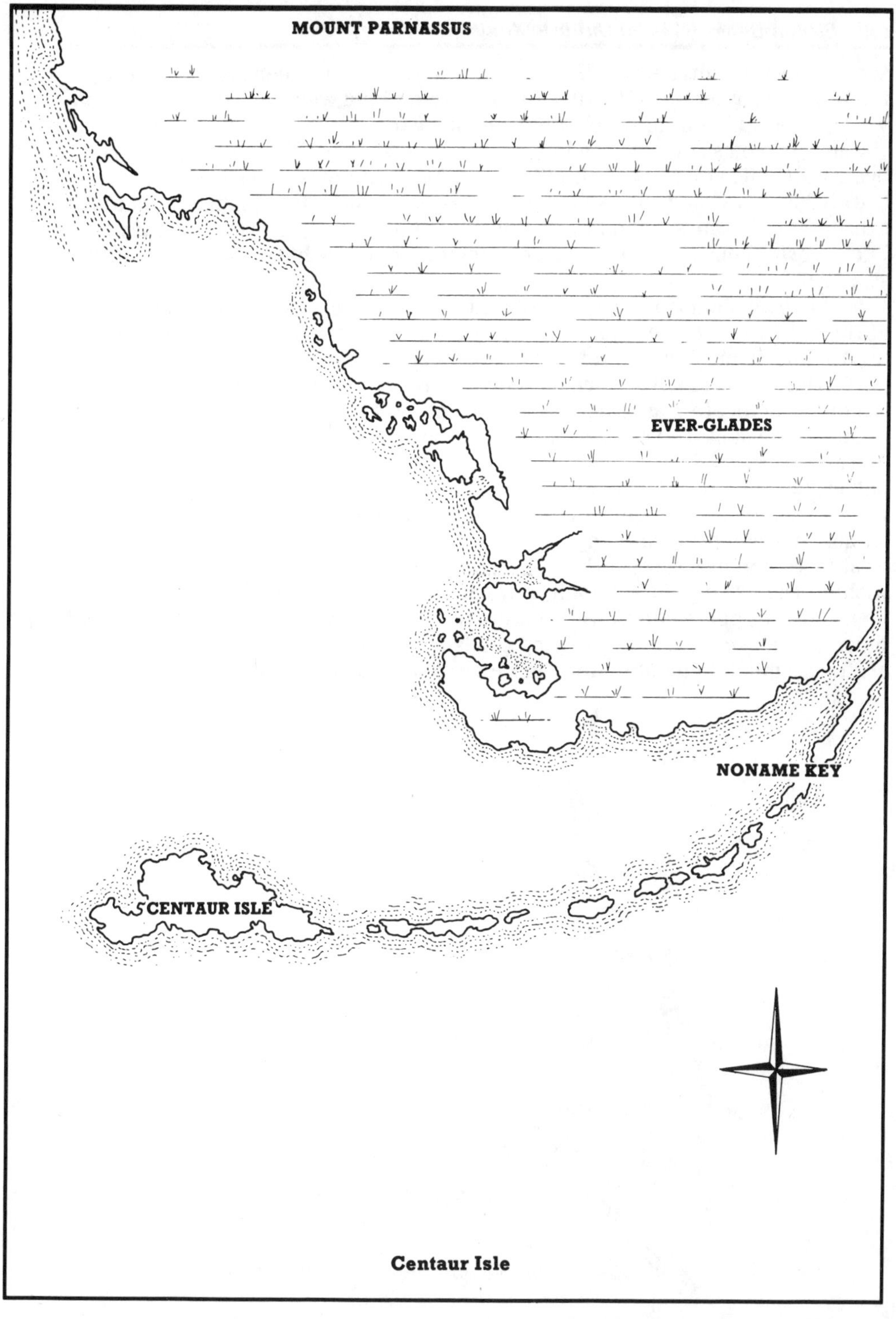

MOUNT PARNASSUS

EVER-GLADES

NONAME KEY

CENTAUR ISLE

Centaur Isle

serve either the intellectual or the physical needs of the centaurs. An entire manufacturing sector of town is devoted to making weapons and armor, and yet the centaurs would prefer not to make war.

Centaur meals are prepared in a communal kitchen. Their dining hall is a beautiful edifice of stone with pillars and high windows to let in the sun and the cool breeze. The table is of striped sardonyx and white alabaster, made tall so that centaurs (who have no need of chairs and eat standing) may eat in comfort. Their plates are of green jadeite. Centaurs have a love of beautiful stonework.

An historical museum displaying centaur artifacts explains the diversities of their culture. The centaurs have an agreement dating from their genesis not to make war. They would rather spend their time studying, crafting and perfecting new skills. The former keeper of records was Arnolde the Archivist, dedicated, asocial, and intelligent even by centaur standards.

One of the skills the centaurs practice (besides the arts of warfare, mathematics, archery, and the study of humans) is weaving. They make battle garments out of iron-curtain thread which is strongly resistant to penetration by foreign objects. But their talent in weaving is not limited to these. They can duplicate any fabric or garment which grows on blanket bush or shirt tree in greater Xanth; in fact, they prefer to make their textiles without the use of magic, which they consider to be obscene and not to be mentioned in polite company. Centaur traders follow routes that lead up and down the coasts of Xanth, carrying goods from the isle all over. Centaur-made crafts are much in demand for their high quality and excellence of design.

A QUICK GUIDE TO PLACES IN XANTH

North of the Gap

Ogre-Fen-Ogre Fen
The Five Forbidden Regions
  Air
  Fire
  Water
  Earth
  The Void
The Kingdom of the Flies
Dragonland
Naga Caverns

Region of the Goblins
The Home of the Callicantzari
Elfland
Region of Griffins
Birdland
North Village
Tsoda Popka Lakes
Half-Baked Bog
With-a-Cookee River

The Gap

The Gap Village

South of the Gap

The Faux Pass
The Isle of Illusion
The Big Top
Good Magician Humfrey's Castle
Castle Roogna
Ever-Glades
Flee Market
Vale of the Vole
Demon Lake
Lake Ogre-Chobee
Faun and Nymph Retreat
The Fountain of Youth
Land of the Basks
New Castle Zombie

The Blackboard Jungle
Spectre Lake
The West Stockade
Isle of View
Isles of Joey
The Gold Coast
Fee
Region of Madness
Region of Cats
Gateway Castle
Mount Parnassus
Mount Rushmost
Centaur Isle

The Gourd

THE GOURD

n Xanth, one of the greatest and most subtle dangers is to accidentally look into the peephole of a hypnogourd, which grow in patches all over the land. These vegetables look completely harmless. A gourd resembles a Mundane butternut squash with an extra dimplelike hole on its upper surface. While the body lies helplessly staring into the peephole, the soul is swept into the world of the gourd, where it wanders lost, until someone covers the peephole. If you return to the gourd, you will always go back to the same place you left. If you are lost there, you will be lost again as soon as you return.

It seems impossible that an ordinary vegetable like a peephole gourd can contain a whole world, but that is the nature of things in Xanth. The most ordinary outside will conceal the most extraordinary inside. Within the rind are several different lands.

The gourd connects Xanth to Mundania via the No Name Key. Unlike the Isthmus, this one uses the gourd for access to the Mundane world, and does not modify the time scale. Night mares and storks make their way through the No Name Key. Turn Key is the Key Holder here.

The first face of the gourd most people see is the region of black-and-white horror scenes, complete to haunted house with shocking doorknob, chill drafts, and ghosts. The house is a horror in itself, with a moving staircase that throws one into an oubliette. The graveyard near the rind is full of skeletons who take great pride in their ability to scare the daylights out of visitors.

Brassilia, the City of the Brassies, is made of shiny gleaming brass. The city is enclosed by a gleaming wall with no perceptible entrance. The long golden streets are set symmetrically on either side with buildings of perfect squared angles and mirror-shiny surfaces, but no doors or windows. Brassilia seems deserted at first, unless you push the brass button set on a pedestal under the moon. The button sets off the klaxon alarm that stirs the city into motion. The metal buildings begin to slide around the landscape, changing location. They move at a tremendous speed, so it is wise to get out of the way.

Black and White Haunted House in the Gourd

J CLOUSE
© '89

There is nowhere safe to hide while the city is on the move. Underneath the buildings are cubical brass holes which serve as anchorage spots for the locking mechanisms which keep them in place. If you can jump into one of the holes and wait, a building will eventually come to a stop over you. It is hollow inside, and there is a corresponding hole in its bottom through which the locking bolt passes. Since there are no doors, this is the only way to get inside.

Brass statues of men and women on pedestals stand motionless inside the buildings until another button is pressed, and then the brassies come to life. Brassies wear brassards or brassieres, and brass hats.

Brassies mass-manufacture certain dreams for the Night Stallion. They are good at mechanical work, when they get down to brass tacks. They do very good work in their specialty.

One can escape from the city by climbing over the wall, or by taking the Luna Fringe Shuttle at the Luna triptych building. It launches one into the moon, which, like the one outside the gourd, is made of green cheese on its near side.

An elevator connects the City of Brass with the Paper World. Green shreds of paper do here for grass. Brown and green constructs of paper form trees. A flat circle of paper pasted on the blue paper sky is the sun, and crepe paper clouds float past it. Houses of cards dot the landscape, each the height of an ogre.

Origami animals roam among the pasteboard plant life. Neatly folded paper bugs crawl in the grass. Cardboard birds pull accordion-pleated worms out of the ground. The rocks, clouds, and even the puddles are paper.

Visitors are not welcome here. Little cardboard boxes with "Tank" printed on them roll out to shoot paper balls at intruders. Paper tigers spring out to snarl at the unwary with a sound like tearing newsprint.

There is a region of the Elements in the gourd, similar to the one in Xanth. The Realm of the Element of Air is lorded over by the Air Monster, a great blowhard, which will not rest until it has destroyed its enemies. This elemental is quite stormy when aroused. It can blow wind or snow or any other inclement weather at perceived threats.

Below the Element of Air lies the Element of Earth. A huge cave-mouth in the floor of the cavern is topped by other features which are the personification of the Earth Elemental. It has stalagmites and stalactites for teeth. It has a long stony tongue on which travelers can walk if they have flattered Earth enough. There is reason to praise this elemental: the region is very beautiful. Bands of colored rock and gemstone line the walls of the caverns.

A wall of flame marks the realm of the Element of Fire. To pass through, a traveler becomes flame. Fire is malleable, so one can change shape, so long as

Paperworld

one is careful not to leave a source of fuel too long. Each of the available fuels have different flavors and colors. Gas is green and flickering, coal blue and even, wood yellow and sputtering.

As Fire ends and Water begins, those who have traveled as flame become fish in the endless lake of the Element. Fish and water-monsters of every type abound here, but they will not bother travelers who stay on the enchanted path.

The Void follows Water. In the gourd Void, shape is not infinite or definite. One can change to whatever shape or configuration one wishes, even change or eliminate the scenery. Since the Void here is merely a representation of the real Void, it is possible to escape without dying. In fact, the representation of the Void itself can be folded up and transported to another location.

In the Desert of the Ifrit, whoever frees the Ifrit in the bottle with the seal marked "Fool" across its cork will die, but is allowed to choose the method. The wise choose old age.

The Mirror World is a maze of endless mirrors set in a hall. Some are straight and show true reflections. Some are bizarrely warped. It is possible to be lost here forever.

A burning iceberg dominates one land filled with amorphous frights. Next to it, stone-masons made of stone work on metal, wood and flesh. They manufacture backdrops and scenery for the worst dreams.

Beyond the masons is a region of boiling mud. This is the best throwing mud, in green, purple, or yellow. It bubbles up from deep underground in messy billows and currents and stinking, flatulent explosions. The mud is impossible to sling without the thrower ending up wearing at least as much as he gets on his target.

The path leads next into a jungle of carnivorous vines and bloodthirsty clouds. The trees are animate, and their branches creak threateningly. Beyond it is a thicket where striking weapons of all kinds grow, along with anything else that might be needed for bad dreams.

Along one side of this path turn huge, grinding wooden gears. These measure out the time for every event in dreams. The length and placement must be exact or there would be gaps, confusion and fuzziness in a sleeper's mind. The dream realm does its best to keep everything on schedule, but even so, there are inaccuracies. Dreams are intended as sincere warnings.

Near the gears, loan sharks, card sharks and poor fish swim in crowded channels. They bluff night mares into fearing them, but they don't dare actually to harm them, for the Night Stallion would punish them if they did. Other travelers have no such protection from the bloodthirsty fishes.

You can see the light in the next region from a great distance. Brilliant beams of light crisscross and wave across the enchanted path. The reds burn anything they touch. Lights of searing white vaporize solid matter. Shimmering black ones turn things cold. Green lights make things sprout leaves. Each beam has a different function. Some make things hot or cold; others turn surfaces bright or dull, and leave them clean or dirty.

On the other side of the lights is Candyland. On either side of the hard chocolate path is a candy garden. Marshmallows lie scattered as if they were

Burning Iceberg

stones. Lollipops grow from the ground like trees and flowers. Licorice weeds do their best to choke out more delicious candy plant life.

Next comes a wooden house with a garden. The house looks nice until you are up close, when you can see that it is filled with every kind of bug and creeping horror. The garden is no better. It looks normal, but as you approach, it changes into one filled with vegetable instruments of childhood culinary torture like turnips, spinach, and cabbages. Near the bug-house lies a placid lake of castor oil. Zombies who enter the gourd usually begin in a zombie garden in which lurks a snake. When it bites, it leaves the flesh healthy instead of infected. The very thought of being visited with health is more terrifying to zombies than the snake is.

Next comes a knife fight, in which hosts of rusty knives bar the way unless a strange knife is thrown among them. They will attack that knife until they all break. From here the path seems to go nowhere, but if a fungus rock of a sickly mossy green is crushed, it will burn away dead vegetation until a wooden platform appears, under which are stairs and a landing.

The landing leads to a lighted cellar, where one finds an enchanted path barred by a gate where one faces one's deepest fear or shame shown on a zombie looking glass. Unless the fear is faced and conquered, the traveler will end up back where he began.

After the gate is a blank wall where one must only picture a door for one to appear. Inside the wall is an exhibition of scenes into which one can pass just by diving through the frames.

If instead of climbing down the stairs to the landing, one seeks a different path which leads to a place where rats run, there is a region where a spread

sheet of surprising springiness makes up the floor. By bouncing on this sheet up and down over and over again, one eventually is propelled through the "ceiling" rind of the gourd, where there is another gourd, approximately man-height in size. This is the gourd within the gourd. The peephole in this gourd leads to Mundania. This is the way that night mares convey bad dreams to sleepers there. On the other side of the peephole is the No Name Key, where Turn Key keeps track of passage between Xanth and Mundania. He has at his command all manner of Mundane "science" which he uses in his job, such as a talk box which speaks both Xanth's language and that of Mundania, a magic boat which is propelled by a box at the back that growls like a dragon, and a watch, which finds the object of one's desire. His house is very nice, with carpets on the floor and windows that look out over the Key.

The Cakewalk, land of confections. Each sweetmeat has a different effect on the eater. Fruitcake makes one silly, rumballs makes one rolling drunk, angelfood angelic, and devilsfood devilish.

Beyond the Cakewalk is a featureless steel floor that forms an infinite plain in the center of the gourd. This is the Pasture of the Night Stallion. The Dark Horse is always in the last place one looks, so one must cover all the terrain of the gourd before ending up here. Trojan is here in one or another of his forms. He may appear as a living stallion with glittering eyes, or as a steel-hard, steel-cold statue of a midnight-black horse. If forced into a duel, Trojan is capable of projecting opponents into visions to force them to concede. This is his turf, the Kingdom of Dreams, and the inhabitants of the other lands inside the gourd work for him.

A specialized application of the gourd was encountered by Prince Dolph: the Terminal. This can be terrifying to Mundanes. It is a large chamber filled with people burdened by baggage and possessions, and running to and fro. The chamber's ceiling is held up by tall square pillars. Halls and walkways lead off in all directions from the main room. Every so often, gibberish bursts from spots on the wall.

Behind a hole in the wall is a very small room which carries passengers up through the ceiling and onto another floor full of hustle and bustle. Mundane men and women dash through here in a hurry to catch their "planes," silver birdlike cylinders the size of a dragon, with flat projections sticking out the sides. They belch steam from their rears.

Magic stairs that move by themselves carry one down to the lower floor again. There are doors that lead to the outside. Once there, you are surrounded by square boxlike things that are jammed head to tail in lines that stretch off into the horizon. They make noises like that of a hungry ogre fighting with a banshee. The moving boxes contain Mundanes that spout nonsense such as "Haybabe!" Large humans dressed in blue whose feet are somewhat flat keep order as best they can, but they can always stop to harass passersby.

Since this is a representation of Mundania, addresses are read backward, not sensibly forward, as in Xanth. A door in the Terminal leads to Angle-Land, which was the last line in the address left by Humfrey.

The Angle-Land in the gourd is very different from the one actually in Mundania. It is populated by angles, both stationary and mobile: dear little acute angles whose horizons are limited, obtuse angles with very little intellect, very correct right angles, humorless straight angles, and philosophical reflex angles.

At the sharpest point of the acute angles lies the gate to Hurts, the next direction in the address. Its bloodstained gate is spiked with broken glass and needlelike spines. Hurts is used by the dream realm for settings to scare dreamers afraid of pain. All its denizens suffer, whether from injuries or diseases or internal emotional distress. The Dungeon Master of Hurts, who manages this set, is a mean-looking human man who wears a black mask.

Hurts is bounded by a swift-flowing muddy river over which several fords are set, each supervised by different creatures. Blood flows into the river at various points, and horrendous monsters, the stuff of which bad dreams are crafted, live in its polluted waters. Upstream from Hurts is Frankford, supervised by a man-sized sausage with arms and legs. Next is Afford, where those with plenty of money might cross. Then Beeford, over which hordes of bees buzz. Next is Ceeford, where all the people looked but didn't touch. An alphabet's worth of fords follow these, ending with Zeeford, supervised by striped horses.

The next lot of fords flock together. Their names pertain to Mundane types of birds: Ibisford, Heronford, and so on to Storkford, which was where storks crossed with their bundles of joy. The storks follow a path through a field of berries, and down near a bury plant, which produces its fruit underground. Every variety of berry is here, from blue and red berries, to Londonberries to Halingberries which call out to passersby. The Big Halingberry has a loud voice, and its offspring, the Little Halingberry, calls in a mere whisper.

Along nearby Main Lane, there are many smaller lanes leading away that have interesting things going on at their ends: Lois Lane, Hot Lane, Cold Lane, Fast Lane, Santa Claus Lane, Derby Lane. After these are the animal lanes, then the bird lanes, where can be found Donald Duck Lane, Sober Goose Lane, and Silly Goose Lane, on which one will get a rude surprise.

Silly Goose Lane is lined with Crofts. Eagle, Handi, Welkin, Mans, Kids, and Dames. Damescroft is a tidy thatched and whitewashed cottage, which is the illusory form of Humfrey's uninterruptible hideaway while he solves his own Question Quest.

The Night Stallion can quickly commission special scenes if he has need of them, intended to torment those he wishes to try for treason. The alleged criminal finds himself in a room with two doors, one marked "Yes" and the other "No," with a question printed on the wall between. Thus the stallion obtains information about the person he is about to put on trial. The questions get harder until the victims beg for mercy, which they will not get. Those found guilty will be executed to find out if they are sincere in their protestations of

innocence. If the executee is sincere, he or she will be restored to employment in the gourd.

Each time someone enters the gourd, the scene is set for that person. If travelers are not in direct contact, they will be thrust into different dream sequences.

Ivy drew Grey Murphy into the Frankinmint Mountain dream sequence when she brought him in from Mundania. The two of them entered through a picture. The mountain is vaguely pyramidal, roughly terraced with sharp clifflike vertical drops and black cave entrances. Perched at the very top is a gourd model of Castle Roogna, so high up that it looks like a tiny toy. Crystal spires point upward from the slopes of the mountain, and fantastic constructs of stone throw long shadows in the sunlight. More than one path spirals around toward the peak.

The mountain lies in a vast empty plain so flat that it resembles the surface of a table. It moves across the plain by itself, carrying passengers to its destination. Once on its way, it passes among jungle trees and a river valley, heading for lofty peaks visible in the distance.

On the slopes of the mountain grow several kinds of mint. Spearmint stabs anything that moves with tiny spears. Peppermint explodes with irritating pepper grains that cause sneezing. Frankinmint merely smells like a nice mint-flavored incense. (Not to be confused with frankincense, which makes people frankly angry). On small ledges stand illusory images of important folks of Xanth. Between some of the ledges the path becomes a narrow span of bridge.

Inside the castle, which is devoid of all life or animation, there is an extra door not present in its outside counterpart. Beyond the door is a lovely green landscape. It is a one-way portal. Anyone attracted by the landscape will

Frankinmint Mountain

become trapped on that side of the door once it closes. The path there leads past a tilting tree to the river of blood that flows from the side of Girard Giant.

Loan sharks swim in the river, looking to take an arm and a leg from unwary swimmers. At the source of the river lies the giant, who lay pinned there by order of the Night Stallion for wrecking several vital dream sets.

Girard originally wandered in through a jungle scene beset by kraken weeds with powerful suckers that drank blood. Once in place, the suckers were painful to remove. Next, he found himself on a halfway flat plain, over which Cumulo Fracto Nimbus blew freezing wind and sleet.

The next peril was a sphinx, followed by a roc. Both attacked fiercely. Girard blundered through the wall of this scene and into the pool of twenty mermaids. Beyond that was the candy house, and on the other side of the candy wall was a pool of writhing tentacles. Next, he found a hillside full of goblins. In the next scene, there was an ogre with a wooden spear which he plunged into Girard's side. These pathways were never meant to intersect.

THE HAZARDS OF XANTH

It seems to be the desire of every Mundane reader to move to Xanth. That's understandable, considering how dreary Mundania is. But not smart. The fact is, Xanth is dangerous. There are more hazards per square circle in Xanth than anywhere else. Since Mundane folk don't have magic, they are at a serious disadvantage in Xanth. The average visitor would survive less than a day, unless he had the advice and protection of a Xanth native.

Oh, sure, things are funny in Xanth. When a harpy swears, the foliage nearby catches fire. When a Xanth couple gets married, zombies may attend. Panty-watching is a great sport, as it is in Mundania. Puns abound. And no good folk ever seem to die. So it seems nice.

But Mundanes are not considered good folk, by and large, so they can die like the brutes they are. Many Xanth creatures who are not main characters can die too. Death is a way of life in the savage jungles of Xanth, and it can come in an impossible number of forms. So the notion of a Mundane reader actually moving to Xanth and liking it is sheer fantasy.

I try to be careful what I write in Xanth. There is only so far you can go saying goblins are horrible and not showing how they are horrible. Many people were surprised at one scene where the children witness a very disgusting goblin atrocity, but even then I made it clear that what they were seeing had happened long before, and they were only seeing a replay. After all there has to be some risk, otherwise the reader can never take the dangers seriously.
— Piers Anthony

But there is one route. A reader can't go to Xanth himself, but he can take the place of a Xanth resident for a while, acting through that resident until he succeeds in making that resident blunder into expulsion. This is the route of the Xanth Gamebooks. The truth is, not many Xanth residents of distinction like having their lives managed by absentee Mundanes, so the usual crowd tends to stay clear of the games, but some can be seen on occasion. If you want to discover just how long you might last in Xanth, go to your dreary Mundane bookstore and fork over some stupid Mundane money for one of those Gamebooks the Nymph has made available. Then you'll know, you fool.

HAZARDS

utside of the stockades, villages and castles, Xanth is wild and dangerous, but in the dark it is doubly hazardous. Only in houses spelled against the supernatural can humans sleep safely, untroubled except by night mares, whom nothing can keep out.

Children growing up in Xanth learn to protect themselves against a variety of threats and monsters which are set to catch the unwary and destroy them.

Dragons are one of the most fearsome species that live in the untamed wilderness that covers most of Xanth. Besides the breed recognized as the Gap Dragons, there are many other varieties. In Xanth, there are land-bound and water-bound dragons as well as those which can fly and those that tunnel. Sea serpents are related to dragons. The ouroboros is a water-dragon, half white, half black, which seeks to drown its prey as it twists around and around with its tail in its mouth. Most dragons have a breath weapon as well as their own armament of sharp teeth and iron claws. Dragons spit smoke and steam as well as the traditional burst of fire.

In fact, the dragons of the earth, air and sea fall into three substantial categories: steamers, smokers, and fire-breathers. The Gap Dragon is the best known example of the steamer; his weapon is invisible steam which turns visible as it encounters the cooler air, making water droplets form. If you want to know how hot that feels, put your finger in the invisible section of steam just beyond the spout of a hot tea kettle: it's about ten times as bad as that. Thus the Gap Dragon doesn't eat raw meat, he eats steamed meat and, if he's feeling like punishment, steamed vegetables. Steam is less impressive than fire, but it does the job, and is more controllable. You never heard of a steamer starting a fire by accident. It is also nice when the dragonlets need a steam bath.

Smokers are effective, too. It is not generally known, but more creatures are killed by smoke than by fire. In fact, smoke inhalation is so effective that it even works in Mundania, where it has a similar ratio of kills. Smoke also blinds the prey and makes it lose its way. The dragon has merely to cock an ear, and it can locate the fleeing prey within the cloud of smoke by the sounds of gasping and stumbling. Then one quick nip does it: smoked meat. In a pinch, a cottage cheese can be smoked; smoked cheese is said to have a special flavor. But sometimes the cloud of smoke is so thick that the dragon chomps on the wrong item, getting maybe the pot instead of the cook. Only a stupid dragon smokes pot.

Fire-breathers are the most illustrious and feared of dragons. Actually, they vary widely; some have only a little jet of fire the size of a human finger, while others have a jet that extends as far before as their tails do behind. But fire is high-calorie stuff, requiring a lot of energy, so dragons must be cautious about wasting it. As a general rule, if a dragon misses its prey with three blasts, it will have to retire to regenerate its heat, because the following blasts will have diminishing effect. There is also the matter of pride: it is considered bad form to miss even once.

However, despite these limitations, it remains true that a good many more men are eaten by dragons than vice versa. Only a fool or an ogre (same thing) would tangle voluntarily with a dragon.

Dragons are good hunters. They are patient, and can outwait most prey. Some can move very quickly, especially the ones that can fly, but others have to stalk their prey and wait at the holes for it to emerge. Dragons prefer to nest on jewels, especially diamonds, which hone their scales to their brightest and sharpest best.

Most dragons are built on long, low lines, with overlapping metal scales on their hides. They are very flexible, very smart, and have an excellent sense of smell. Their spiked tails, which they can use like whips, are dangerous weapons, too. They like the taste of roasted man, though almost any nonpoisonous meat will do. Dragons are very hard to kill or even to hurt. The best way to kill one is to shoot arrows or explosive things down its throat, or slice between its scales with a sword or spear. A dragon's ear twitches when its possessor should listen, and hears things of importance and relevance, so it will nearly always detect pursuit. Should a hunter manage to kill a dragon, or just to cut off one of its ears, he has obtained a useful magic item that can help to protect him. Of course, if he is capable of killing a dragon, he needs very little help from anyone.

Wiggles are part of the greater family of voles, which also includes squiggles, which are ten times the size of a wiggle, and diggles, which are ten times the size of a squiggle. It is the immature wiggle which swarms and causes all the damage, but the majority of swarms never find their way to the surface of Xanth.

Wiggle larvae are tiny spiral worms less than a finger-length long that drill holes in anything. They zap outward in straight lines from their hatching

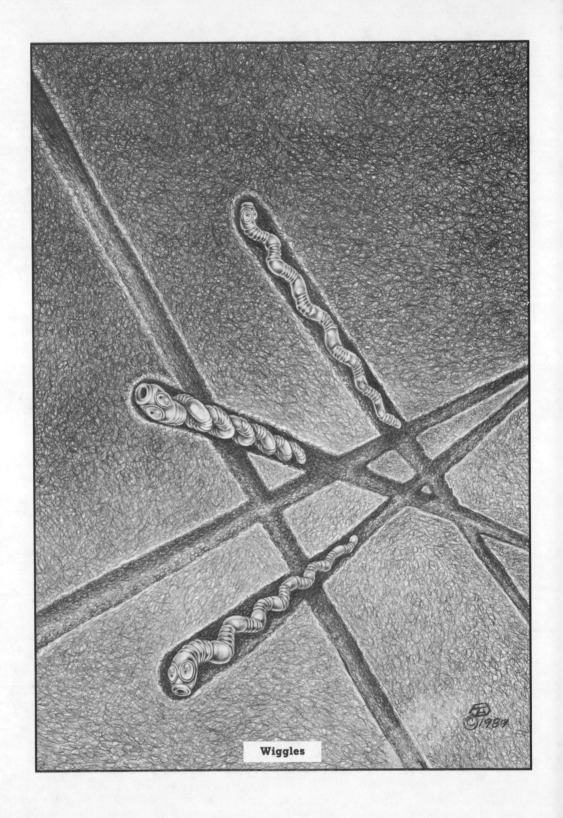

Wiggles

place. By following the path of a wiggle, one can catch it in its still phase and kill it. They move, then hover for perhaps a minute, then move again with a *zzapp!* noise. It is when they are hovering that they are most difficult to find. Unless every wiggle in a swarm is killed, they can breed again and replenish their numbers. If someone stands in the path of a wiggle, the

worm will hole right through them. Wiggle larvae can be killed by crushing them with anything hard, chewing them (although they taste terrible), slamming them between rocks, or turning them to stone.

A female wiggle will mate only once and is sterile thereafter. A male will attempt only once to find a mate. If he is rebuffed by the female of his choice, he will smell of his failure, and can never try again. Voles mate for life. Because of this high selectivity, a wiggle-brood has to be large for the species to survive. There are roughly two swarms a year, most of them underground.

Wiggles are governed mostly by instinct. The females go through color changes when they are ready to mate. A sure sign that a female is ready is that her eyes turn red.

The members of the vole family eat rock. They are highly selective about finding just exactly the kind of rock they like. When a swarm princess is preparing to lay her eggs, she will find a vein of her favorite kind of rock, and eat nearly all of it to give her strength toward the upcoming effort of producing her swarm. It is only once in a while that a princess will find she has a taste for air-flavored stone, which can be found only on the surface.

A wiggle female constructs a special nest made of mud, bones, stones, sticks, sand and other "crud." She crawls into this boxlike contraption, pulls the lid down over her and lays the eggs. When she is through, she has an hour to get clear before they begin to hatch, for the larvae pay no attention to what they hole in their search for the right kinds of rock.

Swarm taste is different from growth taste, so the larvae which hatch must move quickly to find the kind of rock on which they like to feed before they starve to death. Only a few of them will survive. Once they find the kind of rock they like, wiggles become harmless. They settle down to mature, and grow into normal vole shape. Containment spells had been used in the past to keep a swarm from becoming dangerous on the surface, but the practice was not widespread, since most wiggles do not prefer air-flavored stone, so their swarms are confined to veins of rock below ground (see also *Voles*).

Tangle trees have normal trunks, but their branches resemble sheaves of hanging green switches or vines. When prey comes within reach of the nice clean lawn that a tangler maintains around its roots, the vines come to life and snatch up the unsuspecting creature, bearing it to the thorny maw in the heart of the trunk. The maw closes over the delectable morsel, and the tree's digestive juices go to work.

In the early history of Xanth, tanglers were cruder, more Mundane-looking trees with mosslike vines hanging from their branches. Their sly, predatory magic evolved over the centuries. They are tough, mean characters. Few creatures dare tangle with them. But every so often, an ogre is stupid enough to do it, and then there is a glorious fight.

Nooseloops are a relative of the tangle tree. Its branches are narrower than the tangler's. They are actually constricting vines that strangle prey that is then consumed within the trunk. Even the tiny twigs are flexible enough to wind tightly around fingers. The difference between a tangle tree and a nooseloop is that a tangler likes its prey alive and kicking. The nooseloop prefers it dead.

actual size of nickelpede wound

Nickelpedes are nasty little monsters with five hundred legs and one pair of deadly sharp pincers that can magically gouge out a disk of flesh called a nickel. They clamp onto a victim and tear out pieces of flesh until their voracious appetites are satisfied. Dimepedes gouge out bits of flesh smaller than nickels, but they hurt twice as much. These monsters are afraid of sunlight, and congregate in dim and shadowy places. A swarm of them can take down a centaur or any other powerful creature, given time and opportunity. It is a terrible fate to be caught among a swarm of these creatures, and be nickeled and dimed to death.

Quarterpedes are five times as deadly as nickelpedes, because they can gouge out two bits at a time.

Dollarpedes, on the other hand, are an endangered species, kept by Good Magician Humfrey in Pandora's Box. Dollarpedes are made of paper that is dull green on one side and grey on the other. They are not dangerous because they haven't got solid metal backbones. Some of them have enough silver in their flexible spines so the stronger corrugations support each pair of legs enough to move its own weight. This branch of the nickelpede family has been losing strength for decades. Although they are one hundred times the size of centipedes, they're devalued by everything they encounter. Dollarpedes feed on Interest and Principal and Assets, Liabilities and Budgets.

Eclipses: When the moon and the sun collide, it can send huge chunks of flaming green cheese hurtling toward the earth. If one is unlucky enough to be underneath it when the cheese falls to earth, an eclipse is dangerous, but otherwise it is a happy occasion. The cheese is delicious. The best cheese comes from the sky, but it spoils quickly.

The basilisk or cockatrice is a small lizard hatched from a yolkless egg laid by a rooster and hatched by a toad in the warmth of a dungheap. It has the head and feet of a chicken and a gaze that can turn any living creature to stone. Its breath is so bad it wilts vegetation and causes stone to crumble. This little monster is all but helpless because of its flabby physique, but to kill it, the

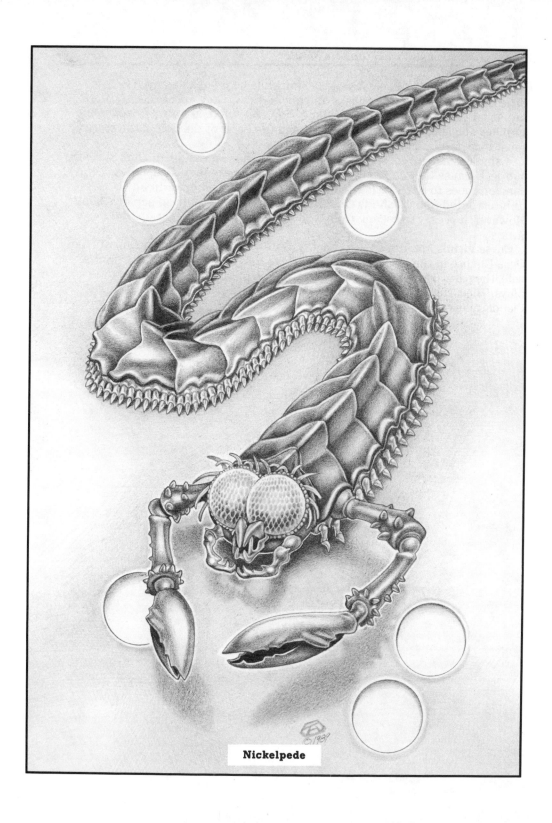

Nickelpede

hunter has to avoid having it look at him while he is sneaking up. There is little difference between basilisks and cockatrices. They are sterile, so there are never very many of them at a time. However, there are a surprising number of cock-, hen-, and chickatrices in the Land of the Basks; the stork must have forgotten about their sterility.

A shade is a half-real spirit, ghost or one of the restless dead. Their threat is subtle, because they can't move from the place where they died, unless someone goes to sleep near where their spirits are anchored. In an uninterrupted hour, a shade can infiltrate and inhabit a living person's body. However, it is easy to escape from a shade. One can always get up and move away.

Curse Fiends are humans that live in Gateway Castle at the bottom of Lake Ogre-Chobee in the Region of Madness. Like the lady who became Crunch's wife, they are actors who are always in search of audiences to watch their plays. Their curses are the result of group effort, a joining of all the Curse Fiends' magic.

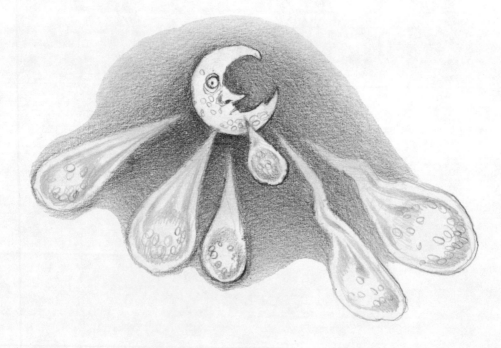

Eclipse

M

Mae One of the Maenads of Mt. Parnassus (see *Mt. Parnassus*). A wild woman who didn't fit in because she didn't like blood. She became a priestess of the oracle. Her eyes glow like a candle when excited.

Magic Dust Village This village was once a normal stockade where humans lived, sacking and distributing the magic dust which welled up from the Source of Magic. Since the time of the Siren (see *Sirens*), many races work together to distribute the magic dust to Xanth.

It is dangerous to use one's talent within the village, for the raw, concentrated power of the dust floating in the air may cause an overload. Accordingly, most of the villagers do their work by hand, and build houses and cook food in the old fashioned way, without the use of magic.

Since the days when the Siren tried to lure all the men away from the village, the headwoman has always been a female troll.

Magic mirrors Very rare mirrors. The Good Magician Humfrey uses them for a variety of purposes: divination, communication, observation. The human Royal Family uses them to communicate with each other over long distances.

Magic-sniffer A knee-high quadruped with a long flexible snout. They react in a friendly way to the presence of magic, snootling in a flutelike voice, and are indifferent where it is absent. They can sense spell intensity. Since they subsist on magic berries, they are considered infallible in judging if something is magical or not.

Magic stones These have varied types of magic proper to stones.

Magic wand A stick that holds a powerful spell.

Magistrate A Curse Fiend official.

Magnifying glass A Mundane device that makes things bigger.

Maiden A pretty girl who comes to the Good Magician's Humfrey's castle for advice about love.

Maidenhair fern A delicate and modest plant.

Manshark Half-man, half-fish with huge toothy jaws that has a giant appetite and two arms to feed it.

Manticora The Manticora is the size of a horse with the head of a man, the body and mane of a lion, wings of the dragon, tail of the scorpion, three rows of iron teeth one inside the other, and a surprisingly beautiful musical voice.

Mare Australe A night mare, after whom the Sea of the South or Southern Sea on the moon (see *Moon*) is named.

Mare Crisium A night mare, after whom the Sea of Crises on the moon (see *Moon*) is named.

Mare Frigoris A night mare, after whom the Sea of Cold on the moon (see *Moon*) is named. She is a three hundred year veteran. She testified at Grace'l's (see *Grace'l*) trial.

Mare Humerum A night mare, after whom the Sea of Moisture on the moon (see *Moon*) is named.

Mare Imbrium A night mare, after whom the Sea of Rain on the moon (see *Moon*) is named. She defeated the Horseman (see *Horseman*) by sacrificing her body in the Gourd. But because she had a soul, given to her by Smash Ogre (see *Smash Ogre*), she was restored to life as a day mare.

Mare Nectaris A night mare, after whom the Sea of Nectar on the moon (see *Moon*) is named.

Mare Nubium A night mare, after whom the Sea of Clouds on the moon (see *Moon*) is named.

Marigolds The blooms of this flower are dazzling balls of gold.

Marquis-of-Queens-berry In the wild, this plant always grows near shadow-boxers and governs their behavior. These acerbic-tasting berries can be eaten as an antidote to locoberries.

Marrow Bones Walking skeleton who was lost on a path in the Gourd. Originally used to frighten sleepers in dreams, he got lost. Like all magic skeletons, he can disassemble his bones and reassemble them in assorted useful configurations. He was chosen by Dolph (see *Dolph*) as his Adult Companion of his Quest.

Marsh-mallow This plant produces edible, sweet, puffy pods much

THE BESTIARY OF XANTH

 his beastiary (sic) shows the true beastliness of Xanth. Most of the creatures make perfect sense, but for some reason critics in Mundania believe that they are egregious puns. Of course they are; what's your point, critics? It isn't as though the beastly cri-tic was neglected; it is duly listed here with the other monsters. Actually, a number of Mundane readers have discovered beasts on their own, and written in about them, and they have been listed here. Xanth is a constant process of discovery.

But if we have to get technical, the fact is that the novels of Xanth are not just funny stories. Xanth is a consistent framework (those who claim otherwise may have misunderstood the nature of its inconsistency) with its own rules, which are subject to change without notice. Those who claim that the novels are poorly written or poorly plotted or without substance are in error; such claims are suspect until some documentary evidence is produced. One reviewer called out Dor's essay on Xanth as bad because it was impossible to tell by Cherie's pronunciation how the words were spelled. The point was that in this land of magic, spelling can indeed be heard; the reviewer had missed the humor, or perhaps didn't like humor much anyway. Each novel is a well-structured adventure, and most are also romances, in addition to the humor. One reader wrote to complain that Xanth was making her laugh out loud in her physics class. Well, that may be a problem — but why was she diverting her attention with a

college class while she was supposed to be giving it all to Xanth? Each Xanth novel is one person's favorite and another person's "Sorry, not up to snuff." Tastes vary, and those who don't like humor are free not to read this stuff.

At one time even the editor became infected with a dislike of punnish things. There were a slew of them in the first chapter of X8, *Crewel Lye*, so he chopped it out, and the novel was published beginning with Chapter 2. This is the problem with listening to critics: it leads to amputation. However, you may read the chapter; it is in the appendix of this volume. But that was not the beginning or the end of the trench warfare with this series. Back in the first novel the editor cut a reference to skeletons in closets: Millie the Ghost must have a pretty one. So in the next novel that pun was so fully developed that it could not be denied, and Millie became a full character, and later even the skeletons of the gourd became characters. The humor of Xanth does not like to be denied.

But there is a serious aspect too. A number of readers, or their parents or teachers, have written to say that Xanth is responsible for their learning to read. They had thought that all books were dull, but discovered that Xanth books were fun, and that provided the motivation needed. Even some adult illiterates learn to become literate on Xanth. Since the ability to read may be the single most important skill for our culture, this is significant.

One young man wrote in to say that he used Xanth to distract him from the discomfort of his chemotherapy treatments. A young woman who had been violently raped found solace in *Ogre, Ogre*, which addresses this subject. Another read Xanth while recovering from brain surgery. It seems that Xanth has a potency of diversion for young folk that others don't appreciate. But if that's the way it works, great! Why zonk out your mind with painkillers or drugs when Xanth will do it instead?

So maybe Xanth isn't great literature. But it does divert folks, and sometimes it helps them cope with the Mundane world, and there can be no shame in that. The fact that it is full of punnish creatures doesn't mean that it is without merit. It is said that man does not live by bread alone, and part of the rest of what he does live by is humor. Enjoy the beasts; they are there for your laughter.

allegory: A green reptile with a long snout filled with teeth; speaks in metaphors.

alligator clip: Strong-jawed hazard secured by a chain to its root.

angelfish: Very nice fish with gauzy wings which allow it to hover and a halo over its head. It dances when it is happy. Devilfish like to pursue angelfish and do something censored to them.

angle worm: A worm which turns corners at perfect angles instead of curving around them as an earthworm does.

Ant-lion

ant-lions: Small beasts with the body of ants and the maned heads of lions. They run in prides, and fiercely roar at any threat. They are powerful fighters, and make good use of their sharp-pointed legs as well as their strong jaws and the stingers at the end of their sharp abdomens.

argus: Land-walking fish with four stout legs that end in flippers, the tusked head of a boar, and three eyes set along its torso in a chevron.

assassin bug: Insect which kills other insects by contract only.

B's: A genus of flying insects, each with its own specialty. There are spelling b's, counting b's, sewing b's, quilting b's. Bumble B makes one clumsy. B's come from a B-have, such as b-hold, b-lieve, b-neath, b-fore, b-hind, b-seech, b-side, b-stir, b-foul, b-devil, b-reave, b-siege, b-set, b-tween, b-wilder, b-wails, and a Queen B, have various effects on the people they sting. They live in a huge have shaped like a lady's bonnet. Worker b's of no special talent repair the inside of the have. Queen B-nign is the ruler of the Bonnet Have. She defeated B's One through Twenty to become the sole Princess of the Have in which she was born.

barbarians: Mundane or primitive men who live by a strict code of conduct requiring excellent coordination with weapons, awkwardness with women, common sense, and faithfulness in completing missions. They have a handbook giving advice on behavior.

baseball bat: Long, thin leathery mammal with wings.

battering ram: Small curly-horned, curly-pelted sheeplike creature who charges straight toward any obstacle with the object of crashing through it. Related to the hydraulic ram, which is stronger.

bear witness: A powerfully constructed quadruped with stubby claws and a protruding muzzle, but no hair on its body. It tells only the truth.

bedbugs: Some sleep in nests that look like comfortable beds. Some bedbugs are shaped like a bed, with four little rollers for feet, springs and fat pillows.

behemoths: Winged creatures so large they can carry whole groups of travelers on their backs. Another sort of behemoth which is mostly mouth acts as the entrance to Gateway Castle.

blister beetle: Its sting raises painful bumps on skin.

blue bottle flies: These insects have blue bottles for bodies. Humfrey uses the bigger bottles for storing some of his spells and demons.

bogey: Orange monster engendered by the bog. Bogeys live in a well-organized, almost military, camp run by a colonel. They are assiduously polite.

bonnacon: A huge, dragonish creature with the horns of a bison, metalbone eyelids, and thick armor on its body. It is more terrible to chase than to confront, for it blasts excrement from its nether portions into the faces of its pursuers.

brown thrasher: Contentious bird that thrashes things.

bugbear: This monster has multiple bug legs and feelers, a horrible bug face, and a huge shaggy bear body.

bullhorn: Creature that threatens to ram its horn into the posterior of anyone in its way.

bull seal: Cephalopod with a spread of sharp horns on its forehead.

bum steer: Four-footed creature with hooves and horns that gives false information and begs for smokes from passersby.

butterfly: Messy insect that oozes butter.

cactus-cat: A feline half the size of a man, with a normal cat face, but its striped green and brown coat is composed of needles instead of fur. The thorns on its ears are large and stiff, and on the front legs are slicing blades of bone. Its personality is just like that of the average cat.

carnivorous rabbits: Harmless-looking bunnies that eat meat.

catoblepas: A hideous monster with snake-like hair and cloven hooves. Its body is covered in scales. Its gaze is fatal, but it holds its head so low that its eyes can seldom be seen.

cat o' nine tails: Except for its rear adornments, this beast looks like a Mundane cat. It will slash fiercely at attackers, but is really fairly timid.

centycore: A beast with horse's hooves, lion's legs, elephantine ears, bear's muzzle, a monstrous mouth, and a branching ten-point antler that protrudes from the middle of its face. The centycore has no mercy.

chameleon: Small, harmless lizard that can assume the shape of any dangerous creature of approximately its own size, though it will not have any of its defensive or offensive capabilities.

chimera: A heraldic fire-breathing beast with a lion head on its shoulders, a goat head on its back, and a snake for its tail.

chipmunk: Natural animal which can conjure tiny bits of food away from hazards and traps.

chobee: Reptile with a long snout with wide nostrils. Its skin is green and corrugated, and it has short fat legs. Its teeth are gleaming white but soft as pillows.

Occasionally one will have real teeth, but there is no way to tell the good chobees from the bad in time.

choke bees: Related to the sneeze bees; a cloud of them makes you choke.

clouds: In Xanth, storm clouds are shaped like dishes full of water, which they sprinkle out when they decide it is time to rain. Most of the clouds are friendly and good-natured; King Cumulo Fracto Nimbus is a notable exception to the rule.

cockfish: This perky fish crows when the sun's reflection hits its pool.

cockroaches: Insects which crow like roosters.

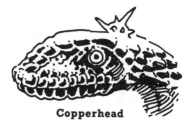

Copperhead

copperhead: Gleaming metal-headed snake with impressive fangs.

copy cat: This feline copies everything one does, but also makes very good copies of manuscripts by sitting on them and extruding the printout from its mouth.

cowboys: Harmless humanoids with the horned heads of bulls, who graze on rockmoss in the gnome-mines. They do not wear clothing, but are fairly furry all over. Music soothes their savage breasts. The cowboys are basically shy and peaceful, but the males are protective and stand their ground to defend their families. The Minotaur is a hero who set out to Mundania to seek his fortune in ages past.

crane: Long thin-legged bird as tall as a tree, cranks its head up and down in slow, measured stages to move heavy burdens from one level to another. They practice rocky-tree, hoisting rocks into the trees.

cri-tic: Loathsome bloodsucking bug of Mundania.

cuttlefish: A white fish with knifelike tentacles that can slash through flesh right to the bone.

cyclops: The fabled Cyclopses are three brothers named Steropes, Brontes, and Arges, sons of Mother Earth and Father Sky. Once they forged thunderbolts for sky, but were deprived of their powers and their job when the sky became jealous of them and drove them away. They remained hidden for ages in caves until they were reunited by Ivy.

deadpan: These creatures have the ugliest faces in Xanth. They live near cooking fires.

deerfly: Delicately furred, four-legged fly the size of a Mundane deer, with antlers and big, soulful, brown eyes.

devilfish: Reddish-colored horned fish that likes to spoil everything for the other fish. It can walk on the surface of the water, using its curving, barbed tail for balance. Its favorite pastime is to chase down an angelfish and do something censored to her.

double-headed eagle: A fierce golden monster. To judge by the coats of arms of many royal houses, several of these were observed in the Mundane world.

dragonflies: Miniature insectoid dragons which prey on bugs and associate with dragons. Occasionally, they adopt a human's garden and keep it free of pests. They breathe fire, and explode in flames when they crash.

dragon horse: A rare creature that has the front of a horse, and the back of a dragon.

drake: Hissing, small, ornate fire-breathing dragon with large, streamlined wings. It is very fierce and highly intelligent.

dung beetles: These beetles magic the contents of chamber pots into sweet-smelling violets and roses.

eclectic eel: It chooses bits and pieces others have made. It does nothing original, but thinks that it is very sophisticated.

fast overland snail: A gastropod that can move faster than most birds can fly. Used to transport messages from one end of Xanth to the other.

feather-winged beetle: This insect has wings made of a single feather each.

fetch: Apparition that shows the dead image of a living person. It was once considered to be death to see the fetch.

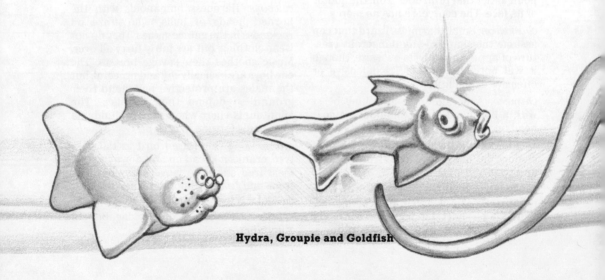

Hydra, Groupie and Goldfish

firedog: Shaped like a Mundane dog, but its sides radiate volcanic heat, and it can breathe fire.

firefly: Flying insect with a flaming tail that can set a forest alight if it is careless. Home cooking-fires can be ignited with the help of a trained firefly.

fireman: Like the firedog, a fireman radiates heat. He can burn down a tree by embracing it.

flatfeet: Mundane demons who patrol the roads.

flying fish: Swift flier propelled by a jet of bubbles coming out its fuselage. Its rigid wings provide sufficient lift, the gills are its air intakes, and the little fins along its sides and belly act as stabilizers.

flying sheep: Winged ovines mentioned in the gourd poem:

> Roes are red,
> Violents are blue,
> Sugar sand's sweet
> And soar ewe.

flying snakes: Mean, unreasonable serpents with wings. Some are poisonous.

friers: Hens that lay fried eggs.

frisbees: Disk-shaped, striped insects that drink nectar and make honey. They spin from flower to flower.

gargoyles: Hideous-faced stone creatures which are frequently used as doors to castles and other magic dwellings, because they can extend their mouths almost infinitely, swallowing up visitors, who find themselves inside the building.

Gerrymander: A shape-changing creature that has the power of surround, select, and conquer. It seeks to trap prey by weakening their power base. In order to defeat Gerrymander, it must be passed, by whatever means possible. Mundane versions exist, with similar traits.

ghastly: Shapeless, slimy creatures like squashed caterpillars with tentacles and many legs. They bite, belch obscenely, and expectorate purple venom. They are very hard to kill, since they can't be squashed or torn apart.

glow-worms: Pale green worms with luminous skin.

gold bug: Similar to the midas fly. It is made of solid gold, and it plates with gold anything it touches.

goldfish: Very pretty fish entirely formed from gold. Not of much value out of the water.

gremlins: Whenever possible, these creatures occupy machinery and make it go wrong. Many gremlins worked for Magician Murphy in the Fifth Wave. Others occupy works of technology in the Demon City.

griffins: Handsome creatures descended from the union of an eagle and a lion. The forepart of a griffin is the head, wings, and feet of the eagle, and the rear is the powerful haunches, claws, and tail of the lion. While their clipped eagle tongues do not allow them to speak the human language, the griffin is nevertheless accepted as an intelligent being.

groupie: A fattish fish with large, soft extremities; if one lets it, a groupie can siphon one's soul out with a seeming kiss.

hal-bird: An extraordinarily thin bird with a body like a pole and a huge, narrow, axe-beaked head.

hedge hog: Mobile brown hedge that is very timid about being chomped.

hephalumphs: Colorful pachyderms that like honey.

holey cow: A quadruped larger than a basilisk, smaller than a sphinx. It is full of holes, including a hole in the head where the brain should be. As a consequence, it is very stupid, but willing to act as a steed.

hoopworms: When frightened, these long, skinny worms coil themselves up, make a noise like a hoop, and roll away.

hoorah bird: Large cheerful bird with colorful but tasteless plumage whose nest is untidy and crowded with debris and collectable bric-a-brac.

hornworm: A trapper that hides in the ground with only its four horns showing like the points of a coronet. If anything disturbs it, it attacks with its corrosive poison which can shatter stone.

horsefly: An insect the size and shape of a horse with fully fledged pinions.

houseflies: These live in tiny houses that they create by magic or have built by sawflies and carpenter ants.

hummers: Unknown flying menace that hums incessantly. It breeds in still, stagnant water. The population of hummers increases the more moist ground is exposed to the air. The sound of hummers drives demons crazy before it even becomes audible to humans, who also find it annoying. They are even worse in Mundania, where demons have meddled with wetlands.

hydra: Multiheaded serpent that draws its strength from water. If one head is torn away or cut off, two more grow in its place. It can be killed with reverse wood.

hypotenuse: Enormously fat animal with a mouth that opens into a triangle.

id: A gigantic, green jelly-skinned creature that swallows anything it likes; it has an oral fixation and is entirely hollow. It is very selfish, complains a lot, destroys carelessly. The id likes to have everything its own way.

imps: Little monsters halfway between goblins and golems, some with a combination of all their bad traits. Some imps are more like fairies or elves, crafting tiny magical items.

J's: These cheery, crested birds come in many colors. There are blue-J's, green-J's, and red-J's in the vicinity of Castle Roogna.

jack in the box: A small serpent with skin like cloth. Some of them can grow to be quite huge. They like to tell rotten old jokes and laugh at themselves.

je-june bugs: Dull and uninteresting insects.

jump-at-a-body: A small monster that is all hair, legs and glower. It is harmless. All it does is jump out, scare folk, and run away. It emigrated from Mundania when people there stopped believing in it.

kingfisher: Bird which fishes for kings among the fish.

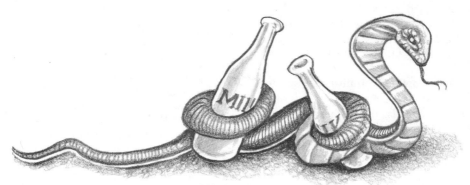

Milksnake

kitty-hawk: Has hawk wings, feathered tail, but its head and legs are feline. When its magic is enhanced, it might chase itself to death.

lamia: A human-headed quadruped with hoofs, a horse's tail, and cat forelegs.

lantern fish: Brightly glowing fish with goggling eyes.

lightning bugs: These insects use miniature lightning bolts to stun their prey.

loan sharks: These look like big fish with flukes and fins and sharp teeth, but they are always looking for prey they can pull in too deep. Loan sharks never help one another. When one is in trouble, the others pull it apart.

the loin: A mysterious force with a good p.r. promoter that puts up signs attesting to its prowess in the jungle. The leader of the pride of loins is Sir Loin Stake.

love bug: Glowing, brightly colored insect.

lutin: Malign shape-changer with a bad temper.

magic-sniffer: A knee-high quadruped with a long flexible snout like that of a tapir. They react in a friendly way to the presence of magic, snootling in a flutelike voice, and are indifferent where it is absent. They can sense spell intensity. Since they subsist on magic berries, they are considered infallible in judging if something is magical or not.

Manshark

manshark: Half-man, half-fish with huge toothy jaws that has a giant appetite and two arms to feed it.

midas fly: It turns anything it touches into gold.

milksnakes: These serpents give milk in bottles.

mimic-dog: An animal that can mimic whatever it sees and hears. It is not intelligent enough to perform original actions.

monkeyshines: Agile, little, brown animals that gleam with their own light.

monocerous: A huge, broad-sided monster that has only one horn.

moose, chocolate: A tasty animal much troubled by ducks which like to nibble it. There are also vanilla mooses in Xanth.

moth hawk: An insect that flies silently and strikes other insects down swiftly with taloned feet.

mudhen: Small, plump bird that spatters mire wherever it goes.

nameless dreads: Unseen monsters with haunting voices. Alister names them Sally, Aloysius, and the Great Fritizini to strip them of their power to terrify.

neon-coral: Brilliantly glowing colonies of tiny sea animals.

netwings: Insects that resemble little nets blowing about on the wind. Their wings are no more than air tied together with a few filaments so that their ability to fly is due more to magic than aerodynamic construction.

nickelodeon: A dumpy box with a slot in its side, which plays music as it eats nickelpedes.

nix: A sometimes-man, sometimes-fish that can freeze or unfreeze water by nixing it.

orc: Huge fat water monster with teeth that overflow its mouth.

owl-fly: A large-eyed, tufted bug that flies silently.

pantheon: A category of gods or demi-gods who fought on the side of Xanth against the Fifth Wave invaders.

parody: A bird with green wings, squat downcurving beak. It talks in an imitation of human speech.

phoenix: The glorious immortal bird which immolates itself on the nest containing its egg and is reborn from the ashes every 500 years.

picklepuss: Cat body with a snout that is green and prickly like a pickle. Its eyes are moist with brine. Whatever it touches gets pickled. Mundanes do the same thing with stuff in a bottle.

picture-winged fly: A small insect, common species in Xanth. Its wings show illustrations rendered in a variety of media and styles. Among those noted by Good Magician Humfrey in his Information Book are the Pastoral, Still-life, Naturalistic, Surrealistic, Cubist, Watercolor, Oil, Pastel Chalk, Pen-and-Ink, Charcoal, and Crayon-Drawing.

piggy-back: Fat pink animal that enjoys carrying other animals on its back.

pilot fish: A variety of flying fish that likes to live in trees, especially plane trees, though they can't fly them unless they have fishing licenses.

pinches: Little birds with outsized beaks.

policeman: A blue demon in the dream realm who chases folks yelling incomprehensible things like "Sendya tothe bighouse!"

Pythia: Innocent damsels who serve as priestesses and speak gibberish for the Oracle at Mount Parnassus.

Python: Guardian of the Oracle on Mount Parnassus. Also in the jungle of Xanth, there is a shape-changing serpent that can alter its form as it chooses into something completely different every few minutes.

quack: A bird with a wide bill, webbed feet, and a bag of patent medicines, who promises miracle cures.

raindeer: Four-legged horned beasts that carry their own stormcloud over them, complete with boomlets of thunder and little bolts of lightning.

razorback pig: Down the spine of this friendly porker is a ridge of sharp razor blades. The spines can be cultivated for shaving.

relevant: Huge, grey animal with four trunklike legs and a nose which reaches to the ground; is concerned with what is current and pertinent.

rhinoceros beetle: Looks like a bulldozer (another big creature of Xanth).

ribbonfish: Enormously wide but completely flat and slick eel-like fish which scoops things up and slides them along its length until it deposits them where it wants them.

robber-flies: These unscrupulous insects will attempt to steal anything which appears unguarded, up to many times their own weight.

robin: Greedy bird, one of the most notorious hoods in the forest.

roc: Largest of all birds. They love rock gardens and rock music. This giant red bird prefers hephalumphs as a snack.

rock hound: A living stone dog. As mobile and flexible as a flesh-and-blood dog, but more solidly built.

salamander: A brightly colored amphibian five inches in length. Salamander fire burns magically anything it touches, even water, except for rock, earth, and salamander weed. It loves to start conflagrations. Its magical fire is one-way, forming its own firebreak.

samphire: Living marshweed with a taste for flesh and blood. It has thorn claws and fangs with which it tears apart unsuspecting victims, and then it drags them under the surface of the marsh to enjoy at leisure.

Magic-sniffer, Fast Snail and Griffin

sandman: Animated sand that can assume different shapes. It puts travelers to sleep.

satyr: A less than innocent relative of the dry-faun.

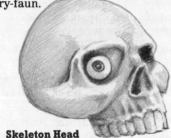

Skeleton Head

sawflies: Use their sharp probosci to saw wood into lengths to build their homes.

scaredy cat: A small feline that spooks easily.

sea cow: Half-bovine, half-fish that makes a loving pet, and is also a useful steed in the water.

sea monsters, lake monsters, and river monsters: Mostly giant serpents that can live underwater. They all have multiple rows of very thin sharp teeth. They honk when provoked.

sea nettle: Roundish plantlike animal that can sting one to death. Its head is gilled like a toadstool, and it has huge stinging tentacles.

secretary bird: Literate avian that writes letters, then carries them itself to their destinations.

sel-fish: Fat-faced fish that enjoys instant gratification, never worries about the welfare of others.

shellfish: Made up of dull, broad, serrated pincers. It fears the starfish in the sky, and hides from them.

shopping centaur: Lady centaur with a big shopping bag.

sidehill hoofer: Mountain cow with short blunt horns whose two left legs are shorter than the two right so that it can run around the perimeter of a hill with ease, and so its horns will be precisely level when aiming at prey.

silverfish: Small metal fish that swim in silvery ponds.

skeletons: In the gourd, skeletons are a normal everyday species. They reproduce naturally by knocking heads together. The female skeleton flies apart, and a baby skeleton is constructed by the male out of some of her bones. She regrows the bones she needs. Skeletons perform in bad dreams, and they dance, developing a sense of perfect timing. They also gamble, rolling the bones to win wagers. They have a talent for cohesiveness, and if knocked apart, they can reform without trouble.

slug: Giant gastropod that spreads slime wherever it goes, and whose breath is fiery.

snake-fly: Long narrow flying insect with fangs.

sneeze bees: Unquestionably one of the most distracting insects in Xanth. Nothing takes your breath away faster than an exposure to the bees' sneeze.

snowbirds: White, cold-loving birds that drop powdery, white snow on travelers which spaces out the mind, producing believable illusions and mind-bending dreams.

snowsnake: White and silent, poisonous, snow-cold serpent that lives in snow. Its bite causes victims to freeze to death. The snake melts when exposed to heat.

spelling bee: It wears a checkered furry jacket, and uses letters from letter plants to spell words. There's nothing a spelling bee can't spell. However, it doesn't necessarily spell the right words.

spider lily: A carnivorous flower that weaves a huge web by its garden to catch prey.

sphinx: Intelligent monsters of various forms that like riddles. They can speak coherently. Some are so enormous that they look like part of the landscape, and one of their eyelashes would serve for a walking stick.

splinter cat: Feline that rubs up against one to deposit painful splinters under the skin.

Swallowtails

spriggan: Destructive ghost that haunts old castles and megalithic structures. It keeps shoving at columns and crosspieces until they fall down. Spriggans holler boo, and appear to be scary, but it is safest to be exactly where they are, for they never pull down stones on top of themselves. A spriggan is only the size of a man, but its arms are huge and hairy, and its face sprouts two giant tusks.

stag beetle: Small insect with a full rack of antlers.

starfish: A brilliantly gleaming water creature on which one may make a wish.

starling: Bird with midnight-black feathers on which can be seen constellations of brilliant silver stars.

stench-puffer: Small beast that emits stinking clouds.

stinglice: Tiny insects that raise painful welts.

stink bug: An insect that emits an overpowering stench.

stink worm: Tastes absolutely awful.

stone dove: Black bird whose protective camouflage closely resembles a rock.

succubus: Alluring female demon who can assume the shape of any woman to attract a man, but cannot stand direct light. Men ought to know better than to dally with her, but men are amazingly stupid about such things.

sucker-saps: Birds that like to eat sweat gnats.

sunfish: Has a rounded fin which projects above the surface of the water. When the fish wishes to, it can light up like the sun.

swallowtails: These birds protect themselves from harm by swallowing their own tails and disappearing.

sweat gnats: Nasty little bugs which cause humans to sweat and then feed on the perspiration.

switchback: Boarlike creature with sharp blades on its sides that it can flick out and slash at whatever the switchback sideswipes. It can instantly charge back the way it came by swapping its head and tail end for end. Switchbacks live on narrow mountain paths where there is no room to turn around.

sylphs: A family of slender elflike creatures: Sylvester, Sylvia, and Sylvanie.

tarasque: Felinelike monster the size of a horse with six ursine legs, head of a lion with a mane, whiskers and tusklike teeth, bright orange eyes, spiked carapace, reptilian tail with scorpion point. Tarasques, technically of the dragon family, are finicky about their food, and do not like to eat carrion, for they fear disease and indigestion. Intelligent, lures prey into a one-way warren-maze to confuse and tire it. The tarasque is vain of its appearance.

tatterdemalion: Large, ragged-coated feline that is addicted to ragweed.

Winged Snake

thesaurus: Very ancient breed of reptile who never uses a single term to describe its actions when many will do.

thunderbird: Makes a huge noise whenever it flies.

tiger beetle: Striped insect that is one of the fiercest bugs around.

tiger lilies: These valley-growing flowers like to eat tender flesh.

tiger moths: Carnivorous insects with striped wings.

tiger shark: Has a tall, striped sailfin and the head of a tiger.

toady: Warty little animal that seeks to advise people of power.

tree hoppers: Small creatures that resemble tiny trees.

tree lobsters: Their protective coloration of leaf-green claws and bark-brown body allows them to hide against tree trunks. They nip with their claws.

trolls: Humanoids not quite as large or as strong as ogres, but very tough. The females frequently eat their husbands after mating.

trumpet swan: Half-avian, half-musical instrument. Its brassy feathers and raucous call make it one of the more noticeable birds of Xanth.

unicorn: Slim, horselike being with the beard of a goat and the tail of a lion, and bearing a single spiralled horn projecting from the center of its forehead. Some unicorns are beautiful, with well-brushed coats and polished horns. Others, less vain of their appearance, are burr-coated and gnarl-horned.

vampires: Members of a human-descended race who cannot bear the sunlight and drink blood to survive.

vila: A hamadryad, territorial protector of the mountain forest who can change shape and cure or cause illness in those who enter her forest. She is tied to her tree; if the tree dies, so does she. Her talents are all functions of her purpose, which is to protect her tree.

wails: Large water creature that looks like a big blue-gray cloud with hundreds of tiny feet that walk on the surface of lakes, leaving a trail of footmarks known as the prints of wails. Its sad wailing can be heard near Lake Wails. Descended from a real whale that wandered out of Mundania, and grew legs to go from lake to lake.

walking stick bug: Ambles on two feet. Several types of these have been noted: silver-headed, Welsh thumbstick, mahogany handled, ivory handled, shillelagh, bamboo-cane.

werewolf: Human whose talent is becoming a wolf. He can be killed or injured only with silver weapons.

whale: In Xanth, they have four feet, the head and tusks of a boar, a rows of spikes along the body, and legs like those of a Mundane lion.

wingcows: Four-legged, two-winged animals that give rich milk from eating leaves in the very tops of trees or grazing on the Moon.

wire-haired cow: Small shaggy bovine that gives whisker cream for shaving.

wood doves: Heavy wooden birds that frequently act as decoys for other birds.

woodwife: Hollow facade of a nymph who comforts lonely men, though her comfort is likely to be empty.

woolly hen: Bird with curly fleece instead of feathers. Not very bright, but trustworthy and a fast flyer.

wyvern: Small dragon with a barbed tail, but only two legs. The wyvern's nest is as fierce as its habitants, and it can fly, too.

yak: Large hairy beast that will talk your ear off. It has lovely eyes, silky hair down its sides, the horns of a sea cow, and the tail of a centaur. The yak is unsilenceable. No one knows how to shut one up, but they can be frightened off. They only talk to people who talk to them first.

Firedrake

©1989

THE BEST THINGS IN XANTH ARE FREE

Xanth culture is rather backward and innocent, compared to that of Mundania. Few Xanth men, for example, think there is anything wrong with chasing and maybe catching nymphs. It is said that a man can have a very good time with a captive nymph, though the Adult Conspiracy prevents this Guide from explaining exactly how. However, once a man marries, he's supposed to leave the nymphs of the wild oats pretty much alone. This is not a law, just custom; for some reason the women of Xanth don't like to have their men chasing off after any pretty pair of legs that dances by.

There are Mundanes who claim that Xanth is sexist. This is nonsense. Anybody can see that women were never meant to have power; they belong at home taking care of the children. Xanth's medieval culture recognizes that. Recently, unfortunately, women, led by Irene, have been getting Notions, and demanding the rights of men. Not satisfied to have nice legs to run with (or whatever), Irene wanted to run Xanth too. She even served a term as King. She finally realized that it was easier to run things behind the scene, while the foolish men thought *they* were running things, exactly as is the case in Mundania. Certainly this is sexist, but until men get smart enough to take control back, that's the way it is.

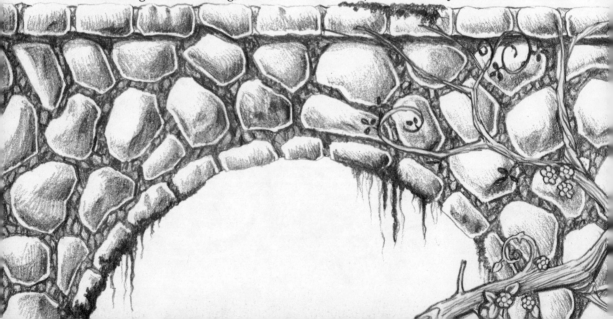

Many of my creatures do not make physiological sense. This is on purpose, to reflect the fact that they are magic. Size and mass are not constant. That's how Dolph can change into a bee or a dragon. With magic, science does not apply, deliberately.

— Piers Anthony

 t is easy to live well in Xanth. There is no monetary system. Everything is obtained by growing it, gathering it, making it or bartering for it. Food is as close as the nearest edible plant, and clothing does indeed grow on trees.

Some of the food plants are very sophisticated. In warm patches, one can often find hot soup gourds, hot potato plants, pie trees, and cocoa-nut trees. Breadfruit trees, which supply fresh loaves of bread, breadsticks, drum rolls (hollow and resonant) grow in several delicious varieties, including white, challah, whole wheat, raisin, Irish soda, and well-bread (good for what ails you).

Refreshingly cool comestibles can be found in jelly-bole trees, soda poppies, and multicolored colorfruit trees, which produce oranges, blues, greens, purples, yellows, and the rest of the rainbow of sweet, pulpy, segmented fruit in thick, nubbly shells. The trees also produce things of limited usefulness, such as door-knobs (some of which can be employed as is; the others, properly cultivated, can grow up to be doors).

Clothing, too, comes from plants. Coat trees produce everything from light jackets to all-weather ponchos. From shirt trees, you can get oxford shirts, football jerseys (brown and white pullovers that moo); from shoe trees and hat trees, footgear and headgear are available in season. Lady's-slipper plants, more delicate versions of shoe trees, are cultivated in stockade gardens.

Dry-cleaning plants exist to mend and refurbish garments which the owners like too much to throw away, though replacements for ordinary garments can be plucked at the nearest grove.

Housing is not a difficulty, either. One can grow, mine, hollow out, or build a home. Bink and Chameleon live in a large hollow cottage cheese. Others favor homes grown from box trees, roof-trees, or wall-nuts, or built from piles of pome-granite stones.

The flora of Xanth partakes of the magic flowing through the depths of the land. Like the rivers and mountains, each plant can evoke situational magic to help it make the necessities of life more available to it: sunlight, protection from destruction, water, fertilizer, and a way to spread its seeds or cuttings to propagate its species. According to need, plants have changed so they have more control over their environment (as the healing springs have), or have been changed to become more useful to the citizens of Xanth. A plant rooted in poor soil may develop laxative magic, to compel passing animals to leave behind whatever nutrient-rich compost they can.

Queen Irene, whose talent is the Green Thumb, carefully documents useful seeds and plants that come into her possession for future reference. The following are excerpted from the journals she has kept since her talent blossomed.

Queen Irene

FLOWERS

African violent: The blooms are small purple clubs which smash out at anything that moves. Good for protection from monsters.

amaranth: Beautiful purple flower that never fades.

begonias: Can't enjoy them long; they're gone as soon as they bloom.

blood lilies: Tall, elegant flowers whose bulbs are filled with blood. Favored by some monsters as a tipple.

bluebell: One of the worst alarmists in the garden. The bluebell is always ringing off.

buttercup: A petal cup on top of a tall green stalk; may contain any one of a number of butters: apple butter, peach butter, creamery butter, peanut butter.

cowslip: Nasty to step on, but its leaves are silky and brightly colored, and shaped like camisoles. Must be cultured to grow big enough to wear.

crocus: Gloomy plant. It utters the most scandalous imprecations.

crowfeet: Wrinkled flowers that look like the claws of birds. (Do NOT grow too closely to Mother's vanity table.)

dandelions: The lion heads roar and bite.

dog-tooth violents: Don't plant near the dandelions. They bite.

fiery love flower: They flame even brighter near people who are in love. (Note: try on Dor.)

foxglove: Too small for me to wear.

gladiolas: Happy flowers that stretch up joyfully as they grow toward the sun. Wonderful for brightening up a garden.

heliotrope: Imitates the sun's rays, can dry things off or dehydrate them completely.

hell's bells: Vines which ring their flowers deafeningly. They can only be silenced by smashing the bells or uprooting the plant.

impatiens: Grows from seed to bloom in a hurry.

marigolds: The blooms are dazzling balls of gold.

moroses: Beautiful flowers in gloomy colors that make one feel sad.

paintbrushes: Brightly colored fibrous blossoms dripping with paint.

periwinkles: Have sly blue eyes that wink.

phlox: Plump, white clumps of flowers that baa-aa-aa.

poppies: The flowers pop loudly as they open. A variety of this flower, soda poppies, gives effervescent drink in many flavors.

primrose: Tall, prissy flower embarrassed by bad behavior.

snapdragons: Vicious little plants with miniature dragon heads that eat other insects and animal pests. They are common in the wild, but rare in captivity.

stunflower: Stuns anything which looks at it in a burst of blistering radiation, while singing "I'm the one flower, I'm the STUN flower!"

sunflower: Until a sunflower goes to seed, its face shines forth with light as bright as day.

sweet peas: Little flower cups filled with you know what.

torch flowers: They resemble sinister glowing eyes, but the flaming flower can light one's way easily, if one is careful not to burn oneself.

violents: Nasty purple man-eating flower. Can be found in a couch potato patch in great profusion. Where violents abound, you must be near a cathode-ray tuber. Originally bred to be planted on the median strip between paths, this one was rejected because they didn't want any more violents on the media. (That would not have happened in Mundania.)

wallflowers: Make good walls unless they wilt. They work faster than wall-nuts, but more ephemeral.

water lily: The flower cups contain sweet water.

xanthemums: Shaggy blue flowers native to the land of Xanth.

Ladyfingers Plant

PLANTS

acid seed: Sour seeds that drop from the acid plant. The juice of its fruit can cut through any substance, including metal.

airplane plant: This plant has stiff wings, an upright tail, and an airscope that sucks in air. When freed from its stalk, it can fly independently.

alumroot: A magical astringent. All soft tissues that touch its juice shrink.

antenna plants: Tall thin trunks with many crossbranches, sparser of leaf and smaller toward the top. They appear to do nothing, but they can broadcast suggestions into the minds of passersby.

ard: The herbs of the ard family are used to season food. Canard, which has a sweet, orangy taste, and mustard, with a stronger flavor, are the most popular, but there are also shouldard, wouldard, and mayard.

armordillo: Metallic plant that smells of brine. It grows the best armor to be had.

arrowroot: Pointing plant that can be used for triangulation.

ascamya: Resilient plant that produces meaty pink below-knee sausages. It will instantly grow back to its original height of a foot or so, even if it is hacked nearly to the ground.

asparagus spears: A good plant for growing in a protective palisade.

bagpipe bush: Grows large plaid bags that wheeze discordantly.

banana: The top banana grows alone on its plant and observes what goes on in the jungle. Nothing slips by without notice.

bananananana: A more dangerous form of banana. Once you slip on this fruit, you can't stop.

bayonet plant: The branches of this plant grow into long, hard points that jab at its attackers.

berry-berry: Double berries that cause weakness, paralysis and wasting away. Their toxin acts as a slow poison. No B's come to them.

bird's nest fern: A plant which grows in the shape of nests to attract birds to live on it; uses the droppings as fertilizer.

bird-of-paradise plant: Looks like a real bird and can fly. Due to its origins, it reacts strongly to bad language or coarse behavior.

bladder wort: Pods which collapse with rude noises when stepped on or crushed.

blind dates: Squarish, waxy fruit that grows on palm plants. Eating one causes temporary blindness.

Airplane Plant

boysengirls berries: The tart seeds look like boys, and the berries look like girls, so they must be eaten together to taste all right.

bug bombs: Grow on bug bomb weed, used for fumigation.

bulrushes: Can be woven into buoyant rafts which may be controlled with any ring through the nose of the raft. They charge forward, traveling best on open water no matter how rough.

burr: A chilly plant parasite that makes anyone it touches very cold.

bury plant: Produces buries, fruit that grows underground. You have to be careful eating them, because of the pits. You don't want to fall in.

Bird of Paradise Plant

candle plant: The top sheds light as the plant grows.

candy-stripe ferns: Pink and white edible ferns.

candy-tuft moss: Very tasty, grows on the north side of trees.

carnivorous grass: This herb throws out hungry shoots, dripping sap-saliva. It reaches up, hooks and grows into flesh, preventing the prey from getting up and going away. It drains away blood and consumes the flesh.

carribean: Vine that continues to bear beans as long as it is moving from place to place. It has bright yellow eyelike flowers that turn eagerly to see new surroundings.

caterpillar nettles: Have all the stinging force of the simple Mundane plant, but they can creep up on their victims instead of waiting for them to approach.

Cobra Plant

catnip: Has paw buds and pussy-willow pusses that yowl and purr, depending on the plant's mood.

cauliflower ear: Thick, white vegetable ear anchored by a heavy green stem. Pulpy around the edges, but solid.

cement plant: A thick white-grey stem topped by a globe of whitish leaves. Squat, low, unimpressive, but very solid.

centipede plant: Mobile creeper with tiny cilia for feet.

chain vine: A creeper with strong linked stems that are almost impossible to cut through. Can be used as a fence.

chokecherry hedge: A good plant for protection. The tendrils throttle anything that tries to force between them.

clatterweed: A plant with low-quality metal or china leaves that bang together noisily.

clutchroot: Low-lying plant that grabs at passing feet.

cobra plant: A hooded vine with sharp thorns that strikes at movement.

coffee beans: When punctured, these beans give strong hot juice that helps wake you up.

colorberry bushes: One of these produces small berries in several colors and shapes on the same branch: red, orange, yellow, green, or even blue berries.

colorfruit trees: Covered with large, round, sweet fruits in every color of the rainbow.

constrictor tentacles: Related to tangle trees. They squeeze the life out of passing creatures and gradually absorb their flesh.

contact-lens bush: Covered with tiny concave disks of glass that magically adhere to the eyeball and improve vision. Contact lenses are so called because they make close contact.

cookie bush: Produces delicious warm cookies. Varieties abound in Xanth, but the most popular are sugar, chocolate chip, oatmeal raisin, and lemon tea.

coral plant: Forms coral on anything it touches.

couch potato: Like the hypnogourd, the cathode-ray tuber can entrance a being's mind, though its soul is not in danger. Couch potatoes feel glassy to the touch, and the eyes are all turned inward. Anyone who stares into the cut half will want to stay and mindlessly watch it forever.

crab-grass: Has sharp-edged pincers and a bad temper.

creeping fig: A mobile plant which likes to stay low to the ground.

currants: Electrically charged fruits that discharge their spark when connected in pairs.

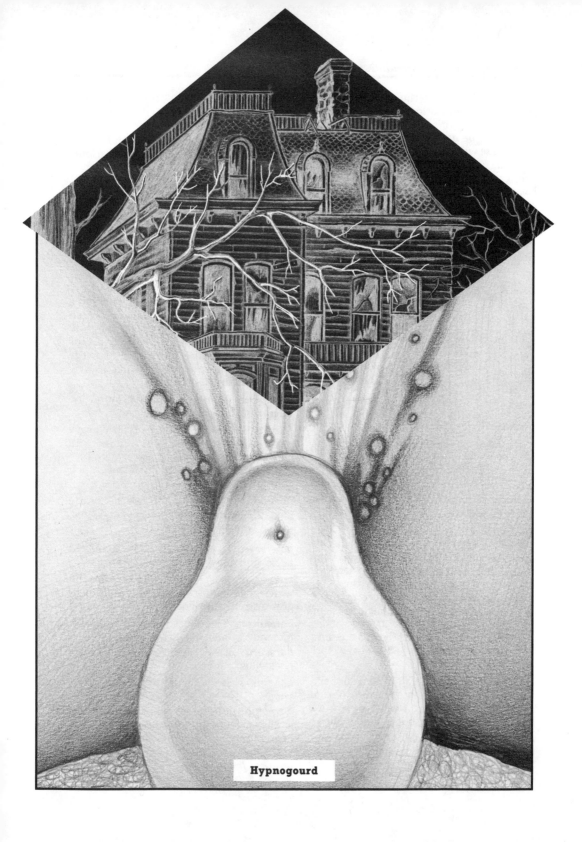

Hypnogourd

curse burrs: One of the most annoying pests of the plant world. The only way to get rid of a curse burr is to curse, and the same curse can't be used twice, though a really good curse will knock off several burrs at a time. In Mundania, they are called sand spurs, and even the best curses don't work because the magic is gone.

curtain plant: A modest plant with slender stalks around which swirl huge sweeping leaves.

Gorgon

cushion cactus: These have soft spines, good for bedding.

daytime cereals: They come from a vast wasteland. Daytime cereals grow amazingly fast, but they are bland and insipid. Even though they are not interesting to eat, they can prove fatally addictive, as the eater must consume more and more of them. There is almost no nourishment in them, but they are very popular among goblins and Mundanes. At night, they shrink into nighttime mini-cereals, which are even more addictive.

devil's tongue plant: A slimy and slippery, foul-mouthed leaf that makes infernal remarks such as calling Xavier "you son of a witch." (Literally true, but unkindly put.)

dog fennel: An eager herb that nips and barks. When it sleeps, it tucks its flower heads under its tails.

dry-cleaning plants: Sharp-smelling bushes whose fumes magically clean garments laid across the leaves.

dumb bell: Big, stalky plant with bulbous growths on each end that rings with a loud, dull bong.

eggplant: Depending on location of the plant, the eggs can be raw, soft-boiled, hard-boiled or, if stolen, poached.

elephant bush: Large gray plant designed by committee.

eyeball fern: At the tips of this fern are seed heads that look like eyes.

eye queue vines: Hanging vines that look as though they've been braided with large eyeballs spaced at even intervals. When they come in contact with a scalp, they sink into the brain, making the wearer smart (or think he is smart, which isn't necessarily the same thing), painless to all but actively stupid creatures, such as ogres.

eye scream bush: On this plant grow several flavors of the eye scream delicacy.

fabric plants: This family of fiber-heavy plants, including flannel plants and corduroy (from cordwood leaves), produce cloth which makes splendid off-the-branch clothing.

false hops: Produces hundreds of miniature kangaroos that are really all leaf and stem.

fireweed: To ignore.

hawkweed: Swoops down on its stem, and pecks and claws with talonlike thorns.

honesty plant: A white-leafed herb around which it is impossible to lie. Naturally, it grows strictly upright.

horehound: The doggy heads of this plant bite only women of loose virtue.

horsetail: Black, ropelike vine that pulls back when yanked.

hose vines: Socks and leggings grow on this vine.

hot potato plants: Tubers which grow hotter as they mature. Hot potatoes send up a jet of steam when they are ready to be picked and eaten.

hunter's horn: Blows a "tally-ho!" note.

Eye-Queue Vine

©1989

hypnogourd: Also called the peephole gourd. Immediately imprisons the mind. Those who peek in the peephole are instantly mesmerized. Their souls are whisked away to the world of the gourd. (See *Hazards of Xanth*.)

ice cream bush: Related to the snowball bush, except the balls are deliciously flavored ice cream.

inkwood bush: Its branches contain the best ink. Splinters of the wood can be used as pens.

ironwood: Grows up like spears, coated with rust. See also ironwood tree, the mature form.

itch weed: Stalky plant whose tiny thorns are shaped like claws.

jeanbushes: Branch of the fabric plant family which produces entire garments instead of lengths of cloth.

jelly bean plant: Mutated shrub of the jelly-barrel tree. Gives variegated beans.

Ice Cream Bush

knotweeds: Long grasses that tie themselves into complicated knots. A growing knotweed can trip up a mobile creature that wanders into its toils while a new knot is in progress. Young knotweeds can only do square knots, but grown ones know all the twists.

kraken weed: Monstrous plant that lives in the sea, feeding on the bodies of men and sea creatures swept helplessly into its tendril-tentacles.

ladder bushes: Useful to those wishing to secure something above them that is just out of reach. Immature bushes consisting of only a few steps are frequently grown in the kitchens of Xanth homes. A very well-grown ladder bush is used by Good Magician Humfrey in his study.

ladyfingers plant: Delicate hands with brightly polished nails. They clamor for attention by snapping their fingers.

lady's slipper plant: Related to the shoe tree, it produces dainty footwear for ladies.

lamb fennel: A primal plant that evolved into blanket bushes.

land kraken: Weed with prehensile tentacles that lives in the jungle. It resembles a harmless vine.

letter plants: Its flowers look like letters, and the whole plant has a smell like ink and musty books.

light bulbs: Surface-growing tuber which glows brightly when healthy. It weighs very little.

lightning rods: Natural reeds that glow brightly and are hot to the touch.

locoberries: Intoxicating fruit that causes those who eat it to go wild.

maidenhair fern: A delicate and modest plant.

Marquis-of-Queens-berry: In the wild, this plant always grows near shadow-boxers and governs their behavior. These acerbic-tasting berries can be eaten as an antidote to locoberries.

marsh-mallow: This plant produces edible, sweet, puffy pods much prized as a treat.

milkweed: When squeezed gently, the pods of this plant yield fresh sweet milk.

mint: A family of plants with some special qualities, as indicated by their names: spearmint, peppermint, frankinmint (smells like frankincense, but without the anger) and such.

mistletoe: Nudges the earth with its toenail and fires off seed pods.

mossquitoes: Vicious lichenous parasites that thrive on sap and bloodroot.

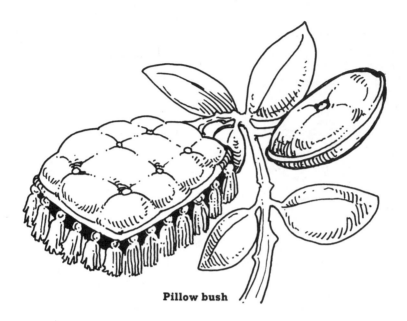

Pillow bush

movie trailers: Transparent vines heavy in cellulose which show a different picture along each inch of their length.

muffin bush: A plant akin to the breadfruit tree, which buds fresh, hot muffins.

mushrooms: Tiny rooms filled with mush. Some contain corn meal mush, some oat mush, and some wheat mush. It isn't very interesting food, but it is nourishing.

needle-cactus: A dangerous succulent which can fling its needles. Its attacks can be fatal.

nosegays: Bouquets of blossoms which clear stuffy noses.

number noodle plants: The produce of this plant is delicious noodles in the shapes of numbers. Alphabet noodle plants are closely related to the number variety.

passion fruit: Causes those who eat it to become passionately inclined.

photogra-fern: Tall, leafy plant that flashes brightly as it snaps away at a victim.

pillbox bush: Grows pills of all useful kinds.

pillow bushes: Plants whose fruits are huge puffy pillows with soft, downy fibers inside and a smooth, cottony skin outside. Pillow bushes tend to be low and hollow in the middle to attract passersby to rest within. The seeds can only be spread if the pillows are beaten and thrown, as they would be during a good pillow fight.

pincushion plants: Low bushes that have a profusion of short, sharp spines which they plunge into the legs of passersby.

pinwheel cookies: Most people hold the cookie by the pin when they eat them. Pinwheels look pretty growing, as they spin in the wind. The Gorgon serves punwheel cookies, a favorite of Ivy's.

pitcher plants: Cuplike leaves filled with liquid that will kill flies. Also plays a game with fly-catchers, pitching fast lobs not fast enough to run away before the plant begins the game.

poison ivy: Can shoot or let go droplets of poison. No relation to Princess Ivy, who isn't like that at all.

popsickle plants: Produces lollypops.

potato-chip bush: The ripe petals of its flowers are crispy potato chips.

potty plant: Makes passersby have a sudden call of nature.

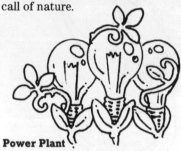

Power Plant

power plant: A plant that grows big fruit in the shape of light bulbs. The fruit makes one stronger than one was for a little while.

pumpkin: A large vegetable whose juices pump up whatever it touches like balloons.

quack grass: Some villagers in Xanth believe that it's an all-purpose patent cure, and use it when a healing spring isn't available. Sometimes it works, sometimes it doesn't.

quats: Edible fruit that grows low, middle, and high on the vine. There are also sasquats, shaped like big feet, which cause anyone who eats them to be sassy. Sasquats give one bad dreams about big hairy creatures and snow.

ragweed: Ragged clothes grow from its stalks. The cloth makes some people sneeze uncontrollably; in fact, some creatures will sneeze their heads off after one sniff.

resurrection fern: Has the property of playing on the psychology of the ignorant spectator. If there is a person standing near the resurrection fern, he or she appears to have the face of some dear departed. If the onlooker knows the secret of the fern, the illusion is broken. It resurrects those precious memories which are etched deepest. In Mundania, without magic, it merely resurrects itself.

sea oats: These stalks of grain swish and gurgle in their patches, following the faraway tides of the oceans. They make a tasty though salty broth, which carries on the tidal characteristics of the grain, slopping some of the contents out of overfull bowls with their waves.

seeds of light: Expand into fat glowing bulbs wherever they light.

serpentine: A partially mobile bush which hisses and undulates like a serpent. The leaves are formed in the shape of little snake-tongues. Pretty, greenish color.

sesame plants: The edible seeds of this plant can only be taken from open sesames, since the petals have sharp stalactitelike protrusions that can effortlessly tear the flesh off a human hand.

shadow-boxer: A plant with buds shaped like little boxing gloves set on springy tendrils. It strikes out at any shadow which attracts its attention. The plant cannot tolerate strong light.

skunk cabbages: Vegetables striped with telltale black and white streaks to warn animals from trying to eat them. They release a horrible stench when upset.

sliding turf: This cross between runner beans and slippery grass is a hazard to travelers. The sod can actually slide along the surface of the ground.

snake plant: Bites only snakes. Can be squeezed to produce snake oil, a vaunted but mostly ineffective cure-all.

snake root: A protective plant that bites any snakes that try to cross it.

snowball bush: Chilly white snowballs just the right size and texture for fights grow on this plant.

speargrass: Miniature spear-tips that grow in sharp-edged ranks.

split rock plant: Its roots split rocks.

spongemoss: Cushiony lichen useful for protecting wounds from the air. Absorbs blood or sap and seals gashes.

stinkhorn: Makes a foul-smelling noise when blown. Also makes children laugh when someone sits on one.

Wild Oats

stinkweeds: They exude a noxious odor that causes anything with a sense of smell to flee.

string beans: Can be unraveled into a ball of tough string, too tough to bite or be cut by any normal knife.

sugar palm: Forms a hand made of sugar.

sweet-bells plant: Like the bluebell, this plant rings a pretty tune.

toma-toes: Modest dancing fruits that blush from green to red when embarrassed.

towel plant: Related to the flannel plant, a source of useful fabric.

trance plant: Anyone who gets too close to it will be dazed.

treasure vine: This trailer bears coinlike fruit and greenbacked foliage on silvery stalks.

watercress: Grows up speedily in a hissing mass that lets off gas with a sound like "cress."

watermelons: These large green-skinned fruits suck in huge amounts of water while they grow. Watermelons have an almost infinite capacity for liquid.

wild oats: Slash and struggle to avoid being harvested. Planted and watered by a young man with his own urine, the mature plant's wild green-haired nymph will be bound to the sower. Parents of young men frown on this sort of thing, for some reason. There are tame oats, too, but for a wild one to behave itself goes against the grain.

wiregrass: Inedible ground cover that wire-hair cows and wire-haired terriers eat to enhance their magic.

witch hazel: It is impossible to see through a hazel copse. The magic fog they generate obscures vision, making it impossible to tell witch hazel is witch. Used for triangulation, a complicated process employed by centaurs for finding unknown locations.

Xanthorrhoed: A thick-trunked growth from which grow long thin grasslike leaves with upright spikes at the top bearing whitish flowers. Primitive, fundamental plant of Xanth.

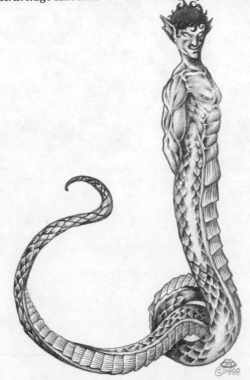

Naga

TREES

The trees in the jungles of Xanth are as varied as any in the wilds of Mundania. All Mundane varieties exist here, but, like anything in Xanth, they have absorbed X(A/N)th's magic, and have changed over the centuries. Evergreen fir trees grow in the cooler reaches, but the fir has softened pleasantly into fur. Other evergreens have mutated and divided, so that everblues and everyellows stand side by side with their ancestor, all three of which can permanently stain anything they touch blue, yellow, or green. Rock maples have evolved until they produce true rocks instead of soft, winged seeds.

acorn tree: Makes acorns. In Mundania, this function is performed by oak trees.

ances-tree: Its big bole branches into two, then two into four, into eight, and so on to infinitesimal branchlets. The bark corrugations resemble tiny words: names and dates.

artis-trees: All are different. No two are alike in color or construction but all are masterpieces, most appealing to behold.

ash trees: Found in blue, white, or black, these untidy trees scatter ash on the forest floor.

baobab tree: Grows upside down with its foliage on the ground and its roots in the air. Inside the hollow of the tree, everything seems to be right side up.

bay tree: A mournfully howling tree from which is produced bay rum.

beerbarrel trees: A variety of brews form naturally in these hollow-boled trees. Beerbarrel trees which look sickly yield Ail, extremely wide ones contain Stout, and ones with twisted, pinched limbs contain Bitter.

blackjack oaks: They bash intruders. Used as part of the defenses of Castle Roogna.

box elders: These trees steal the youth of creatures which blunder into their grove. They are hollow inside.

breadfruit trees: A staple of the Xanth diet. Fresh bread in Xanth is budded, not baked.

buckeye: Rakish trees that wink at passersby. Centaurs make a potent liquor out of the nuts that has a real kick.

bull spruces: These have horns that can tear or gore the unwary.

butternut tree: The soft-shelled nuts contain the best fresh butter.

cabbage palm: A tree with normal-looking fingers, but the palm is solid cabbage.

cedar-chest: This tree produces antiseptic-smelling boxes in which one can store anything safely away from bugs. Some cedars yield Hope Chests, which can contain insubstantial magic.

cheesefruit: Tasty fruit found on cheese-wood trees, out of which cheeseboxes are made.

Wiggles

cherry bombs: Originally ordinary chocolate-covered cherries adapted by King Roogna for the battle against the invading Fifth Wavers. They explode with great force when thrown.

chest-nut: Grows chests of nuts, which contain all manner of nuts: cocoa nuts, P and Q nuts, red, blue and hazel nuts, sandy beach nuts, and soft butternuts. The chests also contain several inedible nuts and bolts.

cocoa trees: Produce cocoa-nuts that contain hot cocoa.

cordwood: Comes from cord trees. The wood can be separated into its component cords. If one wants to make an especially strong object, one would disassemble the cord and re-form the matter into the parts wanted before construction, thereby making use of pre-recorded material.

cough drop tree: Small nuts that make one cough.

coven-tree: Large individual leaves with black markings on them label cages with their inhabitants' names, and give direction. On display are Gi-ants, ma-moths, enor-mouse, tremen-does, gigan-tics, stupen-does, and im-mens, brought here by Xanthippe. When they are freed, all the creatures charge around madly.

crabapple: Snappish fruit with ugly little faces and pinching claws. When steamed, crabapples turn bright red, and are delicious. Crabapple jelly is a popular favorite, though it affects everyone's mood for the rest of the day.

date palm: This plant has fronds for every day of the year. Day lilies grow around it in little cups of earth, but only one blooms each day. In the center of the palm is the century plant, which has long, thick green leaves spread out in a globe. At the heart of the plant are little straight stalks clothed by many round leaves that glitter as brightly as gold. When they are touched, they stop all time, for that is what the gold coins are: thyme, one of the most subtle and powerful plants of all. In Xanth, it appears that thyme is money.

date tree: On this tree grow down-dates and up-dates, which are affected by air waves. The fruit looks like a little 8 connected to a little D, as is proper for a D8.

dead-wringer: A plant so closely related to the tangle tree, or nooseloop, that it is frequently mistaken for one, though it is less dangerous than either.

direc-trees: Yellow-leaved tree which will help with any inquiries for a quarter part of anything. On its leaves are pictures of the things it knows about.

dogwood: A normally friendly tree with teethlike inner branches, though its bark is worse than its bite. Its many leaves resemble the faces of dogs, and its roots are like doglegs. Its fruits are hot dogs.

flying fruits: These fruit flies are tasty and normal. Their leaves act as wings. When they leave their tree, they find nests that resemble large salad bowls.

geome-tree: A three-dimensional plane tree with precisely shaped leaves.

glass trees: The transparent, brittle leaves of this tree and its inner bark provide windows for Castle Roogna. It is wise to handle it with care, for each sharp fragment may cause one pane.

gluebark: Anything which penetrates the bark of this sticky tree is held fast and then engulfed, as the tree slowly grows around it and absorbs it.

hoarse chestnut: A tree which makes heavy breathing sounds when the wind passes.

hominy tree: Produces fresh grits.

hornbeam: Honks and shines brightly.

horse-chestnut: This tree whinnies to attract attention, then tells boring old stories, dropping one old chestnut after another as long as it has an audience. None of a chestnut's stories are ever true. The nuts themselves resemble a centaur's droppings, another expression for blatant untruth in Xanth.

indus-tree: A busy plant with a lot going on in the branches.

infant-tree: Tough babies grow on this tree that wear diapers and helmets, also a little sword or spear. If anyone disagrees with them, they say, "Tough shift!" because in the military, some shifts are harder than others.

ironwood tree: Used for pressing clothes, also a source of the metal; very tough.

monkey puzzle tree: Only someone watching it grow can solve the puzzle. Makes a good refuge when staying in a dangerous place.

multifruit tree: Useful plant on which several different fruits grow at once. Magically adapted where there was too little room for all the different fruit trees to grow.

mys-tree: Its defense is that under its influence an intruder has trouble figuring things out.

nonenti-tree: An unimportant tree, hardly worth this listing.

oilbarrel trees: Citizens of Xanth get their fuel from these trees.

pagean-tree: Very ornate tree. Has marching bands marching through its branches: strips of cloth, brass or rubber with little legs that step out in cadence.

pairs: Fruit of greenish yellow that can only be plucked from their branch in twos.

papershell pecans: The finest paper can be drawn from the shells of these nuts.

Infant-tree

peace-pines: These are more dangerous than they look. If you lie down underneath one, it will lull you to sleep if it can, and keep you there forever.

pepper tree: The spicy bark makes one sneeze.

pie tree: One of the staples of food plants in Xanth. Pie trees can bear any kind of pie, usually several types on the same plant: delicious ones like pizza, pecan, shoo-fly, mince, shepherd's, cheese, chocolate cream, as well as offensive varieties like crabapple, pepperpot, pineapple, pe-can, and so on.

pine tree: This melancholy conifer makes one too unhappy to live. Sometimes to recover from its effects, one needs to seek out a psychia-tree.

pineapples: This fruit grows on apple pine trees in Xanth, unlike Mundane pineapples which grow on the ground. The ripe, golden-fleshed fruits, when dropped, explode in smoke and flame with a force that sends shrapnel-seeds hurtling in all directions.

plane tree: A jet black tree that enjoys flying, and is willing to carry passengers in its branches. They don't care for mocking-birds, who imitate their pilot fish, so many of them have No Mocking sections.

plumbs: Fruit that grows straight up and down on stringlike twigs on trees; they bob on their branches.

pogo trees: Incredibly springy trees that compress vertically and rebound straight up. Can be used as a form of transportation if a crosspiece is attached for the feet to rest on. Pogo trees are found in swamps.

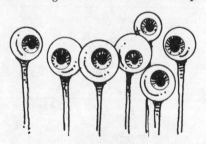

Seeing-Eye Dogwood Tree

pome trees: Pome trees have granite fruit, hard as stone, which can be used for building. It takes excellent teeth to bite into a pome-granite.

psychia-tree: This plant soothes and comforts any troubled person who lies down in its shade.

punchfruit trees: These give bowl-shaped fruits that contain thirst-quenching fruit punch. If allowed to get too ripe, the liquid packs a very solid punch indeed.

reverse wood: Reverses any magic performed within the range of its power. It affects only exterior magic, not inherent magic. In its more primitive state, it also reversed emotions. The bits of it that turn up in Mundania are called "lighter knot" because they burn with magic heat, melting stoves.

rock maple: A tough tree whose fruit is large round stones. Rock maples have a nasty sense of humor, and like to drop their stones on creatures which pass under their branches.

roses: In a special courtyard by themselves at Castle Roogna, five bushes of Mundane-seeming roses grow. They are white for indifference, yellow for friendship, pink for romance, red for love, and black for death. The Test of the Roses is to determine what relationship truly lies between two people. They are enchanted so a person can only pick one of the appropriate color. Any other will stab his hand with long, sharp thorns. The person taking the test must climb a rope ladder to a tile where the rosebushes can examine him to make sure the emotion the roses reveal is directed at him, not at someone else. The roses cannot be fooled.

rubber tree: A very flexible tree whose sap is used to make musical rubber bands.

seeing-eye dogwood tree: This plant looks like a mass of eyeballs on stalks that follow any movement.

sen-trees: These guard parts of the forest where intruders are not welcome.

Pie Tree

shade tree: This tree yields no real shadow, because it has no substance. A shade tree is the ghost of a real tree which died by violence.

shoe tree: The plant from which most citizens of Xanth get their shoes. All kinds of sturdy footwear grow on its branches. The sap from fresh high-heeled pairs can be used as emergency heeling potion when nothing else is available.

Shoe Tree

silver oak: A tree formed of silver.

slash pine: A close relative of the needle pine which brandishes sharp blades instead of small spines.

soda tree: Special hollow tree which when punctured spouts forth soda. Lime soda is one of the great favorites, but the tree comes in many different flavors.

sophis-tree: An animal that looks like a solid tree, but turns out to be an animal masquerading by standing on its thick tail and spreading its limbs out. It covers itself with bits of green to emulate leaves and branches.

spikespire tree: A narrow growth whose branches all point toward the sky in a sharp, tightly wedged spike.

stork-leg tree: Spindly bole with thick, plumy foliage at the top.

symme-tree: Is of perfect bilateral design, each vertical half the mirror image of the other.

torment pine: Just touching this tree hurts.

tree house: A magically enhanced hybrid of a boxwood, wall-nut, and lodgepole pine which grows into a comfortable domicile mounted high atop the trunk.

trouser-tree: On this tree grow nice brown jeans and other pantaloons.

two-lips tree: Its flowers give big smacking kisses on the cheek to passersby.

umbrella trees: These come in two types, the dry-loving umbrella trees, and the wet-loving parasol trees. The broad spreading canopy of the umbrella opens out when it rains because it likes dry soil over its roots. Parasol trees fold up in rain and spread out in sunshine, because they prefer their roots cool. They are not natural companion plants. Budding seedlings of either are called bumber shoots. Anyone can shelter under these plants; they are beneficent magic. An extract of sap from the parasol plant is a sun-shade elixir called parasol balm, or pa ba for short.

waffle tree: A plant that only grows in the Roogna Royal Orchard.

water chestnut tree: If you pick and puncture the chestnuts, you can drink their store of fresh water.

widowmaker: Tree with reddish sap that drops heavy deadwood limbs on those who walk below.

winekeg tree: Depending on the variety, these can contain any color of wine. The saplings yield only sour, immature wine, while the full-grown trees give robust, mature vintages.

You-call-yptus tree: Calls out warnings and can move its branches to ward off danger.

Tangle Tree

MAGICAL THINGS OF XANTH

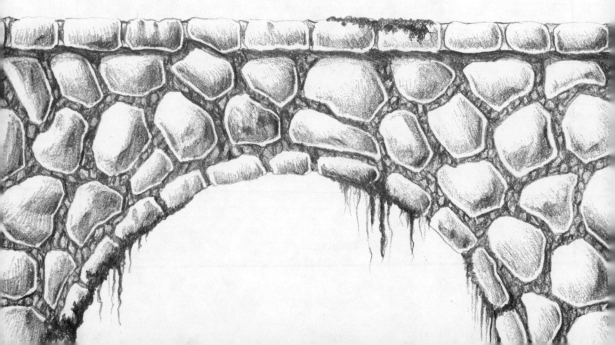

Mundane folks sometimes don't appreciate the fact that the varieties and techniques of magic are as diverse as those of science in Mundania. If you wanted to travel from New York to California (to make up two ludicrous names) and someone told you "Use science," you might be inclined to inquire, "What kind of science?" The science of aeronautics differs from that of automotives and from that of seacraft, and within each science are many subsciences. You might fly by glider, human-powered craft, propeller-driven airplane, jet plane, or balloon. You might prefer the craft of one maker to that of another. In short, it is really no answer to say "science." Why, then, should "magic" be an answer? The laws of magic differ from setting to setting. It works one way in the Adept framework, and in another way in the Incarnations framework, and another in the *Dragon's Gold* framework, and another in the Mode framework — oops, cancel that; you aren't supposed to know about that yet — and yet another in the Xanth framework. So when you say magic, you are merely opening the door to a considerable subject; don't be quick to assume that you know it all.

But for all that, the magic of Xanth is fairly straightforward. After it diffuses from the ambience of the Demon X(A/N)th, it takes a number of conventional forms. Generally, all things either use magic or are magic. Human folks, for example, use magic, each having a talent, while dragons are magic: their magic is built in. But you can never be quite certain where the line is drawn. Some folk seem to be magic, like the Good Magician Humfrey, while some magical creatures, like the centaurs, seem to have magic talents. So the general rule is only an imperfect guideline, like the statement "Mundane women are gossipy." Don't take it too seriously. After all, Xanth women are gossipy, too.

A computer in Xanth would work, but what it would do is not the same thing in both universes. Things of science work; a lever is a machine. Once something enters Xanth, the magic begins to affect the object. What was even more fun was writing about the effect that a program written in Xanth has in Mundania.
— Piers Anthony

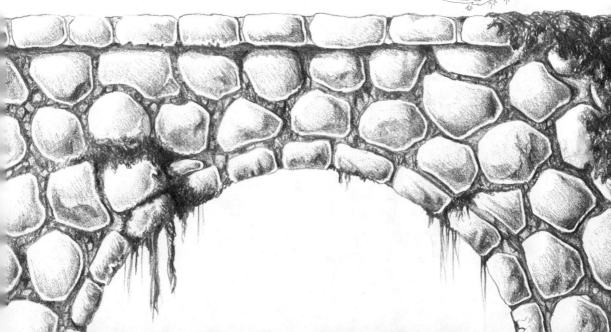

Except for rare occasions, every item of magic has but a single spell: a magic cloak may make one invisible, but it won't make one invulnerable, too. Enchanted items generally are enchanted for a specific purpose, such as a sword which makes the wielder an instant expert swordsman. Naturally occurring items frequently have less obvious uses, such as the midnight sunstone. And the uses of some have been long forgotten, as some items change hands often.

All of the curiosities and puzzles which abound in Xanth are listed somewhere in one of Good Magician Humfrey's collection of magical tomes. Following is a sample of spells, oddities and customs of Xanth from his books which have never been known in Mundania.

accommodation spell: Packaged by a magician named Yin-Yang to make the two who use it compatible in every way physically necessary for interbreeding. It is continually invokable, and does not dissipate after being used once. It is the size and shape of a grain of rice, most suitable for facilitating weddings.

address: Where Good Magician Humfrey can be found, if you can figure it out.

Adult Conspiracy: The secret of summoning storks, kept from all children by all adults. Also, the way adults force children to eat yucky wholesome food, like spinach.

age springs: A trap for the unwary, as water drunk from this spring hastens old age, for what reason no adult will say.

agony column: Tall pillar of marble upon which sufferers lie to cause their pain to abate.

apology: In the gourd, one apologizes by giving a passionate kiss to the person whom one has offended. This pleasant custom has spread out into Xanth.

beachcomber: Giant comb that sweeps all the debris out of the sand of a beach, and piles it up to be moved to a dumping site.

babbling brook: Freshwater stream which can talk.

blue agony fungus: Glows blue and has a dry, pleasant odor, but it turns the body of its agonized victims blue and melts them into a puddle that kills all the vegetation where it soaks in. It used to be used for executions during the early Waves of Colonization.

Book of Answers: Humfrey's gigantic personal tome of Information, which is the ultimate authority on every subject in Xanth.

bottomless pith: Fiber used to make bags with nearly infinite capacity.

castor oil: A vile substance which adults make children eat because it tastes dreadful. It leaks from castors when they roll too far.

chocolithic rock: Veins of tasty brown rock from which chocolate chips are mined.

cloudstones: Stepping stones one can use to cross the sky.

conniptions: Nasty little things that aggravate folks to the point of rage, especially when there is already a problem.

coral sponges: The remains of migratory sponges, they absorb pain and spread healing comfort.

cottage cheese: Large cheese that, when hollowed out, hardens and is quite suitable as a domicile. They grow, but are not plants.

crewel lye: A mixture used to clean the magic Tapestry in Castle Roogna.

D-tails: The hinder parts of bulls and bears, to which Mundanes pay close attention.

D-tour: An illusion that can be planted on an enchanted path to cause a traveler to change direction.

dark lantern: This lamp spreads a beam of darkness.

darning egg: Ovoid stone which nice girls use to rid themselves of curse burrs.

Deathstone: A rare rock which radiates an aura of death. One was used to protect Xanth for centuries from intruders.

dime: Tiny silver object that causes things passing over it to stop. It can only be used 12 times before it wears out, hence the expression, "a dime a dozen."

drying stone: This flat rock generates warm radiation to soothe anything near it that is cold or wet.

ectoplasm: A squishy cloud of formless matter in the gourd. It trails pale, sticky white streamers from its mass, and can stretch just like taffy. It is hard to detach from anything it touches.

Enchanted Mountain: A replica of aspects of Xanth in the dream realm, in the form of a towering mountain. Accessed by the frankinmint plant.

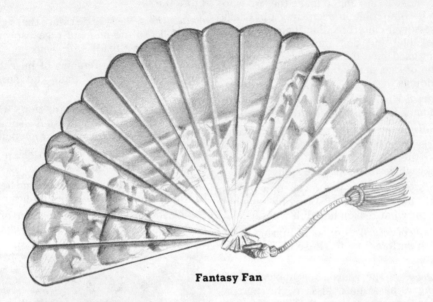

Fantasy Fan

enchanted paths: These trails abound throughout Xanth. They can defy gravity, carrying their passengers high through the air in a loop-the-loop, submerge them underwater without drowning or carry them under the earth. Evil magic can't exist on a charmed magical path, so pedestrians are protected while they remain on one. Some exist only in one direction.

evil eye: Shoots beam of light that can damage or kill.

eye scream, eye smilk: The eyes of these birds are rich and delicious. They may be served frozen as a special dessert treat. Scream birds are skinny and bony. All they eat goes to add size and richness to their great yellow eyes. They feed on eye plants, like eyebright, eye-rises, eye-o'-the-day flowers, and the like. (Demons eat an imitation of this treat which is made from the toe of the fu bird, but frozen toe-fu is inferior in flavor to eye scream.) Eye scream tastes very good served in crunchy pine cones.

Vitamin F: Which puts the F in F-ect if you put forth the right F-ort, and has been lost in the gourd for centuries along the Lost Path. Not to be confused with Vitamin X, which is for X-perts.

fan club: A length of wood with which a fan can place itself in the middle of fandom.

fantasy fan: A bamboo fan that has a magic picture on it when it is spread open. It makes the wielder think that he is cooler than he is, especially when the picture is of a snowscape. Periodically, the fans gather together from all over Xanth for a convention where they shoot the breeze and blow a lot of hot air, and decide who is the secret master of fandom.

fan-tom: An image of a fantasy fan that lacks substance.

figment: An illusory figure. Gina Giantess started out as one, but Girard's love made her a regular dream figure.

firewater opal: Mela Merwoman's prize, which she needs to gain a husband. She enlists Prince Dolph's aid to recover it, because Draco Dragon killed her former husband and stole the gem.

fire, water, sand: A gambling game popular in Xanth, played by simultaneously offering a hand sign indicating one of the three elements: a closed fist means sand, a flat hand means water, and the first two fingers forked represent fire. Depending on who is playing, fire evaporates water, water covers sand, and sand smothers fire; or water douses fire, sand displaces water, and fire melts sand. If both players offer the same symbol, the round is a tie, and play continues. The rules should be discussed before play begins.

firecracker: Flaming cracker that explodes in pretty sparkles when crunched.

firewater: Streams, pools or fountains of orange water which cascade and steam naturally. Firewater is used for cooking, but is too hot for bathing.

fish river: A stream which turns all that drink from it to fish.

fog horns: Tall treelike horns which blast out columns of fog to obscure the forest paths.

foot-ball: Every kind of extremity that there is, hooves, feet, claws, talons, paws, insect legs, growing on the outside of a sphere which rolls by itself all over Xanth.

Forget-Whorl: Piece that has broken off from the Gap's Forget Spell. These wander randomly across the land, causing memory lapses.

Freshman English: A fate worse than death, in Mundania.

wild fruitcakes: Dangerous when cornered, but delicious.

golden fleas: The fabulous metallic fleas of a dragon, sought by Ja-son, a foolish Mundane.

Gorgon-zola: A delicious, half-petrified cheese made by the Gorgon by staring at milk through her veil.

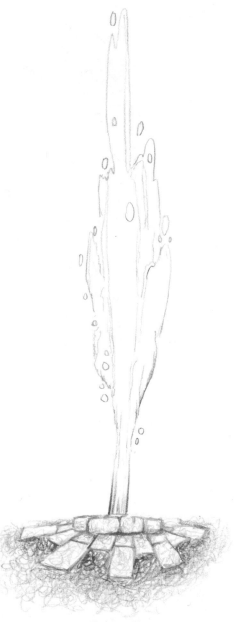

Fire Water

Icicle Forge

hand-ball: Related to the foot-ball, a sphere of hands, paws, wings, claws that rolls around Xanth. Frequently used for games by ogres.

handkerchoo: Delicate square of cloth used for containing sneezes.

hate spring: Makes anyone who touches its water hate the next person seen. Used by the Goblinate of the Golden Horde to torment captives.

hayberry longcake: A delicacy. There is an inferior substitute in Mundania, using short straw instead of long hay.

headstone: Magic rock which takes on the appearance of whoever is buried nearby.

healing spring: Heals completely all wounds, rashes, diseases, bruising, amputations (deliberate or accidental) except for beheading. It may lay a geas on any user to protect the pool in exchange for its benefits.

Heaven Cent: A penny piece that sends the wearer to the place most needed; it can be charged only by Electra.

hem lock: A border plant that can be set at the hem of a dress. Once locked, it will never slip off.

honey comb: B's use this to comb honey from honeysuckle and honeymoons.

honeymoon: The far side of the moon, which remains as sweet as honey, and is popular with the newly married. The near side of the moon, of course, has long since been corrupted to green cheese because of the horrible sights it sees below.

hope chest: A special box that grows on cedar-chest trees. It can safely contain insubstantial magic like hope or love.

hot cross buns: Similar to patti cakes, these inflict warm stripes across the same part of the body that patti cakes pat.

icicle: This sickle is made of the purest white non-melting ice. It has a cutting edge on its inside curve which can be sharpened by honing it over a torch.

Love Spring

infinite decimal: A tiny dot which precisely and impersonally judges the fairness of matters to the smallest degree.

jigsaw puzzle: No two pieces fit together unless requested by the correctly worded plea, which is different for each match. The portions of the picture that show, unlike Mundane puzzles, keep changing.

ladder, enchanted: A useful device that anchors permanently to any wall until someone calls out "weigh anchor!" which causes it to kick loose violently.

lemon harangue pie: A sour little pastry that throws insults around.

lepermud: This dead white liquid clay infects any flesh it touches with leprosy.

lexicon: All the properly forgotten things of Xanth, compiled into a list by three curious Mundanes.

life clay: It can be molded into the semblance of any living creature. It will then behave as such, except that it will not die when cut into pieces; it will merely reform as several small models of the original creature.

lightning bolts: Bolts which fall from the sky during storms. They do a lot of damage if they strike too close to anything. When they cool, they are good for bolting things together.

lines and boxes: A popular game of strategy in Xanth.

living room: A room which wanders about on its own legs, seeking to find itself a home.

Lost Path: The path along which all lost things lie, from artifacts to people.

love spring: This natural pool causes any two species who drink of it to wish to mate (including plant life). This is chiefly how new conglomerate species are engendered.

lunatic fringe: A protective illusion of madness woven out of the light of the full moon to scare off intruders.

magic mirrors: Very rare. Humfrey uses them for a variety of purposes: divination of questions that can be answered yes or no, long-distance communication, and magical observation of distant scenes. Others are used by the Royal Family to keep in touch with one another.

magic stones: Have varied types of magic proper to stones, such as to divert streams up over them or to cause damage to humans.

magic wand: A stick that holds a powerful spell that anyone can use. Goldy Goblin has one that can levitate objects or people.

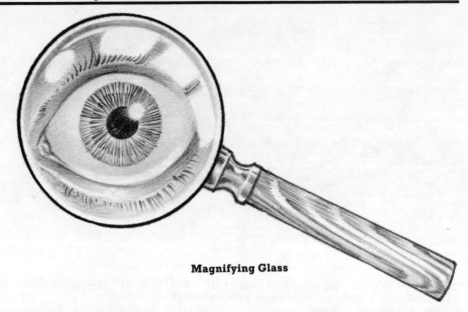

Magnifying Glass

magnifying glass: A Mundane device that in Xanth makes things bigger.

memory crystal: A huge cut crystal resting in a sunny grove where it can pick up the best sunlight. Each of the crystal's many facets reveals a different memory to anyone who looks into it.

midnight sunstone: The rarest of all gems, it glows as brightly as the sun when there is no other light.

milkshakes: Milkweed pods which, when opened, quake and shiver, spilling half their contents.

mocolate chilk: Tasty brown fluid that comes from mocolate choo-cows.

monster cheese: A delicious cheese that makes a human act like a monster. On real monsters, it has no side effects. The more ladylike version is monsterella. Variants exist in Mundania: muenster and mozzarella. (Sorry, we're not responsible for crazy Mundane spelling!) See also Gorgon-zola.

moonstones: Little pocked globes that shine silvery green with the light of the moon. Their outline reflects the quarter of the moon showing in the sky.

mouth organ: Big plant made up of mouths of all sizes and shapes, plays music. Little ones can be picked and played by hand. They are part animal, vegetable and mineral. The organ pipe cactus is a related species.

mussels: Clamlike things that pull shells closed.

oil slicks: These puddles lie on the surface of the ground, the products of tanker trees that have inadequately disposed of their wastes. The oil is slipperier than almost any other substance in Xanth, and can propel a walker headlong into obstacles. They have sentience to a limited degree, and a mean sense of humor.

opposite sex: By order of the Adult Conspiracy, this definition has been censored. What would happen if children found out which one it was?

panties: Object of much speculation in Xanth: exactly what color are they? Boys beneath the Age of Consent are not permitted to speculate. It is part of the Adult Conspiracy.

Paste Orifice: A delivery service that gums things up.

patti cake: You should eat this sitting down, or it will pat you. Fresh patti cakes give pretty fresh pats, so you should protect any part you don't want patted.

pennies: Round bits of metal that fall from the sky. Single penny bits have one delicious perfume scent. Twopenny bits have two scents, sixpenny bits have six scents, and so on. Not to be confused with the Heaven Cent.

pied-piper flute: Once begun, this flute will play itself and attract any creature into following it.

purple bouillon: A delicacy in Xanth, wrung from purple wood by ogres.

quicksand: It speeds you up.

rainbow: A banded arc of color in the sky containing in order every color in the spectrum. Between the bands of visible color are the translucent colors, and some hues lie in patterns, such as polkadot, plaid and checkerboard. Some of the colors have never been imagined by man, such as fortissimo, charm, phon and torque. The rainbow is fussy about where and under what conditions it appears in the sky, and it works on a very tight schedule, so it never remains anywhere very long. It keeps a set distance from those viewing it, so that it is fixed as long as one keeps looking at it. The rainbow is one of the most fabulous sights in Xanth or Mundania, for this is one of the only types of magic which appears in both lands.

red tape: Festoons of red ribbon that prevent movement by tying things up and presenting physical impediment.

Revised Simplified Tax Manual: A source of limitless inspiration for gibberish, used by Mae Maenad for oracles and by Mundanes for annual aggravation in the month of Apull.

rolling hills: Topographical features that can be a hazard to travelers because they really roll.

sad sacks: Gloomy-colored but strong fiber bags that grow on low bushes.

sand dune: A heap of sand that moves onto beaches and takes them over; it rolls over prey and smothers them to eat at leisure. It believes that it is preserving fossils for posterity. It doesn't attack at night.

seaweed soup: Wholesome and nutritious, therefore a torment to children. Mela feeds it to Prince Dolph. See *Adult Conspiracy*.

shadow of a doubt: A deep, dark gloom which dissipates when ignored.

sharpening stone: Casts keen edges on any knife or axe brought into contact with it.

shoefly pie: Filled with shoes, boots, slurpy leathery juices, delicious laces and soles, this huge pastry is a treat fit for an ogre.

shower cap: From this useful hat, water rushes down your person to the ground and back up again, magically washing you clean without spilling the water.

sign language: Understood by animals in Xanth, if people have the wit to approach them with it, and by a select group of Mundanes.

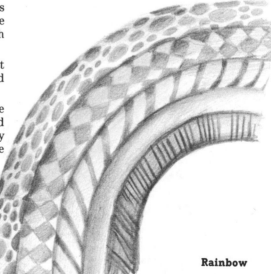

Rainbow

Stares

skeleton key: Needed to find the Heaven Cent. At first thought to be an isle, it turns out to be a rib Grace'l possesses, which sounds the Grace'l note in the key of G. Female skeletons have one more rib than male skeletons, because the missing rib was used by the Demon X(A/N)th to form the first female skeleton for the first male skeleton, who was lonely.

skinflint: Small brass scales from the City of Brassies used for covering and protecting wounds (or dents) until they heal. Can be used on human flesh as well.

slowsand: Prevents one from getting through the region by slowing their progress to a crawl. One can die of starvation wading through slowsand. Even a jump over it can take forever.

soda water springs: Natural effervescent springs that come in several flavors, such as lime, strawberry, cream soda, celery, or orange.

soapstones: These scented or unscented balls of rock lather up nicely when rubbed in the hands with water.

somersault: A seasonal wandering white globe made of salt that explodes into powder if struck.

spec-tackles: Ghostly creatures with glassy eyes and big shoulders.

sponge: Natural cushions that soothe pain and spread healing comfort.

stares: A means of attaining the next level in the Bookworm's cavern. By meeting the gaze of each successively higher statue, one is lifted magically through the air.

stepping stone: Stone which expands in water to provide a broad but not steady step. The top protrudes just above the water.

sugar sand: Found in patches throughout Xanth, it is one of the nicest additions to a meal. Unlike the Mundane equivalent, sugar sand does not cause cavities. Naturally sweet things grow in it.

tail-lights: Fluffy little animals that hop which have glowing cottony tails.

Uroborus

tangles: They start out as tiny snarls in children's hair or horses' tails, but grow into huge tangle trees.

technicolor hailstorm: Puffy and light stones that fall out of the sky that sting when they strike.

There Restorer: Potion used to re-embody ghosts.

tire iron: This mace-shaped weapon tires anyone it strikes so much they go to sleep.

twister: Deadly storm, much like those in Mundania, but these twist houses and trees into corkscrews. Tangle trees are braided, and wheatfields are cornrowed, by these fearful spiraling winds.

Two Minute Replay: A gift to Onda and Max from the Time Being which enables them to replay two minutes of time.

typewriter: Mundane philosophical device used for generating wisdom.

Uroborus: A legend in Xanth about a giant serpent who was so large it encircled the Mundane world and grasped its own tail.

vomit fungus: Found only in the Region of Madness or anywhere a monster wants to liven up his abode with appropriate decoration. It hangs in disgustingly greasy streamers, and looks distressingly real.

washing powder: A useful spell to get clothes clean, but it has to be kept in a sealed container because it is always running out. When it is poured into water, it makes the water wash up and down against the edges of its container.

watch: Magic amulet of Mundanian design which can find things. It is called a watch because it watches things with its single eye.

wood wind: A living plant that can be played as a musical instrument. It is long and hollow, with holes along its stem. It blows out much more wind than it takes in.

Worm: A computer program nominally put out by Vaporware Limited. It promises a lot, if you wait long enough. It installed Com-Pewter's Sending in Grey Murphy's computer. It was sent to Mundania by Com-Pewter as part of a nefarious plot. However, it has ideas of its own on what it plans to do in the future, which has nothing to do with Com-Pewter's instructions. If the computer containing the Worm is running, Xanthians in the vicinity can understand Mundane speech.

worry wart: A wart you may get on your head. When you scratch it, you become worried. Sometimes they are impossible to ignore.

CALENDAR OF XANTH

The months of the year in Xanth (AwGhost, etc.) and their holidays and celebrations

(New ones initiated by Piers Anthony 9 October 1988)

Jamboree

4	Day of the Allegory
8	Hiatus' and Lacuna's Birthday
12	DeMetria Offers Esk Ogre Three Great Experiences
16	Castle Roogna Dedicated
21	Volney Vole Sets Out to Save Kiss-Mee River
25	Faux Pass Created
28	Chameleon's Birthday

FeBlueberry

3	Dame Latia Curdles Water
6	Arnolde Centaur Learns His Talent
10	Night Stallion Takes Over the Night Mare Herd
15	Day of the Zombie
17	Sorceress Tapis's Birthday
19	Grundy Golem Is Constructed
25	Gerrymander Divides and Conquers
30	Simurgh's Birthday (Doesn't come often, so she lives long!)

Marsh

3	Day of the Dragon
5	Chex Centaur Weds Cheiron
6	Marrow Bones Defends Draco Dragon's Treasure
8	Rapunzel Escapes the Ivory Tower
11	Dolph's Birthday
16	Demon X(A/N)th Learns How to Play to Win
21	Humfrey Marries the Gorgon
25	Grace'l Ossein's Trial
29	Magic Dust Village Founded

Apull

2	Nextwave Invades Xanth
7	Prince Dolph's Test of the Roses
11	Blythe Brassie Emerges from Gourd
15	Irene's Birthday
22	The Siren Marries Morris Merman
24	Day of the Secretary Bird
27	Justin Tree Transformed

Mayhem

1   Nada Naga's Birthday
7   Day of the Nymph
15 Smash Ogre Crams Demon Into Gourd
20 Voles Depart Xanth
25 Tandy's Birthday
30 Centaur 500 Race

JeJune

4   Brain Coral Kisses Irene
10 Day of the Elf
15 Ichabod Comes To Xanth
20 Demon Beauregard Completes
    His Thesis: "Fallibilities of Other Intelligent Life"
23 Irene Marries Dor
27 Sorceress Tapis Completes the Tapestry

Jewel-Lye

3   Day of the Goblin
5   Nymph's Mother Frightened By A Pun
8   Mare Imbrium Goes Day Mare
12 Herman Hermit Dies
17 King Trent's Coronation
28 Jewel's Birthday

AwGhost

1   Day of the Ghost
6   Bink's Birthday
10 Gap Dragon Rejuvenated As Stanley Steamer
13 Ivy Conquers Thyme
15 Smash Ogre's Birthday
19 Zora Zombie Finds Love
23 Wiggle Swarm
27 Electra Completes the Heaven Cent

SapTimber

OctOgre

NoRemember

Dismember

AFTERWORD

erhaps the most controversial aspect of Xanth is the pun factor, as mentioned in the introduction to this book and in the intro to the Beastiary (sic), and wherever else they can wedge their way in. Critics pounce on them, seeming to think that though a wart on Miss Universe might not make her wholly unattractive, a pun in fiction destroys all vestige of readability. Readers seem divided, with some even sending in puns, which largess I am trying to discourage. The fact is, Xanth is composed largely of puns, from its outline and geography to its incidentals, so those who would abolish all punnish elements would in fact abolish Xanth — which may be the point.

I harbor a suspicion that it isn't really the puns that critics object to. After all, others have been known to pun without being excoriated. It may be the fact that Xanth has become highly successful. The last seven Xanth novels — #5 through #11 at this writing — have made the *New York Times* bestseller list. I dare say that not many series have that kind of record; offhand I can think of only Start Wreck within the SF/fantasy genre, and that series too is not well accepted critically. So it may be that the critics resent the success of it, and use the puns only as a pretext.

I also suspect that when a critic condemns the stupid puns — and there are plenty in Xanth! — it is because he is too dull to catch the sophisticated puns. Oh yes, they are here, some of them requiring special expertise to fathom. For example, Heavenly Helen Harpy, the one pretty harpy in an ugly flock. Why did I name her Helen? Well, for the alliteration, of course; that's always fun. But also for literature. British poet Dante Gabriel Rossetti of the Victorian Age read about how Helen of Troy dedicated to Venus, the goddess of love, a goblet molded in the shape of her breast. Rossetti, evidently intrigued (as what man wouldn't be?), wrote a poem about it, *Troy Town*. It starts off "Heavenborn Helen, Sparta's queen,/ (O Troy Town!)/ Had two breasts of heavenly sheen,/ The sun and the moon of the heart's desire:/ All Love's lordship lay between./ (O Troy's down!/ Tall Troy's on fire.)" Well, I too am fascinated by the intrigues of history, and have played several times on the ramifications of the Siege of Troy. I am also fascinated by poetry and literature, and the thinking and the art of those who have lived before me. I am also fascinated by life and death and the figures of young women. How I wish I had that goblet on my shelf! So it was natural that I allude to this matter in some way, and I did it punnishly in Xanth, and more seriously elsewhere. Thus instead of Heavenborn Helen, Sparta's queen, and her marvelous breasts, I have Heavenly Helen, Harpy's queen, with her marvelous breasts. This is indeed a pun, and one I suspect few who are not versed in the literature of England have caught on to independently, but it is also an expression of my sincere appreciation for history, literature and beauty. There is more on my mind than puns, but a pun can be the key to the rest of it.

Another cross-jurisdictional pun is a centaur's reference to passing his croggle test. This one cuts across horsemanship and fandom. Those who have show horses must give them the Coggins test, to be sure they will not contaminate other horses; Sky Blue, the model for Mare Imbri, had such a test. Those who are in fandom have a special language to address fannish things, and one of their terms is croggle: to be croggled is to be amazed. So the croggle test — ah, I see you get it now.

The night mares are structured on layered puns, starting with the Mundane term for a bad dream which becomes literally a type of horse, and moving on to the *mares* or seas of the moon, which can be seen only at night. The pronunciation differs, but a little thing like that never stopped a galloping pun. Hence the prints of the hooves of the night mares show the partial circles of the phases of the moon, with each mare's *mare* highlighted.

Then there is the matter of the calendar. A rumor was going around fandom that I was being an ogre at conventions. Since at that time I had never even attended a fan convention, this struck me as unkind, and it accounts in part for the distance I keep between myself and fandom; I prefer to associate with those who have some fairness about ascertaining the truth rather than spreading a false story. But I dealt with it in my own punnish fashion: I wrote a novel featuring an ogre as the hero. That novel, *Ogre, Ogre,* was published in the month of October, and became my first *New York Times* bestseller. I started calling myself the Ogre, especially as I bashed down other fans who sought to spread misinformation about me. I think it is now generally known in fandom that it is not safe to misrepresent Piers Anthony in print. That pretty well set back that rumor! But I couldn't help perceiving the justice of it: obviously that was the month of the Ogre, OctOgre. But what about the other months? My brain began heating, ogre-style, as I pondered, and in due course I came up with an entire calendar of ogre months, and it was published for 1987 by Del Rey Books. It seems that the ogres keep the calendar of Xanth because they are the only creatures too stupid to mind getting their hamfingers sticky on the dates. Now the calendar may become a regular thing, starting with the Xanth PinUp Calendar of 1990, with its twelve luscious females and one unluscious female: Miss Mayhem, an ogress so ugly that the mirror she is looking at is shattering, and she wears a dead skunk tucked in her belt as a deodorizer. So the puns truly abound in the calendar, but it can still be used for Mundane purpose, if you are too stupid to mind the sticky dates. We ogres must stick together.

There is a pun of another kind in X12, *Man from Mundania*: the weird address where the Good Magician is hiding, with its Silly goose Lane and all. The tribulations of wending one's way to this address are detailed in the novel; Hurts is where the painful things of the gourd are generated, for example, and that region bears a passing similarity to the Mundane Hell. But this address is actually that of a lady named Pamela with whom I have been corresponding for several years, and sometimes phoning, and I even give her ten to fifteen percent of the money my books earn overseas. No, I am not the only man in her life; she has a number of other clients, for she is a professional. What, you may be wondering, does my wife think of this? Well, my wife is tolerant, for Pamela is the mistress of my foreign sales. That is, my overseas literary agent. If you want an agent and are willing to search through Hurts itself . . .

I have been called a pun master, and folks inquire how I do it. The answer is, I don't know. I was never known as a punster, and it hardly manifests outside Xanth, and indeed, critics do not find me funny at all, except when I speak of writing well; that they find hilarious. But I do have an analogue type of mind, seeing analogies in everything, and this in its basest form seems to result in puns: analogies between horses and seas of the moon, or between the breasts of a harpy and those of Sparta's queen, or between horses and fandom. In its more elevated form, this way of seeing things helps me to be a better writer, as I contemplate the human condition and the meaning of the universe, and seek to make sense of some part of it for myself and for my readers. This is true even in Xanth, and I hope that my readers derive some of their pleasure from that wider perspective, even if the only hints of it are in a mare's hoofprint or a heavenly harpy.

The Chronicles of Xanth

CREWEL LYE

(A Caustic Yarn)

CHAPTER ONE

Retyping of deleted chapter from carbon of original, said carbon donated to Clarion West for scholarship fund.

TANGLEMAN

t was the month of Octogre, when the ogres were tromping about and ugly forebodings stalked the land of Xanth. Or so it seemed to Ivy, for a number of annoyances had settled about her like knick-gnats. For one thing, her mother Irene was getting quite fat in the tummy, but kept right on eating and pretending it was wonderful, and didn't seem to have much time for Ivy anymore. For another, her father King Dor had ordered a baby brother for her, and they were expecting to find him under a cabbage leaf any day now. Ivy did not need or want a baby brother, but nobody had asked her. How could they have been so thoughtless as to order something like that without consulting the one most concerned? What good was a baby, anyway — especially a boy?

Well, she could go out to the orchard and throw cherries at glass trees. That was always fun for bad moods, and the explosions created a nice commotion, not to mention the breaking glass tinkling down. Of course the adults tended to raise a fuss, but that was part of the excitement. Yes, that would do for a start!

She jumped off her bed, landing just beyond the reaching grasp of the monster-under-the-bed, and ran for the door. "Pooh to you, monster!" she cried nastily, sticking out her tongue at it as she slipped out. The thing growled, but could not reach her, and had to retreat back into its shadow.

Grundy the Golem intercepted her as she passed into the hall. "Where are you going, Princess Tadpole?" He always called her that, ever since hearing the fable about the princess and the frog; he liked the story, but refused to grant her the status of a full-grown frog.

There was another annoyance! They had sicked Grundy on her as a baby-sitter; she couldn't sneak out anywhere without him tagging along. "Nowhere, ragbrain," she said shortly.

"Then we might as well get on to the North Village, Sweetpea." He always called her that, ever since — never mind.

"The North Village! I'm not going there!"

"Yes you are, Snippet. To visit your grandpa King Emeritus Trent for a few days."

"Grandpa Trent? Why?" Actually, this sounded interesting; still, she felt obligated to protest, on general principle.

"To get you out of the way, Cutie-pie, while your baby brother arrives, of course." He always called her that, ever since she had climbed into a pie and pulled the crust over her for a blanket. The castle cook had made a fuss, for no reason.

Ivy wasn't thrilled to be reminded of that. "I'd rather stay at home and build a deadfall to trap him. Do you happen to know which cabbage leaf —?"

Grundy considered, seeming to find something funny. "You could ask the zombies to do it. They keep an eye on the garden, and they're good at deadfalls. They use them for their deadstock."

"Good enough!" She ran down the hall, heading for the zombie graveyard.

The golem zipped after her. He could move surprisingly quickly for such a little creature. "But we haven't time for that right now! King Trent is waiting."

"Oh, pooh!" she said, skewing around a corner in the manner only she could manage, spooking a ghost who happened to be drifting through. "He's not here yet!"

"Really?"

Ivy skidded to a halt. There stood her grandfather, at the head of the stairs, awesomely stern and grave.

"Oopsy!" she exclaimed.

King Emeritis Trent smiled. Like most adults, he was subject to mellowing by cute displays. "Are you ready to travel, Ivy? What form of bird would you like to be?"

Ivy brightened. She liked flying! "A blue-J," she decided. "And Grundy can be a green-J."

"Coming up," King Trent said. He never gave her cutesy nicknames; he treated her with the dignity due royalty. Ivy had a high regard for grandparents; sometimes she wished she could eliminate the middleman and just be her grandparents' daughter.

"Wait, Grandpa!" she cried, remembering something. "What about Stanley?"

"We'll fly down and fetch him," her grandfather agreed indulgently, aware that children always wanted to take their pets with them. Then Ivy became a blue-J, and Grundy a green-J, and King Trent himself a red-J.

At which the green-J did a doubletake. "You can't transform yourself, Your Majesty!" he squawked at the red-J.

"I can when I'm only present in illusion," the red-J replied.

"Live and learn," the golem-bird muttered. "He's here in illusion — and can still do transformations. Isn't magic marvelous!"

It occurred to Ivy that it would be great talent to be able to transform oneself to any other form. Grandpa Trent could only transform others; it was Grandma Iris who handled the illusions. So she was projecting Grandpa Trent as a red-J instead of himself; he wasn't really here. Ivy envied those who had such obvious talents; her own talent of enchantment was subtle, and tended to do others more good than herself, so people didn't always recognize her as the Sorceress she was. That could be most annoying at times.

They flew out a window and looped down to the moat, where Stanley Steamer was snoozing on the bank and a young moat-monster snoozed in the water. The young dragon was somewhat smitten with the female monster, and at times got fairly steamed up about her, but Ivy knew her for a tease. Males of all kinds tended to be foolish about females of all kinds; this was a fact Ivy noted carefully for future reference. One never knew when such information might come in handy.

"Come on, Stanley — we're flying north!" Ivy called.

The dragon peered up at the J's, perplexed. He flapped his vestigial wings, as if to show that the spirit was willing but the flesh inadequate. He recognized Ivy by her voice and smell; sometimes Grandpa Trent had transformed her to other forms, so Stanley was used to that. But as for flying — he was a half-grown dragon, far too massive to get airborne.

Then he became a green dragonfly. He buzzed up, looking startled, and more than a little nervous now about the birds. "It's okay, Stanley," Ivy called. "The others are just Grundy and Grandpa Trent; none of us eat bugs."

The dragonfly remained uncertain, for a real bird might say anything to lure a tasty dragonfly within reach. Ivy saw the problem, for she perceived herself as a bright child, and unlike her grandfather she could apply her magic talent to herself as well as others. "Maybe if you were bigger —"

"No problem," Grandpa Red-J said. Stanley became a larger dragonfly, more massive than any of the birds, with six big bright wings and twice that many teeth. Now he had much more confidence. He buzzed loudly and shot out an experimental jet of fire, pleased. In his natural form all he had was steam.

They looped above the castle and headed north toward the Gap Chasm. Ivy was thrilled to see Castle Roogna and its environs from above. It looked so small, almost like an elaborate toy castle. The trees of the orchard resembled bushes. The whole landscape of Xanth was a tapestry of greens, with fields and forests alternating intriguingly. Here and there were the houses of people and the dens of dragons and the warrens of unidentified creatures. She had explored some of that on the ground once, two years ago, and met a nice goblin-girl and a cyclops and of course Stanley Dragon himself. She'd have to that again sometime!

Soon they were over the Gap. This was a huge, deep fissure that extended across the peninsula of Xanth. For centuries it had been forgotten, not even appearing on maps, because of the Forget-Spell on it, but now that spell was mostly gone. Ivy wondered where that monstrous spell had come from, and who had made it, for she was curious about everything. No one seemed to know about that Forget-Spell, which she found very frustrating. Ivy liked to know everything that caught her passing fancy, especially things that were secret.

A gleam caught her eye. There was a lake perched at the edge of the Chasm; in fact it overlapped the Chasm slightly, but refused to drain down. The perversity of the inanimate showed in various ways in Xanth; if a lake wanted to hold its position, it used magic to do so. Ivy knew that Mundane lakes lacked that sort of determination. That was just one of the squintillion things wrong with Mundania.

She peered more closely at the lake — and saw that the gleam was in the shape of a star. It was a starfish in the water! Ivy knew what to do with a starfish.

"Star light, star bright, star-fish shining bright, I wish I may, I wish I might, have this wish for my delight!" she chanted according to the magic formula. "I wish I knew who made the Forget-Spell!" She waited expectantly, but nothing happened.

"Dummy!" Grundy said. "You didn't specify when!"

Ivy squawked with dismay. Magic always had to be nailed down tight, or it slipped away. The starfish might wait till she was a mean old woman of sixteen or seventeen to grant her wish, and there was nothing she could do about it.

Now a shape loomed ahead, in the air above the Gap. It was too large for an ordinary bird, and too small for a dragon. This creature was extraordinarily thin, with a body like a pole, and a huge, narrow, axe-beaked head.

"That's a hal-bird!" Grundy exclaimed, alarmed.

"That's awkward," Grandpa Trent said. "Though I am here in illusion, I still must bring my apparent identity within my normal reach of a creature in order to transform it. That battle-axe could go after one of you before I reach it."

Indeed, the hal-bird looked as if it were considering which one of them to chop up first. "Transform Stanley into a griffin," Grundy suggested. "He'll tear the hal-bird to dripping pieces." He glanced at Stanley, who seemed to be fascinated by the Gap. This was hardly surprising, since he had once been the dread Gap Dragon, and some day would be again, once he got over his rejuvenation.

"Don't you dare!" Ivy cried fiercely. "It's not right to hurt exotic wildlife!"

"That's my grandchild," Trent said approvingly. "Mayhem should never be practiced unnecessarily, and that creature is on the Rare Species list, as is the Gap Dragon. But what alternative do you recommend, Ivy?"

Ivy realized she was being tested. Her father was easy to manage; she had learned how to do that from her mother, Irene. But her grandfather was of sterner stuff, and though he humored her in little ways, he also expected her to come up to princessly standards. That awed her when she happened to think about it. Grandpa Trent expected her not only to be a sorceress, but to be smart too, and even with her talent that was more of a challenge. "Uh — maybe we can distract it —"

Trent was silent, and the hal-bird loomed nearer and larger. Its razor-sharp blade-beak glinted. She had to figure out a distraction — and the pressure of the situation distracted her. That was the problem with a real-life challenge; the details interfered with being smart.

Then she saw a puff of vapor to the side. "Hey, isn't that your breath?" she called to the hal-bird. "You'd better go catch your breath!"

The hal-bird turned its axe-head and peered at the puff, which accelerated its drift. Horrified, the bird flapped off in pursuit of his breath. The rest of them were left unmolested.

"That is the way for a future King of Xanth to do it," King Trent murmured approvingly, and Ivy felt very good. She had come through.

They completed the Gap crossing and flew to a region of clouds. Ivy looked around nervously, remembering the evil cloud, King Cumulo Fracto Nimbus, her nebulous enemy, but there was no sign of him here. Relieved, she relaxed and enjoyed the company of those more gentle clouds. Certainly it would be unfair to judge all clouds by a few ill-winds. These ones were fabulous, displaying themselves in many fleecy forms and types; indeed, the cloudscape was more phenomenal than the land-scape below. There were cloudy puffballs, toadstools, trees, anvils and cliffs. One cloud was shaped like a Mundane pig, with a slot in its back. "A cloud-bank!" Ivy exclaimed, recognizing it.

She flew to the left, to get in the middle of the formation. "I'm part of the cloud!" she exclaimed.

"Princesses are never part of the cloud," Grandpa Trent said. Embarrassed, Ivy dropped out and flew right.

Soon they closed on the North Village. This was a small collection of houses arranged about a central large tree.

"Good ol' Justin Tree," Grundy remarked. "Ever since you transformed him, fifty years ago, Magician Trent!"

"Transformed him?" Ivy asked, peering down at the tree. This sounded like something she hadn't known about.

"Back before I was King," Trent explained. "Then I was known as the Evil Magician, because I transformed anyone who got in my way. Ah, the impetuosity of youth! In the Time of No Magic, about thirty years ago, he reverted to manform, but he insisted that I return him to tree-form. He likes it that way."

"He's really a man?" Ivy asked, uncertain whether this was humor. Adults had funny senses of humor, and could laugh at incomprehensible things while frowning at what was really funny, like someone accidentally sitting on a stink-horn.

"He started as a man," Trent agreed.

"And there's no other tree just like him?"

"No other," Trent agreed. "He is unique."

"Then he must need a woman-tree," she decided.

"Your ma's probably got a seed to grow one," Grundy said. "From the Tree of Seeds."

"She's too busy for me," Ivy said, pouting. Her bird-beak wasn't very good for that, however.

They swung down toward Justin Tree, coming in for a landing. Then Ivy saw something interesting to the side. It seemed to be a mass of eyeballs that waved about, peering up at the party. Ivy abruptly swerved to fly closer.

"Oh, that's nothing," Grundy said disparagingly. "Just a seeing-eye dogwood tree."

"I want a branch of that!" Ivy insisted.

"Wait, Ivy!" Grandpa Trent called after her. "Things are not always what they seem!"

But she was already dropping down to perch on the seeing-eye tree. "This will only take a moment —" she began.

Suddenly a tentacle reached up and grabbed her. "Eeeek!" Ivy screamed in the manner of her mother. There was a right way and a wrong way to scream; it was one of the things a girl had to learn early.

"That's no dogwood!" Grundy exclaimed. "That's a tangler in disguise!"

Indeed it was! Now the illusion puffed away, and the dread tangle tree, one of the worst vegetable monsters of Xanth, was revealed in all its horror. The tentacles wrapped around Ivy's naked-J-bird body and drew her down into the mass of it, where the terrible maw in the trunk awaited with its wooden teeth and dripping saliva-sap.

Ivy screamed as piercingly as she could, no longer bothering with mere polite eeeking. She was, after all, five years old, and this was business. But the tree only slavered thicker sap and carried her in toward its orifice.

". . . can't reach her in time!" she heard Grandpa Trent saying in the distance beyond the barrier of tentacles. "Have to transform the tree instead . . ."

Then the tangle tree became a man. He was big and bare, except for a tangled mass of green tentacle hair and brown root boots that maybe were his feet. He was holding Ivy by her wings, about to cram the tasty blue-J into his mouth — but now his mouth was too small. He paused, startled.

The green-J flew up. "Put her down, Tangleman!" Grundy cried.

Tangleman focused on the golem-J. "Why?" he demanded in a windy voice, for that was normally all any tree had. Then he did a double-take, as if nearly blown over; it was the first time he had heard himself speak.

"'Cause if you don't, tentacle-top, Magician Trent will turn you into a skunk cabbage!" Grundy said with gusto. He liked bullying a tangler, when he had the chance.

Tangleman, horrified, bolted, carrying Ivy with him. He had forgotten her, but lacked the wit to put her down before he panicked. He wasn't used to being a flesh-and-bone creature, and wasn't good at it; he still thought of himself as a block-head. He charged into the deepest available jungle of Xanth, where he felt most at home. The green-J and dragonfly followed, but the tangler's progress was so swift and erratic that they couldn't catch up. Magician Trent, present only in illusion, had more trouble; he veered the wrong way, unable to reorient effectively on such short notice.

Ivy managed to keep her wits about her, after almost dropping them, and realized she was in no right-now-immediate danger, since the green giant was paying no attention to her. She began to watch the scenery, to see if there was any way to help herself. She spied a cabin with legs; it scrambled up to avoid the charging tangler. Actually it was just a single room, a living room, that hadn't yet found a home. No help there. In a moment they left it behind, the poor thing seemed nearly dead from fright.

Tangleman charged up to a four-footed creature who had hooves and horns but did not look aggressive. "Who you?" the green man demanded.

"I'm a steer," the creature replied. "Can I bum a smoke?"

"Where there's smoke, there's fire," Ivy remarked wisely.

"Where's the fire?" Tangleman cried, alarmed. Trees could get quite nervous about fire.

"That way," the bum steer said, pointing with its tail.

"That's the wrong way," another four-footed creature said. This one was powerfully constructed, with stubby claws on its feet and a protruding muzzle, and no hair on its body.

"Who you?" Tangleman asked.

"I am a bear."

"I see you bare!" Tangler said. "Who you?"

"Not bare. Bear," the creature said with dignity. "Bear witness. Don't trust the bum steer; you won't find any fire where he tells you."

"No fire!" the tangler agreed, and charged off in that direction.

The bear witness was right; there was no fire there, which was exactly what Tangleman was looking for. Instead there was a deep, dark shadow. The Tangler paused just outside it, distrustfully. "Who you?"

"That's the shadow of a doubt," the bear witness called. "Ignore it, and it will go away."

Tangleman stepped into the shadow, ignoring it, and sure enough, it faded away and a beam of sunlight shone down.

Bong! The sound was dull but loud, startling them both. "Who you?" the green man demanded, glaring about, but all he saw was a big stalky plant with bulbous growths on each end.

This time Ivy knew. "That's just a dumb bell," Ivy said.

Tangleman scratched a wart on his wild head. "I not dumb bell," he protested. "I worried."

"That's what happens when you scratch a worry wart," Ivy said. She had made that mistake once herself, so she knew. The trouble with worry warts was that sometimes it was almost impossible to ignore them.

omething clamped a pincer on his big brown toe. It was some crab-grass, and it was really crabby. Tangleman leaped up with a vegetable roar, and the grass let go. He landed in a bush — and a flock of screaming meanies burst out, startled. Their screams buffeted the tangler like the stings of B's, and he took off again.

This time the green man charged into a strange region. It was characterized by sound. There was a constant, stiff wind there, and the trees had many radiating spokes that angled into that wind and generated sounds from it. Each spoke had its own sustained note, and each tree had its own typical pattern of notes. Large trees had complex chords; small trees had simpler sounds, and saplings had but single notes.

As Tangleman charged through this forest, he moved past the trees, and the sounds Ivy heard changed. The dominant chords shifted, forming a kind of melody. "It's playing music!" she exclaimed.

Now that music became more pronounced. Definite themes developed, governed by the progress of the listeners through the forest. Their motion affected the music, and the effect was enhanced by Ivy's power. Ivy's attention was enough to bring the qualities of anything out; now that she perceived the music of the trees, the music became louder and more interesting than it had been before. The forest became an orchestra.

Tangleman slowed, hearing the music, trying to face it. "Who you?" he demanded.

"That's music, silly," Ivy said. "It's not a who, it's a what." She had realized that the tangler wasn't such a bad man, even though he had been a bad tree. He was just wild and confused. A little guidance could make him a decent companion.

He stopped, peering about, still trying to face the music. "Moo-sick?" Naturally the music stopped when he did; now it was merely fixed sound, no notes changing.

"Well, it used to be music," Ivy said. "You have to move to make it."

"Move," he said. "Move-sic." The concept was a real problem for him. He took a step — and stumbled, for clinging vines had grown about his feet. He ripped his legs free and charged on.

There was an earsplitting screech. Startled, Ivy looked down. Tangleman had just stepped on one of the tails of a cat o'nine tails. The other eight tails were swishing angrily as the cat got ready to pounce.

The tangler reacted in his natural manner; he grabbed for the cat with a dozen tentacles and gaped his wooden maw. Of course in manform he didn't have tentacles, so it was merely a one-handed grab, and his wooden maw was just a fleshy mouth. But the ferocity of the gesture alarmed the cat, who retreated.

The green man took another step — and waded into a huge web. Immediately several spider lilies swarmed down from their garden — and paused when they saw the size of their prey.

Tangleman grabbed at a black rope, pulling himself out of the spider's range. The rope yanked back, jerking itself out of his grasp as he stumbled into the marsh surrounding it.

"Silly — that's a horsetail!" Ivy exclaimed. "Now we're stuck in the mud!"

Indeed they were. The tangler lifted one foot out with a great sucking noise, but the other sank in deeper. Meanwhile the horsetails continued to swish angrily at being disturbed, and one of them rose out of the muck to reveal a broad brown hide. "A horse chestnut!" Ivy said, thrilled. She had liked horses ever since encountering the night mares and day mares, but they were evasive and fleeting. A genuine chestnut horse, however, suggested solider possibilities.

Tangleman sloughed his way toward firmer ground, but spied a bright metal object there. It was copper, wrought in the likeness of a reptilian head, complete with impressive fangs. It was mounted on a serpentine neck. As the green man approached, the snake reared up on its coils and hissed menacingly. "Better stay clear of that copperhead," Ivy advised.

He heeded her advice and squished to the side — only to come up against a bank bristling with green claws that snapped alarmingly. "More crab-grass," Ivy said. "Stay clear; you didn't like the one that champed your toe."

Tangleman was getting confused. Ivy realized that he just wasn't ready for the flesh-folk's world. She wondered what it was like to be a tree, just soaking up sunshine and grabbing whoever came near. She pictured herself as a tangler. If any of that crab-grass scuttled near, she'd just snag it with a tentacle, and —

She paused. There, at the corner of her consciousness, was the day mare Imbri, who had brought her the day-dream. "Imbri, you're out of your gourd!" Ivy exclaimed happily.

Startled at being discovered, Mare Imbrium bolted. But Ivy wanted to tell her about the horse chestnut. "Follow that mare!" she told Tangleman.

He tried, but his feet couldn't keep up. He started to fall forward. "Idiot!" Ivy cried. "Don't fall on your face; you'll hurt the ground, not to mention getting my nice blue feathers all gunky!"

If Tangleman thought it strange to be taking orders from a captured blue-J, he didn't indicate this. He reached out desperately and grabbed the nearest thing, which happened to be a cabbage palm. The huge fingers were normal, but the palm was solid cabbage. Great leaves of it tore away, leaving Tangleman holding a handful of green — and still falling. It was never wise to trust a cabbage-leaf, Ivy knew.

Tangleman grabbed again, this time catching hold of a giant ear. It was a cauliflower ear, pulpy around the edges and not very pretty, but it was well anchored, and finally the tangler managed to pull himself out of the muck.

There stood Grandpa King Trent and Stanley Steamer and Grundy golem, all in their natural forms. They had caught up while Tangleman was bogged down.

"Now —" Grandpa Trent began.

"Oh, don't make him change back here, Grandpa!" Ivy exclaimed, abruptly returning to her own form as his magic touched her. "This is no place for a tangle tree!"

Trent paused, not making the transformation. "What did you have in mind, Ivy?" He always encouraged her to think things out and make her own decisions, because that was what she would have to do when she eventually became King of Xanth.

"Tree?" Tangleman asked. "Me no tree!"

"Well, you started as one, vegetable-brain," Grundy said.

"He means he doesn't want to be a tree again," Ivy explained.

"I'm afraid we can't leave him as a man," Grandpa Trent said. "He would not survive long, with his lack of man-experience."

Ivy knew not to argue with her grandfather, but she tried to divert his intent. "Maybe we can find him a good place to be a tree, a better place than he had before —"

"I'll ask the top banana," Grundy said. He trotted over to a plant that bore a single monstrous banana, and made silent noises at it. Grundy could talk to anything; that was his talent. "It says to ask the big potato, whose eyes see all," and he trotted across to the potato that sat on the ground and had eyes all over. "It says it saw a lot of real peaches and tomatoes not far from here," he reported. "They're young and sweet and really nice company."

"No doubt," Grandpa Trent agreed. "Very well — we shall plant him there."

They started toward the promising spot. Tangleman, responsive to Ivy's talent, had calmed down considerably, and went where she directed without protest, still carrying her though she was now a regular girl. Unfortunately it wasn't a simple walk, because Ivy was not only a Sorceress, she was a child, and she remained interested in things. She spied a hem lock growing beside the path, and quickly had the tangleman set her down so she could unlock it and put it on her dress, locking it in place there; it looked very nice as a border, and of course it would never slip.

Then she found a honey comb that the B's were no longer using, and used it to comb out her tangled hair. She paused at a small silvery pond to look at the silverfish swimming in it. She reached in to pick one up, but it turned out to be a goldfish, very pretty and heavy metal, but not much value out of the water. She plucked a golden rod growing at the bank and used it as a staff, though it too was quite heavy. So she threw it in the water, making waves, and the waves were enhanced by her presence, spreading into the air, and the air waves shook a nearby date tree so that the down-dates quivered and some of the up-dates at the top were shaken loose. Ivy grabbed one; it was in the shape of a little 8 connected to a little D, as was proper for a D8. She nibbled on the 8 part, as that was all of it that could be ate.

Meanwhile, Stanley's attention was wandering, so he sniffed along a brown hedge and finally took an experimental bite out of it. The hedge threw up its limbs, scattered leaves all around, and scurried away. It was a hedge hog, and didn't like getting chomped by a dragon, even a small one.

They moved on, past a clump of hypnogourds. "I looked into one of those once," Grandpa Trent remarked. "Back in the days when they were less common, before I was King. I —"

But meanwhile Ivy had spied something bright lying on the ground. She picked it up. It was a glass disk with a handle on it. "What's this?"

Grundy peered at it. "A magnifying glass. They have them in Mundania."

"You mean it makes things bigger?"

"Sure, Pipsqueak. You just look through it, and —"

"Oh, goody!" Ivy held the glass up and looked through it at the nearest gourd, which grew under a canopy that was anchored by several mussels that seemed to enjoy stretching themselves.

Immediately the gourd became much larger. In fact, it swelled to monstrous, with a peephole twice the size of a port-hole. Startled, they all looked at it — and into it, and were caught by the spell of the gourd.

They stood in a haunted house. The walls were rickety, covered with badly faded and peeling wallpaper, and the light was gloomy. There were handsome spider webs in the upper corners, and a mouse squeaked with surprise and scooted into a hole.

Ivy was delighted. "What's this?" she asked.

"We're in the gourd, dodo!" Grundy said. "You magnified it so we all saw into the peephole, and now we're stuck until someone breaks our eye-contact and lets us out."

"Which may not necessarily be soon," Grandpa Trent said heavily. "We're deep in the jungle; no one knows where we are, or what has happened."

Grundy glanced at him curiously. "Say, King Trent — you're only with us in illusion. How come you got caught?"

"I'm not sure," Trent confessed. "I have not had a great deal of experience with gourds, and all of that has been involuntary. I presume that if I can see about me in illusion, I can also be trapped by the gourd in that state."

"But since the Sorceress Iris generates the illusion —"

Trent shook his head. "Evidently my wife doesn't realize. She's not as young as she once was, and doesn't always pay close attention. In any event, I am not eager to remain here longer than necessary. Let's try to find a way out."

"But getting out from the inside of a gourd has never been done before," Grundy protested. "It has to be done from the outside. Only the night mares can pass out of the gourd freely."

"There is usually a first time for everything," King Trent said positively, but he looked slightly negative. He wasn't as young as he used to be, either; this was evidently a strain.

Meanwhile, Stanley was sniffing around. He hadn't been in a place like this before. In a moment he spooked a ghost, who had evidently led a sheltered life and never seen a green dragon before. The ghost floated up, considered, and then tried to scare the dragon by making a horrendous face. Stanley was not scared; he was annoyed. He responded with a jet of steam. The ghost zipped out of the way, alarmed. Now it was angry; it drifted close to a dragonfly ear and yelled "Boooo!"

Furious, Stanley leaped at the ghost, trying to chomp it with his teeth. Naturally they closed on nothing. He crashed into the wall, breaking through it.

Two more ghosts, a haunt, and a spectre started up, spooked. It seemed they had been napping in the wall. Stanley pounced on them, too, snapping violently for their backs. But none of these were tangible. In the process he stirred up something else. Something strange.

It lifted from a crevice and spread out above the dragon in a somber cloud. Pale white streamers hung from it. "What's that?" Ivy asked nervously.

"It looks like ectoplasm," Grandpa Trent said. "Generally harmless, but it would be best to leave it alone, as it can have unusual properties."

"Stanley, leave that icky-plasm alone!" Ivy ordered the dragon preemptorily.

But already Stanley was leaping at it. His jaws closed on the cloud. It squished, and its streamers wrapped around the dragon's snout. He tossed his head about, trying to get the stuff off his face and into his mouth, but it just stretched like taffy and clung. Stanley smacked his head into the wall, trying to knock the ectoplasm free, but merely succeeded in bashing another hole. Finally he leaped right through the hole, carrying the stuff along with him, streamers of it trailing back.

Tangleman, convinced something was going on, charged after the dragon, knocking out more pieces of wall. Grandpa Trent winced. "The Night Stallion will never forgive me for this!"

"Who?" Ivy asked.

"He runs the gourd-world," Grundy explained. "You know — the boss of the night mares. We're ruining one of his best sets."

"Oh." Ivy hadn't thought of that. She had considered the wall-bashing interesting; now she realigned her reaction. She hurried after dragon and tangler. "Boys! Boys!" she scolded. "Stop that this instant! What do you think this is, a battlefield?"

Grandpa Trent rolled his eyes — adults did that every so often without apparent reason — and followed.

Ivy's reprimand was effective. Dragon and Tangleman drew up short, looking abashed. Stanley had finally scraped most of the ectoplasm off his snout. The stuff quickly floated elsewhere, having had enough of the dragon.

They were in a chamber with a table, and on the table was a box. On the box was a small green plant. "Oh, goody!" Ivy cried, reaching for it.

"Hey, you don't know what's in it, Turnip!" Grundy warned. He always called her that, knowing she hated both turnips and turndown. "Might be a hobgoblin!"

"No, Rapunzel wouldn't do that," Ivy said confidently, lifting the box down to the floor.

"Rapunzel?" Grandpa Trent inquired warily.

"My pun-pal," Ivy explained, admiring the box. She liked wrapped packages.

"Pun-pal? Perhaps my ancient brain is ossifying. If you would explain —"

"It's simple, Grandpa! We can't read or write yet, so we can't be pen-pals, so we're pun-pals instead. We send each other punny things. Or she does, anyway; I send her regular things like flowers and pebbles, and she seems to like them very well."

"Flowers and pebbles?" Trent asked. "They're rather common, don't you think?"

"Not where she lives," Ivy said. "She's in an ivory tower or somewhere, and she can't get out. Her guardian's an old witch who never lets her near any of the good stuff like mud or peanut butter."

"I can't think why," Trent murmured, smiling in that devious way adults had.

"'Cause it gets in her hair," Ivy explained matter-of-factly. "She has real, *real* long tresses she can dangle right down to the ground outside the tower, but she can't get down herself. So I send her all the things she can't get, and she sends me puns 'cause she's a pun-dit."

"That does sound like fair exchange, now that you have explained it," Grandpa Trent agreed gravely. "But shouldn't you tell your father, King Dor, about this person being held captive in a tower? We don't encourage that sort of thing in Xanth, you know."

Ivy considered. "Maybe I should. But Rapunzel says she's of elven descent; maybe she doesn't count."

"She counts," King Trent assured her.

"How do you know this box is from her?" Grundy asked. "Or that it's for you?"

"I know what her boxes look like, silly! See, it's a tress-ract."

"Tesseract?" Trent inquired.

"Tress-ract, 'cause of her tresses," Ivy explained patiently. It seemed that her grandfather had not been fooling about his brain mossy-fying; he was pretty slow on concepts. "And it's for me 'cause it's got my ivy on it."

"So it does," Trent agreed.

"How's it get here in the gourd?" Grundy asked. "And how'd she know to send it here, right where you'd be? Does she live in the gourd?"

Ivy shrugged. "Course not, silly! She's in an ivory tower. I told you. She's not in the real world, really. She just sends the box to where I am, and here's where I am."

"Perhaps we had better see what's in the box," Grandpa Trent suggested. "I note that it says O-PUN on the top."

"And PUNDORA on the side," Grundy said. "Are you sure it's safe to open Pundora's box?"

But Ivy was already opening it. She reached in and brought out a thin cylinder, pointed at one end. "A pun-cil," she explained, waving it about. As she did, a line appeared in the air, remaining in place. She turned it around and rubbed the other end along the line, and it disappeared. Then she lost interest and gave the pun-cil to Tangleman, who waved it about, admiring the lines of it. They did vaguely resemble tentacles.

Ivy reached in again and drew out a bundle of sticks. When she untied them, they sprang out into an enclosure like a play-pun, but messier and a lot worse smelling. "Oh, a pig-pun," she said, losing interest again. She was, after all, only a little girl, so her attention span was no longer than she was.

Tangleman climbed into the pig-pun and sat, satisfied. He liked rich soil.

Next she brought out a soft-ball that radiated small shining rods. "A pun-cushion," she said, and carelessly tossed it in to Tangleman, who tried to chew on it. He thought the puns sticking out of it were thorns.

Then Ivy found a basket of warm-smelling pastries. "Hot cross puns!" she exclaimed, delighted. Indeed, each had an angry face painted with icing on its top, and fairly steamed when touched. Ivy ignored the frown and bit into one, whereupon the icing-face smiled. "They don't like waiting to be eaten," she explained around her mouthful. "When they wait too long, they get cold. That's why they're so cross." She handed them out to the others. Soon everyone was eating them, and all the pastries were smiling. They tasted very good. "Rapunzel is pretty good with baking-puns," Ivy explained.

"Upun my soul," Grundy agreed, munching his own pastry, though it was as massive as he was. Fortunately he had a big mouth.

When they had snacked, Ivy brought out the rest of the items in the box. There were two doll-like figures identified as Puns and Judy, and a pair of snake eyes on small cubes that must have fallen from the Ivory Tower, and a couple of miscellaneous spells locked in globes. Grundy looked at these, and identified them as captured noises; one was an outcry, the other a sound-of-mind.

That was it; the pundora box was empty at last. Ivy grimaced. "Not much, this time. Well, I'll send her some stuff back." She walked about, picking up pieces of plaster, wood and wallpaper and tossing them into the box. A poltergeist wandered through the room, rattling its chain; Ivy grabbed the chain, starting a tug-of-war, till Grandpa Trent interceded.

"That chain belongs to the ghost," he explained. "It's not right to take it."

"Oh, all right!" Ivy said with bad grace, suddenly letting go of her end so that the ghost shot backwards through a wall. "But I don't have enough things for the box yet."

Now they all cast about, scavenging for fragments, until there was a fair selection. Then Ivy snapped off one of her hairs and tucked it in the top of the box, in this manner addressing it to Rapunzel of the long tresses. She clapped her hands, and the box vanished.

"Live and learn," Grundy remarked. "I never heard of a pun-pal before."

"Lots of things you don't know, golem," Ivy said smugly.

"But our problem remains," Grandpa Trent said. "We need to find some way out of the gourd, and I don't believe walking about will do it."

"This is probably the gourd Mare Imbri was heading for when the tangler chased her," Grundy said. "As a night mare, she can travel in and out at will. Maybe we can get her to carry a message to the Sorceress Iris —"

"Imbri doesn't use the gourds anymore, silly," Ivy said. "She's a day mare now. She won't come here."

"Anyway, Peanut," Grundy said — he always called her that — "we have to break the eye-contact we have with the peephole of the gourd from the outside, not the inside."

"Which means we'll have to be creative," Trent said. "Let's see what we have here." He assembled the remaining items from the pun box. "Here —let's pass these out and let each person try to fashion what he has into a device for escape."

No one seemed to be very positive about this, but each accepted a couple of puns. The green tangler got the two noise spells, because they seemed the least promising. He tried to eat one, but the globe resisted his teeth; he shook one, but the noise merely swirled around inside. Finally he bashed the two together, hard.

They cracked and the sounds escaped. There was a halfway deafening shout — and suddenly the group was standing outside the huge gourd. Tangleman, startled, pushed his fist forward into the gourd, shattering it.

"We're out!" Grundy exclaimed. "But how?"

"The only one of us to act was Tangleman," Grandpa Trent said. "But I don't see how cracking the noise spells could have —"

"Ask the mussels," Ivy suggested.

Trent looked at her. "The mussels?"

"They covered up the peephole," she said. "Why?"

Grundy asked the mussels, who had indeed contracted and drawn the canopy down over the peephole, breaking the people's line of sight and freeing them from the gourd's spell. The mussels replied that they had reacted to a mind-jolting outcry from within the gourd, that had so alarmed them that they had immediately contracted.

"So it *was* Tangleman!" Grandpa Trent exclaimed. "He smashed the sound-of-mind into the outcry, and the result was so loud it reached right out of the gourd!"

"That's the nature of outcries," Grundy said. "They've got to get out of whatever they're in. Only the magic of the spell kept that outcry contained before, and when that cracked —"

"Now let's get on to my house," Grandpa Trent said a trifle grimly. Adults were like that, their moods changing inexplicably. "Before we get into any more mischief."

"But what about Tangleman?" Ivy asked. "He saved us, by being the most creative, didn't he?"

Grandpa Trent sighed, then quirked a smile. "I suppose he does deserve credit for that. Perhaps he'll work out in our society after all, if he wants to. Very well, we'll bring him along too." He glanced about. "We can't risk any more of this jungle trek," and he transformed them all back into birds, including Tangleman, and they flew in a flock to the North Village.

They had a wonderful time at Grandpa Trent and Grandma Iris's house, and Grundy took over the management of the tangler, perching on his green shoulder and telling him what to do to get along in the strange world of flesh folk. The golem was good at that sort of thing, and it did get him off Ivy's case. So all problems were neatly solved.

But two days later, when Ivy returned to Castle Roogna, and her parents heard about the great adventure, they acted in the truly inexplicable manner of adults. They grounded her, for no reason at all. It was very unfair.   ●

Other deleted sections from the book:

(and one paragraph deleted from p. 435 of manuscript:)

The "creative" effort our heroes made to get out of the gourd derives from an exercise we were given when we attended our daughter's Cheryl's gifted class summer program, and were given envelopes containing an assortment of things like paper clips, beads, paper and yarn, and told to make something creative from this. Naturally I botched mine, since I had a truly fantastic notion that fell apart in practice, exactly as my novels do, but I thought the idea worth salvaging. So here's the yarn!

(And from manuscript p. 432)

. . . But since this is getting out of hand, I don't promise to do this indefinitely, and will try to close down Pundora's box. So those of you who remain out there, bursting with puns — stifle them, because there's only so much of this nonsense anyone can take. One fan even sent me the first chapter of his *Dictionary of Puns*; I used none of those, because he hopes to have that published independently; he just wanted marketing advice. By the time *Lye* sees print — please, no remarks about what kind of eyes it has to see anything — I should have completed the following Xanth novel, and plans are inchoate beyond that, so any puns you send are apt to be wasted anyway.

(Some of this duplicates the published Author's Note; I just wanted to have a record of what I did originally say about the cessation of puns.)

Todd Hamilton, Jody Lynn Nye, and Piers Anthony

OUR GUIDES TO THE LAND OF XANTH

Piers Anthony is the bestselling author of the Xanth series, The Tarot, Bio of a Space Tyrant series, The Adept series, The Incarnations of Immortality series, and more.

Jody Lynn Nye is the author of the *Encyclopedia of Xanth, Ghost of a Chance, Dragonlover's Guide to Pern, Dragonharper, Dragonfire* and contributor to *The Fleet.* Her new novel, *Mythology 101,* will appear in March 1990.

Todd Hamilton is a John W. Campbell award nominee for his novel *The Gamesman.* He and Jim Clouse are also the artists on *Roger Zelazny's Visual Guide to Castle Amber* and the *Dragonlover's Guide to Pern.*

James Clouse has previously collaborated with Todd Hamilton on *Roger Zelazny's Visual Guide to Castle Amber* and the *Dragonlover's Guide to Pern.* Clouse has had maps and artwork appear in products from TSR, Inc. and Mayfair Games, Inc.

Piers and Carol
Anthony

Jody Lynn Nye, Todd Hamilton,
and Piers Anthony

Author and
Night Mare